CW00766398

THE BREAKDOWN

BOOKS BY ARIANNE RICHMONDE

The Wife's House

The Newlyweds

The Guilty Sister

THE BREAKDOWN

ARIANNE RICHMONDE

bookouture

Published by Bookouture in 2022

An imprint of Storyfire Ltd.
Carmelite House
50 Victoria Embankment
London EC4Y 0DZ

www.bookouture.com

Copyright © Arianne Richmonde, 2022

Arianne Richmonde has asserted her right to be identified as the author of this work.

All rights reserved. No part of this publication may be reproduced, stored in any retrieval system, or transmitted, in any form or by any means, electronic, mechanical, photocopying, recording or otherwise, without the prior written permission of the publishers.

ISBN: 978-1-80314-177-0
eBook ISBN: 978-1-80314-178-7

This book is a work of fiction. Names, characters, businesses, organizations, places and events other than those clearly in the public domain, are either the product of the author's imagination or are used fictitiously. Any resemblance to actual persons, living or dead, events or locales is entirely coincidental.

For my readers.
Thank you with all my heart; you mean so much to me.

THE DISAPPEARANCE

It is when the thunder cracks a second time, Lizzie screams. The person taking Lizzie is clutching her tiny soft hand and leading her to a place Lizzie hasn't been before. She has no idea where she is going, or why. *Why is she out in the pouring rain, at night, in the middle of a wild storm?* She asks but gets no reply.

This is what makes the little girl most nervous.

The unknown.

Lizzie is only four years old. A normal kid who enjoys playing and laughing, someone who trusts easily. She loves to do somersaults on the lawn, and to gobble ice cream cones faster than they melt, and her favorite color is blue.

This August has been so perfect up until now. She's had such a fun summer, playing on the beach with her brother and family. Building sandcastles for her princess doll, teaching her teddies the alphabet (even though they haven't all been as smart as she hoped).

But now, out in the dark in the rain, in her pajamas, it doesn't feel like fun. She asks the grownup where they are going again, but the person gripping her hand and pulling her away from home doesn't respond, just carries on humming. The tune, barely audible on the person's lips, competes with the howling, hissing wind. The deafening roar of air.

Lizzie throws her skinny arms around the adult's legs and squeezes tight. Maybe if she clutches hard enough those legs will turn back home. "I'm scared. Where are we going?"

But her question is swallowed by a flash of lightning, faster than a blink and whiter than snow, sizzling over the restless ocean, casting its talon-like prongs into the raging water.

If anybody hears Lizzie cry out, nobody will ever say. There will be denials and lies and deceit. In her four innocent years it doesn't occur to little Lizzie that somebody wants her dead. How could she at such a young age understand the wicked thoughts that invade the minds of certain adults? Evil things they think and say and do? She knows nothing of this.

Just today Mommy read her *The Happy Unicorn.* Just today, she was collecting seashells for her princess castle.

The adult doesn't look behind but now grapples little Lizzie by the elbow instead of her squashy, small hand, and shifts her up above their hips in a piggyback ride. But this isn't a fun ride, not with the rain, the thunder, the crash of lightning above.

And the fog. Oh, the fog. You wouldn't think it was possible to have fog and thunder and rain all mixed together. But then you wouldn't know unless you lived by the savage coast of Maine, you just wouldn't know.

Lizzie's eyes fill with tears. "Where are we going?" her tiny voice peals out again above the smash and lash of rain.

Again, the grownup doesn't answer.

Just keeps humming a spooky tune that Lizzie doesn't recognize.

CELESTE

Nine days ago

We come here every year apparently.

Apparently, this is our summer house. It might as well be a vacation rental, because that's how it feels. Strange. Unfamiliar. Like it has nothing to do with me at all. Nevertheless, it's a beautiful place. The house sits on the edge of the water, the backyard a sprawl of lush green grass that rolls down to the cliff-side, which meets the ocean. The house is all wood and creaky old windows and floors. It's so romantic, otherworldly, and the sense of peace is extraordinary. The lap of waves, the jingle of boat bells, the birdsong. But when the tide comes in and the waves kick and smash against the jagged granite rocks, it makes me remember little slices of my life, and my past, and then it comes back to me: we are on an isolated island. Anything could happen, especially with the weather. Things could change in a single blink.

There are buried secrets here. Rumors whisper amongst themselves about ghosts and centuries-old ships sailing in the fog and mist.

The dead still live on, some say.

It's hot. Summer. Tomorrow August begins. I can hear the children running around, squealing with joy. The baby is in the bassinet, next to my bed, sleeping soundly. I would have her cozied up next to me, pressed close, flesh on flesh, but I keep dozing off and I'm terrified of rolling over and squishing her. So I wait until Max is around so he can bring her to me and sit with me on the bed, while I hold her in my arms. I'm not breastfeeding because... well, just because. I have a nurse who helps me with the bottle, with the feeds. She's been invaluable.

My baby's extraordinary. So innocent and pure. So new. I love to smell her scalp, breathe her in, inhale her baby scent. Is there anything in the world more beautiful than a baby? When I hold her, my eyes fill with tears. How can anyone be so precious? And she's all mine. Although, that's another thing I can't remember. I can't remember giving birth. I can't remember... anything. Can you imagine? Not remembering one of the most important days of your life?

I had a head injury, you see, with the car crash. They told me I was driving. I was pregnant and a few days away from giving birth. They got the baby out by C-section. And we both survived. Lizzie survived, too, in the child seat, at the back of the car. My beautiful little Lizzie, only four years old. Another love of my life, a spirit so warm, so divine... nothing beats the love you have for a child. It was a miracle she survived the car wreck.

Everything seems to be a miracle.

So here I am, convalescing in bed. Max is here, of course. He's taking a couple of weeks off work. Although one of those weeks is up already. Marjorie, his sister, is here too. She came all the way from California to be with us. To help me. Well, at least to help with the kids, the running of the house. I can tell already it's too much for her. The au pair is coming tomorrow. A girl from England. Well, not a girl, she's twenty-three years old, but still, she looked young in her photo. Jayne is her name. Will she be responsible enough? But we need someone with a lot of energy to help out.

It's a strange thing when your memory goes, when it becomes ambiguous, because you do recall other things. Futile stuff. Like that TV program *Supernanny*, for instance. I remember odd things like that. It's what gave me the idea to ask the agency for a British au pair.

Certain meals, tastes, and smells are also as familiar as my skin. I know who my husband Max is—on a good day—but other things turn into a blur. I remember them for a second... and then they're gone again. My brain is constantly snatching and losing and reaching and dropping. Like a beautiful butterfly you can't catch. It's exhausting to think, to grasp at the past, so I try not to think at all and simply accept the situation for what it is. What else can I do?

It was Dr. Stephen who suggested I keep this diary. To keep tabs on my thoughts. Use it to jog my memory. He's my psychotherapist. He's been coming here three times a week. He takes the ferry from the mainland. When the weather's calm, that is, which it has been for the most part. He's always here on time. Unwavering. Dependable. Which is more than I can say for my state of mind. Max is dependable, too, but he works so hard and can't always be here, even with his time off. He must feel as bewildered as I do. The way he fusses over me demonstrates to me how loving and kind and caring he is. I couldn't wish for a better husband. Everybody agrees. I feel really blessed. So lucky I'm still alive, and more than anything, grateful. Grateful for my baby. Every time I think of a name for her, I then forget. A forget-me-not is purple, isn't it? A flower. I can grasp onto the name Violet. Violet. That's her name.

I swear I feel as if a stork delivered her. That a great big bird brought her along and plopped her in my arms. I don't feel equipped, and I can hardly believe that Lizzie and little Liam are my children too... shush, this is my secret. Because the thought completely horrifies me. I am a *mother*. A mother of *three* children! I'm meant to feel completely whole and delighted and fulfilled. And I do, I love my children, how can I not? But I am overwhelmed by confusion. Dr. Stephen says this is completely normal, that on top of the head injury I'm probably suffering from postpartum depression.

But I can't shake off the thought that I'm a bad person, because I have these feelings deep inside me that... I'm wrong. That the damage to my brain was already there before the car crash.

JAYNE

Eight days ago

The ferry journey to the Wainwrights' house on Cliff Island is less picturesque than I imagined, simply because I'm surrounded by fog. Our boat smashes onto crashing waves, lurching, swaying, churning up my insides. I can hardly believe it is summer. The ferry is pretty big so I don't feel the impact the way you do with a smaller boat, but still, it rocks from side to side, and I end up tripping over myself and lunging for the railing, sucking in a lungful of air to steady my nerves. The smell of brine makes me heady. I don't look up but hear a seagull swooping overhead, crying its angry-baby cry. It unnerves me all the more. I taste the fog on my tongue, and salt, too, from my hair whipping across my face. My eyes are smarting from the wind, causing them to stream tears that make rivulets down my cheeks.

God knows I must look a real state. I'm dressed all wrong, in my 1950s rockabilly dress, one of my charity-shop finds. I'm not quite sure why I hadn't thought to google "weather in Maine." I was so desperate to get away from London, I hadn't researched things properly. That's what happens when you've got demons on your tail: you run without thinking, without preparing yourself.

"Is it normally this rough?" I say to a bystander: a man pacing about the deck who happens to observe me half bent over the railing, my face green.

He takes a step closer, his legs parted to balance himself from the rocking vessel. "It can be. We Mainers have a saying, *There are two seasons in Maine: winter and August.*"

Wrapping my cardigan around me, I pull my lips into a smile, or try to. I think it might come out as a bit of a grimace. Foolishly, I packed my jacket in the suitcase and it's too much trouble to find it amongst the other luggage.

The man has blondish hair and he's tall, muscular, with a slightly weathered face as if he has spent a lot of time outdoors. Friendly. Attractive. Probably, I'd guess, in his late thirties, early forties. But the last thing I'm entertaining in my head is any kind of romance. Getting involved with anybody or even flirting is not on my agenda. Besides, I feel too seasick to give him anything more than a woozy smile. I can tell he's looking at my outfit like I'm a mad person in a vintage dress on this windy boat.

He goes on, not put off: "It was August nineteenth, what, thirty years ago when Hurricane Bob passed through."

The man is actually *very* attractive on second glance. His voice is husky, mature. And I'm wondering how old he was thirty years ago when that hurricane happened. In my twenty-three years I've probably seen more hurricanes, earthquakes, volcanoes, and floods than any other generation previously, although thus far only on TV. Trust my luck if I run into a real live hurricane.

"Hurricanes?" My voice is wobbly. "I didn't know Maine had hurricanes!"

"Don't worry, it's very unlikely to happen again. With these cold ocean waters, it never really rises above sixty. Hurricanes don't generally hang around these parts. They like warmer water. By the way, I'm Eric. I like your accent by the way. British?"

I nod.

"Let me guess... London?"

"How do you know?"

"I lived in London for a while, when I was an exchange student."

I've sworn myself off men, so I stop myself from asking him who he is or what he does, which is unusual for me with my nosy, curious nature. But I can't help wondering what *does* this man do? And why is he on his boat? And where is he going? I feel that about everybody. Like when I'm in a traffic jam I want to get out of the car and interview people and ask them, *Where are you going, what are you doing, why are you causing this traffic jam?* I don't know why I like to stick my nose into strangers' personal business, but I do. I've been that way all my life. I want to know everybody's story. It gets me in trouble. So that's why I am determined to keep my mouth shut now. Because if I ask him too many questions he'll want me to reciprocate, won't he? And I really don't want to share any personal information about myself. And with jet lag, I'm not exactly on the ball right now, so I'd better not risk too much conversation.

The boat heaves again and I feel—looking into this void of white with nothing to focus on—like I might throw up. "The mist?" I ask. "Is this normal?"

"Sure." The man gives me a smile. "It'll be gone in an hour and then we'll have gorgeous blue skies, you watch. It's a southerly wind and that often brings fog, and haze, and heat."

I shiver. "But it's cold. Much colder than I thought it would be."

"Don't let that fool you. It'll be a hot day today, you wait.

But sure, we get summer storms sometimes. Winds can reach sixty miles an hour. Maine summers never come without a little bit of risk."

That's all I bloody need. *Risk.* I give this man a weak smile and bend over the railing again.

He seems to want to snag my attention though, as he says in a loud voice, "I was just kidding about risk. Hey, have you heard the story about *The Dash*, Casco Bay's ghost ship?"

"No."

"Fishermen have spotted her—she still sails at full mast. There are ghosts in these waters. You know what? I think I see her now. No way! There she is coming through the fog!"

Despite myself, I look out to sea and then can't help but giggle. "You almost had me there."

"So, is this a day trip?" Eric asks.

"No, I've got a job as au pair for a family called the Wainwrights."

Eric makes a face.

"You know them?" I inquire.

"Could say that."

"Are they nice?"

"Nice? Well"—he laughs—"'nice' is not exactly a word I'd use to, er... well, you'll see for yourself."

My stomach folds. *Oh, God, what have I got myself into?* "Why, what are they like?"

"Told you the fog would lift. Well, good luck," and Eric nods towards our destination.

I need luck? I follow his line of vision and spot an island ahead, and by the way everybody begins to shuffle around, I realize it must be our stop. I feel dread gather in my veins and a little voice inside me tells me not to disembark, that something is going to go horribly wrong. *Don't get off this boat,* it says. *You know what your luck's like... do not tempt fate.*

But the fog starts to slowly dissipate and the atmosphere turns less ominous. The sky heats up as the sun shines above like a spotlight lasering through the white air. It's such a relief to see land again, even a small amount of it. I shake the warning voice away. *It'll be fine*, I convince myself.

Cliff Island looks like it's a couple of miles wide. One end of the island has a smooth sandy beach—at least it appears that way from here—and the other, jagged rocks. Wooden clapboard houses are dotted about in different muted colors: olive green, beige, off-white, weather-worn blue. It looks pretty rugged, but civilized, since people's manicured front lawns are spread out in front of their homes, extending towards the cliffs dropping below, with a smattering of small boats moored on the water. I wonder what it's like when the tide goes out.

A frisson of excitement and dread simultaneously run up my spine. I have no idea what awaits me with this job as au pair, looking after two of the Wainwrights' three children, especially after what Eric insinuated. Or was he teasing? I have memorized the kids' names. Liam, six, Lizzie, four, and the newborn, Violet, only a month old, who, thank God, I will not be responsible for, although they did ask me if I had experience with newborns and if I could lend a hand if need be.

Scanning the people waiting for the boat on the dock, I spot a man who I assume is Mr. Wainwright, waving at me as our ferry approaches—I think it's him, I saw his picture online. I feel relieved that he's come out to meet me in his golf cart. His wife—Celeste's her name—had a terrible car accident, apparently. They didn't tell me any details, but I know what's expected of me. To look after the children for as many hours a day as I can, to relieve her of responsibility. *They need entertaining*, Mr. Wainwright told me in an email, *and at all costs don't let them exhaust their mother. She needs all the rest she can get.*

Eric offers to help me with my suitcase. I thank him and tell him I'm fine... it has wheels. Knowing this is the last stop on the line, I realize he must live here or have some kind of business, and now I wish I'd asked and pressed him on what he meant about the Wainwrights not being nice. But when I turn around to ask him, he's nowhere in sight.

CELESTE

As I lie in bed I reread what I wrote in my little diary-slash-notebook, and I smile remembering that one day, all of this, all of it, will make sense.

This I what I wrote:

Things are coming back to me, too, like meeting Max for the very first time. It was at the dentist. I was going in for a root canal and was terrified. Dentists have always frightened me. I suppose I am not alone in this. Who wants a drill put in their mouth?

Max was in the waiting room. I remember how well-dressed he was, in a suit, his wavy dark hair flopping over his brow. And he glanced at me and gave me a small, itsy-bitsy smile, and said, *You look nervous, don't be. Dr. West is one of the best.*

I laughed. *That rhymes*, I said. And he laughed too. *It does, doesn't it?* and then we both cracked up as if we'd known each other for years and had some silly, private joke. We talked for quite a while—I can't remember what about. He was so kind and uplifting, so by the time I was called in for my root canal I'd forgotten all about fear, and in its place there was hope. Because

Max had asked for my number, and I sure didn't waste any time giving it to him. I was overly eager, I admit. A smart girl would have played it cool with a guy as handsome as Max, but my heart was bulging out of my sleeve. I couldn't believe such an attractive man wanted to ask me on a date. He didn't call for a few days, and I thought, *Oh well, that's the way it always is, isn't it? Disappointment is something I know well.*

But when he did call, he invited me to a charity benefit for children with cleft palates. He had spent a fortune: bought the whole table for... I don't know how much, at least ten thousand dollars. There were a couple of other women there around my age, all Max's guests, and I didn't think much of it except how pretty they seemed, and I wasn't the only one who liked him. I had competition and almost gave up even contemplating the possibility of him being my boyfriend. Who was I kidding? He was polite to us all, and I didn't feel like his only date, which was crushing, it was. Because I was beyond smitten with him and had already fallen a little in love, the way some women do fall in love at first sight, despite what their head tells them. We know it's ridiculous, and it is, isn't it? Love, pretty much at first sight? How foolish is that? Fantasizing about marrying someone you've only just met? But all women seem to do it, even if only in secret, even in denial. We women are all guilty of fantasy, aren't we? We are all susceptible to being weak when it comes to love, for falling hard for someone we hardly even know. But I didn't need to worry, after all. Because Max called again.

Anyway, that was it. By the time Max invited me to dinner and the ballet, a week later, I had made up my mind that he was the man for me. I had never met anyone who paid for everything, who opened taxi doors for me, who sent me flowers. And even more romantic, he mailed me a postcard every day, by snail mail. That was the clincher. Those postcards. Always with some meaningful place we'd been to or something we'd talked about. He was a bit flashy with money, I couldn't help noticing.

We married three months later. Me, with my stringy hair and pale, skinny arms and legs. Max, like some kind of dashing white knight.

It's a strange feeling to think about your husband and pain in the same thought, but of course I do, and always will.

JAYNE

Being summer, I am traveling light and only have the one suitcase. I've been hired for six weeks. Strange, that they'd go to all the trouble of hiring someone from the UK when there must be thousands of young people desperate for a summer job right here, not only in the States, but New England itself. Lucky me! That's all I can say. This family has saved my bacon.

We set off in the golf cart, me sitting by Mr. Wainwright's side, his long longs spread wide. I hate that, don't you? The way men feel they have a right to spread their legs and take up space, yet we women are supposed to keep our legs neatly together? Even when women are wearing jeans, you don't see them doing the "spread." I see it on the Tube and public transport all the time. I think it's a mark of arrogance. However, I have to say that in every other way Mr. Wainwright is punctiliously polite, asking me about my trip, my journey on the boat, and if I'm tired. I lie and tell him I slept on the plane, but I am tired and can't wait to go to bed. I'll need to wait, though, until at least nine o'clock, or I'll never get into the rhythm of the time zone.

"I'll take you to your cottage first, so we can drop your case, and then if you like you can come to the main house and I'll show you around."

"Great," I reply.

As Mr. Wainwright drives the golf cart off he begins to tell me about the island.

"In the olden days this island was very popular with summer tourists. There were once lots of inns everywhere, but there aren't any hotels left now. Some islanders have rented out places on Airbnb in the past, but not this year, you know, with all the troubles we've been having lately."

I nod, assuming he's referring to all the previous coronavirus lockdowns.

"Truth be told, the island's very empty right now. I hope that won't bother you, Jayne."

"I doubt it. I'm looking forward to a bit of peace and quiet after London. You know, with all the traffic and pollution and fumes? This will be a lovely change."

And I mean it, I have been looking forward to a little bit of "me time." Well, usually "me time" means, for a lot of women, doing their nails or going to the hairdresser, but for me it'll be reading, catching up on novels I've wanted to read for years, going on walks in the fresh air, that sort of stuff.

I shoot a glance at Mr. Wainwright to see if he's in the mood to chat some more, but he's quiet now, his mind somewhere else. He's lean and tall, with a face that's very classical and old-fashioned in a way. Thick, thick eyebrows, and brown eyes that are very deep-set. His hair is dark and wavy and on the longer side, but not long, just a regular cut. He must be about forty. Truth is, he's very handsome. And I would say "handsome" not "good looking," because he looks like he's from a different era. Much like this place. I feel like I've stepped into another century.

"The roads aren't paved here," he suddenly pipes up. "It's all sand tracks. Sometimes they talk about paving, but we islanders don't want that, we don't want cars and noise and traffic. That's why we came here in the first place."

"Been in the family a long time, this house then?" I ask.

"Yes, for several generations. There's about eight miles of coastline in total here, so you can't really get lost, it's only small, this place. Most of the land is in conservation easements, which protects it. You know, keeps it rural, keeps it safe from construction, from hotel chains. There's a tennis court here, if you play, and a store with a café, and even a library, but not much else for entertainment except swimming or lobstering, and looking out for porpoises. I hope you won't get bored."

"No. I'll have plenty on my plate with the kids, I'm sure."

"You'll get time off, though, of course. You know your hours, right?"

"Oh, yes." I am being contracted to work no more than thirty hours per week, including babysitting. One and a half days free each week. Which works out at roughly five hours a day. They paid my airfare here, of course. God knows why they particularly wanted somebody from Britain.

"So can you tell me a little bit about the children's schedule?" I ask. "You know, what time they get up and go to bed, any foods they're allowed or not allowed... Oh, and the kind of things you expect me to do to entertain them." I remembered his email about "entertaining" the children.

Mr. Wainwright, one hand on the wheel of the golf cart, turns to me in surprise, and with a laugh, says, "Oh, we're not very strict, we go with the flow, you know?"

No, I don't know, I think. I try to pin him down. "If you could be a little more specific, that would be really helpful for me, so I know what's expected."

"Oh, just use your imagination."

My imagination? This is going to be really awkward. "What time do they get up? And if I'm in my own cottage, what should

I do? Come collect them in the morning? Hang out with them at the main house?"

"Marjorie's been giving them breakfast every morning, with Ms. Sharpe, the nurse, keeping a watchful eye over her."

"Marjorie?"

"My sister."

"Oh yeah, that's right, your sister's staying with you, I think I remember you mentioning that in an email."

"You do understand, don't you, that my wife is... well, her mental state of mind is very, very fragile. Marjorie isn't only here to keep an eye on the house and children but to help Celeste's business. Run her website. Take and ship orders."

I remember looking up Mrs. Wainwright's website when I got the job. "She sells French linens and stuff, doesn't she?" I ask.

"Exactly. Quality sheets and towels, scented candles, luxury items to do with the bedroom and bathroom. It was doing extremely well before she had the accident, and orders have really piled up with her absence. I wanted to keep it in the family, didn't trust just anybody to look after my wife's creation. She started it about five years ago when she was pregnant with Lizzie. It was a way of her being able to stay home and look after the kids at the same time. It took off and did extremely well. I'm only telling you this so you understand the extent of it, the gravity of the situation. Before, she was working night and day on this business, and now she can't even get an email together. Poor love, she's..." He trails off, his eyes misty, as if this has blown their world apart. It's endearing that he seems so proud of his wife's achievements.

"Is she likely to get better anytime soon?"

He sighs. "I really don't know. All cases are different, the doctors say. Anyway, Marjorie needs to be close to the family and take over the running of Celeste's business. And either she or the nurse gives the kids breakfast. Usually around seven, they're up pretty early."

"And then should I come over and collect them?"

"Good point, that's not something I've really considered."

"Well, what do you usually do? What did you do before..." I was about to say "before the accident," but I don't want to get too personal, too prying.

"Why don't you come and pick them up around eight a.m.?"

"Okay, will do."

"Then you can take them away, take them to your cottage, get them out of the house, anyway."

"So I'm to give them lunch, cook for them in my cottage?"

"Yes, that's a point, I need to get some extra food for you at the cottage so you can give them their meals there. At least lunch, that would be great."

I realize, talking to Mr. Wainwright, that he hasn't thought through any of this. I did try to get this clear in the emails but had no luck. It's all very casual, and this makes me nervous. He's the kind of parent who might say go "with the flow" and then could end up screaming at you when you get something wrong. "Use your imagination" is not a very useful thing to hear.

"Any specific allergies or diet requirements that I should be aware of with the children?" I inquire.

"Diet?"

"Not 'diet' exactly. I'm not talking about a losing-weight diet, but you know, is anybody allergic to peanuts or shellfish or anything like that?"

"No, no, nothing like that."

"Any medical issues I should be aware of?"

"No, Liam and Lizzie are both incredibly healthy. Well, you'll see, very boisterous, very healthy, very noisy, and too damn curious." He smiles at this. *Proud dad*, I think.

"Can they both swim?" I press on.

"Oh, yeah, they're both excellent swimmers, even Lizzie. But obviously they're not allowed to go swimming alone."

"Well, that goes without saying," I agree.

We ride on in silence for a couple of minutes. Then I ask, "So you don't have a list for me of any sort of rules or regulations?"

"Heck, no, what do you take us for?" He laughs again.

"You'd be surprised. Most parents are kind of helicopter types these days. They hover over them, wanting to know exactly what's going on every second of the day—some even have cameras set up."

"Well, that's not our style. We believe in freedom and letting the kids be a bit wild. Here, anyway, while they're on vacation. This is our summer home. We like them being outside in nature, with the birds and the bees, the whole nine yards."

"Okay, that's great to know. Anything I should know about... *anything* at all? I want to make sure I get it right."

He stares at me for a second, his eyes burning through me. There's something a tiny bit fearful about this man, a little mysterious, like he has a secret to hide and I'm nosing too much.

"Just enjoy yourself here, Jayne. We like to think that you'll be able to have a bit of a vacation, too, while you're here."

I mull over everything he's said, probably overthinking it. Maybe I will have lots of fun. But as I gaze around my surroundings—the golf cart trundling along dusty roads—I feel the isolated island vibe beneath me, along with the rough journey getting here, and knowing I won't be going back to the mainland in a hurry I am suddenly panicked that I'll be living on my own in such an unfamiliar place.

I ask, "By the way, does my cottage have a phone?"

Mr. Wainwright frowns, his dark brows meeting. "No, no telephone. Sorry about that, but you have your cell phone on you, right?"

I take my mobile from my bag and take a snap of the seascape. "Of course." The sun has risen high and the sky is a sharp, crystal blue. That guy on the boat, Eric, was right; it's turning out to be an amazing day.

"Then if there's an emergency or you're needed at any time, we can call or text you, right?" he checks.

"Oh, yeah, course," I tell him, feeling a little worried. What if there was a fire? A hurricane? But I don't ask him this, I don't want to sound overly fussy. I've only just arrived, after all. I've already grilled him enough.

As if reading my mind, he says, "There's a list of emergency numbers on your fridge, but don't worry, this place is incredibly safe, nothing ever happens here."

We carry on in silence for a while longer.

Then I ask, "So when will I get a chance to meet the children?"

"Good point. Tell you what, why don't we change course?" He swerves the golf cart in a U-turn. "We'll go to the main house first, meet the kids, I'll show you around, and then I'll drop you back at your cottage. Good idea?"

I turn my phone into selfie mode and look at the state of my face and hair, ravaged by the ferry journey. I want to say, *No! Please take me to my cottage so I can clean up a bit*, but he's already driving towards his house.

I suppose getting the meeting with his wife over and done with is a good thing, so I find myself nodding in agreement, saying, "Okay."

I'd prefer to look more like a bona fide nanny/au pair when I meet Mrs. Wainwright than how I am now... a ragamuffin. Never mind. Too late. Something tells me it's not Mr. Wainwright who's in charge of hiring me, judging by his cluelessness, but his wife, so it would be nice to make a good impression.

We bumble along in the golf cart on the sandy, rather potholed road until we reach the driveway of their home. It's a big wooden clapboard house, pale green, the paint peeling rather, slightly rundown, but lovely. There's a sweep of lawn rolling down to the cliffs below, to the water, which has calmed. The waves are lapping at the shore. Amazing how quickly the weather changed as soon as the sun started shining. The house looks very romantic, like something out of a novel. *Little House on the Prairie* but by the sea.

"We'll leave your case here," Mr. Wainwright announces, pulling up outside the house. "Come meet the family. And by the way, you can call me Max."

I follow him into the house, although we go in by the back, by the kitchen. He pushes open a screen door. I guess to keep mosquitoes out. Americans are always clever about things like this, always very practical. I step inside. The kitchen is beautiful. Like something out of *The World of Interiors*. The opposite of glitzy or flashy, because it appears all original, as if there have been no upgrades or remodeling for decades. I have never seen a place like this in real life. The stove looks like it's from the 1950s, with rounded edges, the color a dreamy, baby blue. A real vintage gem. In my dress, I have instant fantasies about being the perfect fifties mom, baking maybe. I could do that here with the kids. Play the perfect housewife. As a child, I used to see mums like that on telly: reruns of American TV series, and I dreamed of *my* mum baking me something, to scoop me out vanilla ice cream with a homemade slice of apple pie. But I was always alone, making my own food, even at six years old. Stale Rice Krispies, a heel of moldy bread. Never any fresh vegetables or fruit. But we did have that old TV going twenty-four-seven. Anything to keep me out of her hair, to make me shut up, and that's how I survived really: dreaming of one day being somewhere else, in a real home with a real family. I suppose that's what attracted me to being an au pair in the first place.

I gaze around this gorgeous *Marvelous Mrs. Maisel* kitchen

and sigh. Or is it *I Love Lucy*? It has one of those lovely old ceramic sinks, also antique, not imitation. It's rare to see real vintage stuff these days. The cabinets are wooden with glass doors, and also look they look like they've been here forever.

"As you can see, this is a no-frills kind of house," Max tells me. "Mostly falling to pieces, but that's the way we like it."

"It's perfect. Excuse me, um, Mr. Wain... Max, would you mind if I used your—"

"You need the bathroom? So sorry, I should have thought after your long journey."

He shows me where the bathroom is, and with a wild burst of relief I rush in and close the door behind me. I take a needed pee, wash my hands and then look at myself in the mirror with horror. My hair is all over the place. Wild and unruly, mascara halfway down my face. Far worse than I thought. I feel so, so embarrassed. But at the same time angry with Max for not having taken me to the cottage where I could've cleaned myself up a bit. I rummage around in the bathroom cabinet and find some face cream, slap it under my eyes, wipe off the smudged makeup with some cotton wool I find in a drawer. Apart from my handbag, I've left everything in my suitcase in the golf cart, so I can't do a touch-up. I dig into my bag, pull out my hairbrush and do my best to neaten up my hair, then tie it into a neat ponytail. I won't win any beauty contests, but at least I look a bit more respectable. Ready to meet Mrs. Wainwright.

As I exit the bathroom and head back to the kitchen I hear a rumble of footsteps and two children come charging downstairs, racing in front of me through the corridor, off in another direction.

Max bellows from the kitchen, "Liam! Lizzie! No, come back here. Mommy's resting."

"But we want to see her!" the little girl shouts out.

The duo tumble into the kitchen, their little faces disappointed, especially the girl's.

"There's somebody here I want you to meet," Max says.

I enter the room, then bend down to their level. "Hi, I'm Jayne, your new au pair."

Lizzie yells excitedly, "We know! We know you! We saw your photo!" Her wild persona doesn't quite match her doll-like looks. Long blond hair and big, round blue eyes—porcelain blue, clear like the sky. Liam looks like a mini Max.

"You must be—"

"Lizzie!" the little blond girl shouts with gusto. She's strutting around in a pair of her mother's kitten-heeled shoes, a six-inch gap between her tiny heel and the back of the shoe. "I got a gift for you!"

"Oh, have you? How lovely."

She grabs a round thing from the table, and I see it is some kind of animal made from papier-mâché. "It's a piggy bank!" she cries out.

"Me, my name's Liam," the boy says with equal bravado. "I'm making you a painting, but it isn't finished yet."

"How lovely to receive presents from you both. How kind."

It's refreshing to see boisterous children with personalities. They don't seem to be shy at all, not like most children are when I first meet them. Lizzie grabs my hand, and Liam looks up at me from under his impossibly long eyelashes.

"That's great," I say. "We're going to have such fun this summer."

Lizzie touches the material of my dress with a sticky hand covered in something pink. "Love your dress. I want a pretty yellow dress with flowers."

"You know what, Jayne?" Mr. Wainwright blurts out. "I won't show you the house right now. Celeste's resting and I'd rather not disturb her, so why don't you two kids come with Jayne and me in the golf cart, and we can take Jayne to her cottage."

Liam shouts, "Yay! I want to drive."

"Okay, you got it, buddy, but be careful."

"So I won't be meeting Mrs. Wainwright, after all?" I ask.

"Please call us both by our first names, we're not formal around here."

"So I'm not going to meet Celeste now?"

"She's weak, she's not being very sociable at the moment. I hope you understand."

"Course," I say, wondering how bad she is. I'm desperate to know more but don't want to be impolite by asking. I turn to Lizzie. "You're going to wear those shoes outside?"

She clicks them together. "Sure. Actually, no. I don't want to get them dirty." She carefully lays her mum's shoes by the door and tears outside, barefoot. Liam, I notice, is also barefoot.

I feel a bit disappointed not to meet Celeste, but never mind. I traipse out of the front door after Max and the kids, a little miffed that I haven't been shown around the house. Still, I'm keen to be on my own for a while, get myself showered and unpack. God, I hope the water's hot. With no telephone and things, who knows what my cottage will be like?

Lizzie holds my hand most of the way. Liam sits on Max's lap and steers the golf cart, his dad's arms encircling him. My cottage is about half a mile away from the main house, and also sits on the edge of the water. There's a rowboat outside. It's so picturesque. Very small, but it'll be perfect for me. I notice the door is unlocked, and the kids charge inside as if it's their own place. Well, I suppose it is. I follow behind. Max takes out my suitcase from the back of the golf cart and brings it into the cottage.

"You should be pretty comfortable here, Jayne. As you can see, it's nothing swanky, just your basics, but there's a coffee maker, and there's milk in the fridge. Celeste told me that you'd need milk, being English. Um, or should I say British? I never know what to say." He laughs awkwardly as if he's worried about offending me.

"Well, all English people are British, but not all British people are English, put it that way," I explain. "But I happen to be English, I'm from London."

"That's where the Queen lives!" Lizzie yells.

"That's right, the Queen does live in London, at Buckingham Palace. She also has other houses in different parts of the country. And a place in Scotland."

"You know what?" Max says. "Why don't I leave the kids with you... for... I don't know, an hour or two? Then I can pick them up later."

This is not a request or a suggestion but more like a fait accompli. This was not in our contract. It's my very first day and I'm meant to be dealing with the kids right now? I have jet lag, I'm tired, I need a shower, but I find myself too exhausted to argue and too intimidated by his unibrow and domineering personality to say anything to the contrary. And I do want to seem like I'm willing and not some drama queen, or difficult to work with. Yet I'm also fully aware he's taking advantage of me. If it carries on like this, I'll have to speak to the agency. Never mind, these kids seem really fun and sweet. No big deal. Might as well jump in the deep end now.

"There's some bread, breakfast cereal, coffee, tea, and basic foods, pasta, cans of stuff, olive oil, salt. Things you can be getting on with to make spaghetti or whatever, so you can cook yourself your own dinner, if that's okay?"

Again, he's telling me, not asking.

Max goes on. "Tomorrow I'll be going to the mainland to buy some extra provisions, so let me know if there's anything in particular you need? Anything you want I can pretty much get it. I usually shop at Trader Joe's."

"Thanks." I frown, not knowing anything about Trader Joe's. "So just to be clear, you'll come and pick the kids up in an hour?"

He nods. "Sure. Nice to meet you, Jayne. Good luck with these two little devils."

"Dadd-eeeeee, I'm an angel not a devil!" Lizzie protests.

I look the two little ones in the eye and smile at them. "I'm really looking forward to getting to know you, Lizzie and Liam." I turn to Max, about to recap, "In an hour," but he's already out the door.

I get that uneasy feeling again. That feeling that something's off. That agreeing to this job was a mistake.

But I shake the thought away and give the kids a big grin.

DR. STEPHEN

It takes sixty minutes, or double that, to get from Portland, Maine, to Cliff Island by boat. The "Calendar Islands" they're called, because when they were discovered they said there were three hundred and sixty-five, one for every day of the year. Cliff Island is small, just two and a half miles long and one mile wide. Nothing eventful happens here. Meeting the noon mailboat is, for the residents, a kind of social event, it seems. There's a tiny post office, a shop that sells some basic provisions, but in the summer months plenty of swimming and beachcombing. Sometimes whales pass by, and porpoises. Its remoteness is its attraction for the few families who have houses here. I was coming to the Wainwright residence three times a week by ferry to treat my patient, Celeste Wainwright. At first, I enjoyed the picturesque journey to this out-of-the-way, H-shaped island, but it began to exhaust me. Not so much the travel time but the worry of missing the boat, delays, choppy weather. So when the Wainwrights offered me one of their cottages for the summer, I wasn't about to say no—not when it comes free of charge with the job. The Wainwrights own a whole group of cottages that they normally rent out for the summer. "The Blue Cottage" is where I'm housed. Max didn't flinch at the cost of hiring me, and, let's face it, with the insecurity of my salary and my recent state of affairs, I snapped up the employment opportunity.

So here I am. Doctor at large, trying to repair Celeste's broken mind, doing my best to help her heal. In my professional opinion, she should be at a care facility in Portland, but because of the never-ending threat of another coronavirus outbreak, that's too risky and neither Celeste nor Max will hear of it. Celeste and the baby were monitored in the hospital for nearly a month. She was miserable there, wanted to be home, though she had quite forgotten where she even lived, so here she is at her summer residence, under her husband's and my supervision.

When I was told about the car accident it was in hush-hush tones. Reading between the lines, it seems it was attempted suicide, and that Celeste was suffering from prenatal depression, taking her car and her pregnant self, and little Lizzie, off the road and into a lake at full speed. She had stopped taking her meds, Max told me, didn't want to "poison her body" with anything while pregnant, apparently, and that's why her mental health began to suffer again. This I gleaned in a roundabout way from Max. "I don't like to brandish around the word 'breakdown,'' he told me, "but... well, you kind of need to know."

Celeste herself is in such a daze she doesn't know what's going on and can't remember anything about taking medication for depression. I need to find out more details, more specifics. I'm not a psychiatrist so am not qualified to prescribe her meds myself, and luckily they've hired a nurse, Ms. Sharpe, to help her, especially with the newborn, so Ms. Sharpe is in charge of all that. The local papers described the car crash as an accident. Intent on covering up the family name, Max asked me to step in, because we go back a ways, were at college together, and he wanted someone he could trust. We in the medical field never disclose private details about patients; it is part of our oath as practitioners, so he shouldn't have been so worried. I was wary of being responsible for a patient whose recovery was way beyond the type of treatment I'm able to offer. But right now, after certain private issues that, thankfully, the Wainwrights have no idea about, I am not in a position to turn down work.

It's a funny place, Cliff Island. Sandy roads. Like time has stood still. It's the last stop "down the bay" on the Casco Bay Lines ferry, the outermost island. There's a few hundred people, tops, living here in the summer. In the wintertime, only a handful of year-rounders. There's a one-room schoolhouse, with only three students, the last, I believe, of its kind in America. Cliff Island is remote, cut off. Just a mom-and-pop grocery store. You have to lug enough food to last a while from the supermarkets on the mainland. People have freezers and generators in case of power cuts, which I imagine happen often.

Nurse Sharpe also lives in one of the Wainwright cottages. We're all on first names here, except for Nurse Sharpe. Odd she likes being so formal. She can't be more than forty-five years old.

There is a smattering of these waterside cottages—all owned by the Wainwrights—dotted at a distance from each other along the shoreline. Mine, luckily, is set the furthest away, atop a jagged rock. I enjoy utmost privacy yet have a great view. It's a twenty-minute walk to Max and Celeste's house, so it's easy to pop by any time to visit Celeste. It's nice and casual here.

Easy.

Perfect for me, in fact.

CELESTE

Six days ago

"Where's Violet?" I scream. The horror of what has happened sucks all the air from my lungs as I race around the house frantically trying to find my baby. She's not in her crib. She's missing. A pain sears through my midsection. My fingers fumble over the flimsy fabric of my nightie: the scar of my C-section. I gave birth to my beautiful daughter only a month ago. We survived a car crash. She was meant to be. She is my world. My life. Something has happened.

"Calm down, Celeste."

I stare at Marjorie, my eyes wild, my hair a tangled, Medusan mess, I can't see straight. Violet disappeared while I was sleeping. "The au pair," I yell. "Where is she?" It occurs to me that this happened after the au pair's arrival. "Where's Max? Where's my husband? Where's the nurse? And my doctor, Stephen, where is he?"

Someone did this. Someone is at fault. Not me. It wasn't me.

I break down into sobs.

Then the realization hits me like a sledgehammer: it *was* me, it *is* me. That it's me who is the guilty one because I am her mother and I should have kept my baby safe. She was sleeping beside me. I should not have let her out of my sight. It's too late. It's all my fault.

Did I crush her? Hold her too tight?

"What happened? Where. Is. Violet?"

Marjorie doesn't speak. Opens her mouth to say something but nothing comes out. Her brown eyes brim with moisture. She's hiding something. She's trying to protect me from the horror of the truth. "You need to get some rest," she whispers. "Everything will be okay."

I push past her, stumble into the kitchen and collide with my nurse. She's holding Violet in her arms, her tiny body swaddled in a blanket. "Ssh," she whispers. "Everything will be fine. The baby's resting, you need to rest too." She's curling her arms around my baby, her chin nestling on Violet's head as if Violet were her own, not letting Marjorie near, and shielding her from me. Violet is silent. Still. *Oh my God, is she even breathing?* And there is a man in a white coat, holding a clipboard. A doctor? I stumble toward him, reaching out for my baby. A foggy haze envelops my brain. And then I remember. My nurse gave me an injection, ten minutes ago. My eyelids flutter. I sway on my feet, my knees buckle.

Marjorie intercepts my drug-induced fall.

I am like a rag doll. Helpless. I collapse in her arms.

JAYNE

Five days ago

Yesterday, all hell let loose. Violet died. Just like that. A beautiful newborn, hardly a month old, dead. I'm in shock. We all are. It's so tragic. I hardly got to know the poor baby, as she passed away only two days after I got to Cliff Island. SIDS, some say, yet nobody is confirming anything for sure. You know, Sudden Infant Death Syndrome? Others speculate that it was the car accident, the impact while Violet was in Celeste's womb, that it took a toll on the baby, after all. Violet was delivered by cesarean, apparently, so it can't have been an easy birth. Luckily, I haven't been hired to look after the baby herself, or maybe they would've blamed me. I wanted to pack my bags and leave, but with a possible storm brewing and dangerous choppy water, I couldn't. I'm still here, weighing up my options. Mourning a tiny soul, a mini life that was snuffed out almost before it began.

"How are you settling in?" It's Stephen, the therapist, or psychiatrist, or whatever he is. I'm scrambling along the rocky path from the local café-slash-shop to my cottage, trying to get my bearings on this weird island that seems to be in the shape of the letter H. I'm in my fifties dress again because it is actually very hot. My legs are scratched, my nails bitten to the quick with nerves, and I feel more than ever that I don't belong here. The kids are having their afternoon nap. I have taken this time to find my bearings, explore a bit, get away from the drama.

Stephen grins at me, waiting for a response. He's an odd-looking man, Stephen is. Late thirties, early forties. There's something too eager about him. Slightly turned-up nose. Beady brown eyes. Looks like someone you might not trust. Though when he smiles he's actually quite charming. He's got that shiny, bright, American smile. Like a lesser Matt Damon. Matt Damon in *The Talented Mr. Ripley*. First impressions, anyway. I still haven't decided if I like Stephen or not. His smile seems a bit off, considering what has happened. I am still reeling from the fallout of the tragedy with the baby. It's heartbreaking.

"Okay, I suppose, under the circumstances," I reply, nodding towards the main house.

He looks down at the ground. "So sorry about what happened. Unfortunate you'd only just arrived. I mean, horrible. Simply horrible what happened. Celeste is beside herself."

I nod, standing there uneasily. And it freaks me out, too, that Violet passed away after I arrived. If I'd known what I was getting into... if I'd had a crystal ball I wouldn't have come. And I did have that premonition on the ferry after what that guy Eric said, didn't I? I can't *believe* she died only two days after I bloody arrived!

As tempting as it is to leave, I'd feel terrible abandoning this job when the family needs me more than ever. I only wish I felt up to it, wish I had more confidence about my abilities to deal with this kind of trauma. Plus, let's face it, I need the money. I *need* this job. I didn't fly across the pond to turn back and chicken out now. I'm not looking forward to staying here for another six weeks though. Mrs. Wainwright ("Call me Celeste," she said, when I met her) should be in the hospital, sedated. But she wants to stay here and is totally freaked out at the mention of any hospital. What do I know? I don't get a say in this, I'm only the temporary au pair. Mr. Wainwright thinks it will be more healing for Celeste to be here, but I think he's just pandering to her. He's obviously going along with whatever she wants to keep her happy. I feel terrible for her. Unequipped to help. In deep water, in more ways than one.

"You took me by surprise," I say to Stephen, realizing I'm clutching tightly onto my handbag. That's what comes of living in a city for too long. Taking the Tube to work. Waiting for the bus at dark. You get eyes in the back of your head. I must look like such a city girl in my makeup and vintage dress. I brought all the wrong clothes here. I need some wellies to navigate these rockpools, not strappy sandals. Even if it is summer.

Stephen steps closer. "Sorry, didn't mean to alarm you. I'm heading over to the main house. I have a session with Celeste in ten minutes." He smiles his Matt Damon Ripley smile again. "I guess this place must seem a little alien to you, the seas so rough, the wind up like this in the height of summer?"

"Yup. It does feel... I do feel a bit out of place. It's pretty remote here, that's for sure."

"Nice to meet you finally," Stephen says. "Celeste is so glad you're here."

"Yeah," I reply, feeling uneasy, and guilty for my fantasies of escaping this job, of letting the family down. "Which cottage is yours?" I add out of curiosity.

"The pale green one. You can't see it from here."

I'm balancing on a pointed rock. I steady myself so I don't slip. "Mine's that one, there. The blue one with the rowboat outside."

"Nice. Mine's, um, a bit more rustic than yours."

"I'd no idea we'd be so out in the sticks," I remark.

"Well, see you around," Stephen says, heading in the direction of the main house.

I survey the ocean, the jut of land. This place is in the middle of bloody nowhere. There's f-all to do. I'm only contracted to look after the kids for five hours a day, but how am I meant to occupy myself the rest of the time when there's nowhere to go? Nothing to do? One little shop/café. If you want anything else, you need to catch the ferry to the mainland. When it's running, that is. Don't get me wrong, it's beautiful here, very picture-postcard, but there's only so many novels I'll be able to read. Dodgy internet. Ice-cold water for swimming. Brrrrrr. I mean, I saw Stephen this morning wearing a wetsuit. That's how freezing the water is. You won't catch me in there.

The kids are all right. Those rascals speak their mind. Quite entertaining really. If you're in the mood. Which of course, nobody is, considering what happened to the baby. Lizzie looks like an angel. Long blond hair. Dollish blue eyes. Liam looks like his dad. Tall and skinny like his legs have been stretched. A thatch of dark hair. A wild look. Max is what Heathcliff might've looked like. In my mind, anyway. Max has got eyes you can fall into. Brooding. Quiet. Doesn't say much but makes you feel you need to respect him. Well, he is my boss. His sister's a snotty cow. Don't like her. Cold. Makes me feel like I'm a servant in an oh-so-subtle way. Which I'm not, thank you very much. But they're paying me really well so I need to stop the negative thoughts in my head and just get on with it and be as helpful and understanding as I can. I'm lucky to have a job at all for the summer, considering.

But a chill runs up my spine. Something is off with this weirdo setup. The baby dying so suddenly. Oh, and don't get me started on Nurse Sharpe. Gives Mrs. Danvers a run for her money, that woman does. She's in her mid-thirties, I'd say, but gives the impression of being older, not physically but because of her sour expression, her serious face, and especially the way she doesn't trust anyone around Celeste. A real jobsworth type of person, Sharpie is.

Something is definitely not right around here. And I'm not only talking about the baby dying, but everything surrounding the misfortune. The vibes I'm feeling, the oddball cast of characters, the place itself.

Something is scaring the living daylights out of me. Yet I still don't know what it is.

CELESTE

I don't think I've ever been so bursting with love as when I first started dating Max. Everybody tells you that your children are the ones you love more than anything in the world, and it's true, but it's a special kind of love. Passion is a different animal, you never get over something like first love, first unremitting passion. There are so many clichés, but they wind up being true: emotions, like your heart about to explode, feeling breathless, or your pulse beating faster. All of these things are true and overtake you completely. Nothing can prepare you for the love you feel when you fall for the first time. And that's what it is: falling, it is *falling* in love. There's no better word for it.

I'm thinking all this as I watch Max from the comfort of my bed. Lizzie and Liam are with the au pair, and I take this moment to absorb my husband, take him in, observe every small detail, every nuance that makes Max who he is. I see the back of him, his strong, handsome stance, as he gazes out of the window at the ocean, at the view. I don't know what's going on in his head, the thoughts he has. Maybe, how I've disappointed him, how I've not been the woman he wanted me to be, how the accident has changed me forever. I feel an overwhelming sadness that things have ended up this way. I want to reach out to him, *If only we could make it the way it was at the beginning, if only I could turn back time and stay in that oblivious little pocket forever, wouldn't that be nice?*

He turns and sees me staring at him, a tear rolling down my cheek.

"You're awake," he says.

"I was so in love with you, Max, I could hardly breathe. Do you remember that? How I could hardly speak, hardly remember to breathe?"

He nods. "Yes, I remember."

"What happened?" I ask, knowing the answer but wondering what he will say.

"You had a mental breakdown," he tells me, in the softest, calmest voice. "You drove your car into a lake with Lizzie strapped in the back and you..." He saunters toward the bed, his arms out, but it's then that Nurse Sharpe races into the room, shoving him out of the way with her bony elbows.

She claps her hands as if to ward him off. "It's time for your medication, Celeste."

"I was just..." Max says, and he goes to leave, taking his tall frame of a body with him as if collecting himself, as if he had momentarily forgotten who he was.

"It's all right, Max and I were reminiscing, having a romantic moment, weren't we, darling?"

But he has gone.

After Max is out of earshot, Alex barks at me. "Snap out of it!" She pours me a glass of water and readies my pills. "You look like you've seen a ghost."

"I have," I say, raising an old silver hand mirror to my face as I check my hair. "A ghost from the past."

THE DISAPPEARANCE

Now

Lizzie has been gone for almost two hours. There is a blood-curdling howl and it's mingling with the sheets of rain as it pelts against the windows. Celeste is raging through the house like a character in a Greek play, yelling, her eyes round with terror.

It is déjà-vu.

Her child is missing.

Lizzie is missing.

Celeste is soaked through, holding a teddy in one hand. "Where is she? Where is Lizzie?"

The nurse holds Celeste by the shoulders, trying to calm her down. "She's gone," she confirms. "It's now in the hands of the police."

How long Celeste was outside, nobody can be sure. She is wearing rubber boots. Her legs are dripping with seawater, an old jacket hangs off her shoulders. Underneath the jacket, her nightie is drenched. It's a wonder anyone could navigate their way around outside in the dark, only illuminated with intermittent slashes of lightning, while the ocean groans and tumbles its merciless surf against the jagged, ragged rocks.

Max is away. Where is Marjorie—how can she sleep through this? Celeste sweeps through the house, inspecting the rooms, throwing open doors, even closets. Lizzie's bed is empty. Celeste wants to scream at Marjorie, *It's all your fault. What have you done, what have you done?*

But then she remembers. Marjorie is not here. She is with Max on the mainland.

Celeste can only look inside herself for answers.

DR. STEPHEN

Four days ago

This morning I found the thing I have been searching for, for years. You see, one of the main reasons I took this job is because of the sea cave. This secret is something I don't think many people know about. Not even the islanders. There was a *National Geographic* photographer a decade back who was also hell-bent on finding it, but he seemed to disappear and never return here. I can't even remember his name. Anyway, proof that it wasn't just me who was obsessed with discovering it. This sea cave was a legend that nestled somewhere in the back of my mind for years. And legends can be based on truth. It had been haunting me all my life, this particular cave. The story goes it was used by smugglers who stashed their booty there, a couple of centuries back, after ships were wrecked on these ragged rocks of Cliff Island. The islanders used to play a cruel trick, waving lanterns in dangerous places so the oncoming ships thought they had a safe landing, when the opposite was true. Many a ship was wrecked in those days, crashing against the rocks, spilling their wares, not to mention their vulnerable crew.

The lantern-wavers would then pick through the dead and wounded and the wreckage, collecting the valuable cargo—sometimes treasure, sometimes spices. Is this true? I really don't know. I know it was true on the Cornish coast in England and in many other places in the world. Did it happen in Maine? Perhaps.

Anyway, they spoke of a sea cave here on Cliff Island and I found it this morning on one of my long swims. You have to swim for about ten feet underwater and then you come up into an opening the size of a small chapel. You can't do it when it's rough, of course, it's too dangerous, you could get trapped in there. I packed a dry-bag with a couple of powerful flashlights, strapping the bag to my body so my arms were free to swim and hold the underwater flashlight I needed to find the opening. Once inside, I discovered the cave rising up before me, the water knee-high at first, the ground steadily rising until you reach a sort of shore and then the higher part of the cave, which is dry. You could stash anything there.

Needless to say, I didn't find any treasure, but the sea cave itself *is* treasure. I felt like a small boy again on excursions with my dad. The adrenaline rushed through me and I yelped for joy, knowing that not a single soul could hear my cries. It was exhilarating. I didn't stay long but I'll be back again tomorrow.

Then, on my way over to the main house, I briefly chatted with the new au pair, Jayne. Poor thing looked so out of her depth. So young, so fresh-faced and foreign, dare I say it, with a look of panic in her naive blue eyes. I wanted to make her feel at ease, but I think I made her more nervous. There'll be time enough to get to know her.

And here I am now with my patient, Celeste.

I find Celeste eating lunch in the dining room but still in her robe. She looks pale, yes, but polished, clean, her eyes bright. Not the wreck of a woman I saw yesterday. She turns and smiles at me and scoops a mouthful of boiled egg into her cherry-red lips. My God, is she wearing lipstick? This is not the same woman I observed yesterday screeching like a banshee, clawing her nails against her scalp, screaming that she wanted to kill herself and everyone in the house with her, after she discovered her baby had died.

As I walk in through the door, she locks her eyes on me and tips me an innocent smile. As they say, *pure as the driven snow*.

"Celeste, you're looking very well rested," I say.

"I slept like a baby lamb." She grins at me and dips one of the toasted soldiers into her soft-boiled egg.

"You're feeling much better than yesterday?" I say uneasily.

"Yesterday?"

"Yesterday you were in a terrible state about the baby." I say the word "baby" with trepidation, unsure of what's about to unfold.

"Baby?"

"Violet," I offer.

"Such pretty flowers, violets are," she replies, as if she is touched with the madness of Shakespeare's Ophelia, and it dawns on me she doesn't remember a thing.

And then she comes out with, "I was thinking of going for a swim today, Stephen. Is the water warm?"

"I think perhaps you'd better stay home and rest," I suggest, pulling out a chair and sitting down at the table. Marjorie is clanking around in the kitchen next door, washing up pans or something. The nurse is nowhere to be seen. "Celeste, you don't remember what happened?"

"Of course I do," she says. "I had a car crash."

"Yes." I am relieved she remembers because she's never going to get better if she can't piece together the events of last month. "Yes, you did have an accident, you had a terrible, terrible car crash and were in the hospital, and you gave birth against all odds. You survived, and your baby survived."

"What a thought." She gives out a trilling laugh. "I've got

quite enough to deal with, with two rowdy children. I've never wanted a third child. Ask Max, he'll tell you."

"Your scar," I say. "Below your stomach."

She fumbles her fingers through her negligee and underneath her robe, and I am momentarily embarrassed that she isn't dressed yet. I'm sitting so close to her it feels far too intimate for my liking. She's my patient.

"Yes, I have a scar, true, although I don't think that's any of your business. I had my appendix out, must've been about twelve. That's the scar you're talking about, isn't it? You saw it when I was swimming? Although, quite frankly, I think that's rather personal, isn't it, Stephen... pointing out a lady's scar." But she's smiling, almost flirtatious.

I sigh. This situation is impossible. One minute she remembers something and the next she's quite forgotten, and I have no idea how I'm meant to deal with this. I'm a regular therapist, not Freud or Jung or some hot-shot New Yorker who charges five hundred dollars an hour.

"Would you like some breakfast, Stephen?" Then she shouts toward the kitchen, "Marjorie, is there any toast left? Stephen's here and I'm sure he's hungry—would you mind bringing out some coffee?"

But Marjorie carries on clanking around in the kitchen as if she hasn't heard. Celeste is in a sort of Blanche DuBois mood, all coquetry and smiles and lady of the manor.

"It's fine," I tell her. I've already had breakfast, and no more coffee for me today. I like to stick to one cup, very early. It's not good to drink too much caffeine.

"All that swimming, Stephen, you must get hungry though. How about some fried eggs and bacon?"

"No," I tell her, trying to make my tone stern. "I'm here for a session and I'm here to work."

"I'm sorry I feel like 'work' to you, I thought we were friends." She gives me a faux pout.

"We are. But that doesn't mean we can't work through stuff."

"Stuff?" Her eyes hold mine with what feels like a challenge, and for a second I see a glint of menace in her pale blue eyes. But then she smiles.

"Your mental health," I clarify.

"But I'm perfectly fine. I don't need any help. It's always wonderful to have a chat with you, but really, I'm absolutely fine. As I was saying, I thought I'd have a swim, take the children out. It's their sailing lesson today, did you know that? You're never too young to start learning how to sail, are you?"

"I don't know, I'm not a sailor."

"Well, I started to sail when I was a tiny thing, and I want the children to be proficient and have confidence. Who knows? Maybe Lizzie will sail around the world one day. Anything is possible if you give kids hope and courage, don't you think? Give them special attention?"

Again, that barb in her voice, which she covers up with a smile. It's as if she's quietly accusing me of something. And, for the first time, I fear what she might know.

About me.

CELESTE

I watch Stephen as he slopes out of the dining room, and I'm relieved he's gone. I don't know how much more of this I can take.

"What are you doing up like this?" It's Alex, bursting into the room from seemingly nowhere. She's dressed in her nurse's uniform. Nurse Ratched comes to mind.

"Ever heard of knocking, Alex?" I say in an easy drawl. Today I'm feeling more chipper, or at least I was until now. Her scowl tells me her mission is not complete. She has a job to do, and her job is me and everything that concerns me.

Her white Crocs squeak on the wooden floorboards, an assault to my ears. "Don't. Don't," she instructs, "don't call me by my first name, please."

I let out a titter. Her pursed lips amuse me no end. "Oh, come on, aren't you going overboard with this formality, Ms. Sharpe?"

"You know the rules."

"*Nurse Sharpe,*" I repeat, and I want to roar with mirth this time. It's an absurd name because it's so fitting for her, especially as she looks now in her fussy uniform, that silly hat she wears, the impossibly thick, flesh-colored pantyhose that are designed to keep varicose veins and thrombosis at bay. I shouldn't jeer and joke, but it's true that Alex's pointed name suits her. The infamous character Becky Sharp, of Thackeray's *Vanity Fair*, was, apparently, going to be called Becky Frost but the author decided Sharp was better. I think of this as I regard Alex—Ms. (not Miss or Mrs. but *Ms.*) Sharpe, with an E.

"You need your rest," she instructs, and I dutifully get up from my chair and glide back to my bedroom and slip into bed. I really don't know why I have to be "the invalid" since I feel perfectly well. This whole fiasco seems crazy. But this is what I have to work with and I need to accept the status quo. But then a wave of doubt washes over me and I have a sudden urge to burst into tears—that all-too-familiar wondering *What exactly is going on*, wondering where Max is and what Marjorie is up to, and asking myself why they hired Stephen, in particular, and what, if anything, he is hiding, because there is a shiftiness about him I don't like. And why am I even here? *What am I doing here? In this house!*

Alex is fluffing up my pillows, straightening the sheets around me. "Do I need to remind you, you nearly died? Do I need to remind you that death is circling you like a pack of wolves? If you don't follow my instructions and do as I say and stop behaving like an unruly child, things could get completely out of hand. Things could go horribly wrong."

Tears smart my eyes as I shimmy down into the bed and bring the sheet over myself, feeling weak again, confused, powerless. My good mood of earlier shifts into a morose, dejected desperation. Things are coming to me in snapshots, things I would rather not remember.

"Marjorie," I complain, "I don't—"

"I don't want to hear it! I don't want to hear about Marjorie," she hisses at me, finishing whatever sentence was on my lips, which not even I myself am sure of. What was it I wanted to say? Alex has a habit of cutting into my thoughts, into my insecurities. She finishes, "I would keep all your dangerous thought processes to your*self*. Damn, can't you be trusted at all?"

Alex, arranging the mosquito net around me and peering through the muslin, her eyes like dry pebbles glaring through the gauze, goes on: "You need to be *nice* to Marjorie. She's running around, helping out with your business. You need to *remember*." She punches at the word "remember" as if I could suddenly wave a magic wand and pretend everything was normal.

"It's so difficult, how can you not understand that?" I protest, fluttering my eyes closed, willing sleep, because quite honestly what else *is* there to numb my mental anguish? My mind is like a dark, long corridor, doors reaching into myriad rooms, all of them offering nefarious possibilities. At least sleep can make me forget.

"Of course I understand," she murmurs through the netting. "But you need to snap out of it. Remember why you're here. Remember what happened. God knows what you might get up to if I weren't here to keep an eye on you. Who knows what you'd do next!"

"Maybe I don't *want* to remember," I nip back, my eyes flying open as I try to snuff out a burst of images: the car sailing into the air in slow motion, the seat belt too tight for my belly, the screams from Lizzie, strapped into her child seat in the back. The sound of the wind as the vehicle sliced through the air. "Maybe this is all too much for me, lying in bed like an invalid, when I need to know that Violet—" I slip my hand through the netting, clutching at my nurse's wrist. I pull her closer—"I need to know what happened. Was she... is she—"

"Shut *up*!"

Marjorie suddenly appears, standing stock-still at the doorway of the bedroom, caught midway, one leg placed gingerly in front of the other as if she's not sure whether to come in or slip back out in reverse. I wonder what she has heard, if she was witness to Alex's verbal attack on me. "Sorry, am I interrupting something? Can I get you anything?" she offers in a sweet voice. She is so like Max in her behavior it's uncanny. But she looks uneasy, as if she shouldn't be here, as if she doesn't feel she belongs.

Alex marshals herself into action, fussing with various vials, pouring out a large glass of water for me, then replies in her efficient, knife-cutting tone: "I'm going to give Mrs. Wainwright her medication now. She needs to rest."

"Thank you for everything you're doing," Marjorie answers. "I'm going to meet Max on the mainland. Is there anything I can bring back? Anything you all need?" Her deep brown eyes search our faces. She gives me a small smile. Sweet, helpful. I wonder what is going through her mind, seeing me here so helpless in my bed, and I'm curious as to how she feels taking over my business.

I shake my head.

"No," Alex says. "Thank you for asking. I have everything under control here."

I eye up my window, surreptitiously... exercising my peripheral vision. I'm plotting in my head how I'm going to climb out of it and go swimming. Join Liam and Lizzie for their sailing lesson. Nobody is going to stop me, whatever the consequences.

I need to see the children. I need to see them in the flesh. Make sure they're real, make sure they're still alive.

DR. STEPHEN

Three days ago

I meet Max at the midday mailboat ferry, to give him a hand. He has been buying provisions in Portland, along with Marjorie. It's nice those siblings are so close. I always wanted a sister, always dreamed of having someone I could share my secrets with. Being an only child was a burden, not a blessing. I had to entertain myself. Max and Marjorie seem to have an easy, chatty relationship. With their dark brown eyes and dark glossy hair, they really look like they came from the same pod. It's very kind of Marjorie to have come to the island to help out. She left her house and her life behind in California. I guess some family members are very close to each other and really step up to the plate when it comes to it. I wish I'd had that kind of family. I wish I had a real family.

We load up the golf cart with various boxes, food probably, and treats for Celeste. Last time Max bought her a beautiful bicycle with bells and whistles and a lovely wicker basket in the front, painted sky blue. He'd put a child seat on the back for Lizzie.

"How was the trip?" I ask Max.

"Oh, you know, got lots of boring stuff done. Lawyer's meetings, shopping, business, those kind of things."

I still haven't had the gall to ask Max exactly what he does. You know when you're meant to know? When you've already been through the details of what somebody does and then you forget because their job is… well, rather boring. Something to do with commodities. He appears to have a lot of meetings anyway.

Max wipes some sweat from his brow, fixes his gaze on me. "How's the patient doing?"

"She's, well…" I'm about to tell him about the scene I witnessed yesterday, after I left breakfast, after I thought she had gone back to bed, but I stop myself. Max is the one I should feel allegiance to, he's the one who's paying my wage, but I can't divulge Celeste's secrets, I'd feel like I'd betrayed her confidence, so I say, "Good. Better, I think."

I feel so bad for poor Celeste. Yesterday I spotted her staggering around on the beach, waving frantically at the children. And then she plunged into the water in her negligee, wading out to join them as they were taking a sailing lesson with their instructor. Her joy was evident as she splashed toward them, the fabric of her nightie trailing like silky fins, like she was some kind of mermaid. She looked so beautiful, I thought, so ethereal. But along came Alex Sharpe and broke up the party. Not just Celeste, but the lesson too. I have no idea what's going on, and I'm going to keep my mouth shut, but was it a case of *When the cat's away the mice will play?* Does Max know about these sailing lessons she arranges for the children? Lizzie is only four. Can Lizzie even swim? The water was far too rough for sailing yesterday, for a child at least. The kid could drown, couldn't she? I mean, good Lord, Celeste drove them into a lake. What *is* it with Celeste and water? You'd think she'd be fearful after what happened. Does she have a death wish? The children's little dinghies were dragged ashore by the instructor. Lizzie was crying, the instructor carrying her in his arms. Max would have a fit if he knew what had been going on behind his back. But I'd feel terrible spilling the beans. Surely this won't happen again, though. Isn't that what the au pair is for?

Come to think of it, I didn't see Jayne at all yesterday. That's right, it was her day off. Which reminds me. I owe her an answer to a question she asked me.

I turn back to Max. "Do you need a hand unloading this at the house?"

"No, it's fine, thanks for the offer."

He and Marjorie jump into the golf cart, and I head off on foot toward my cottage.

There's a dark bubble of cloud on the horizon.

A storm is brewing.

JAYNE

Three days have passed since Violet died. I feel useless, ineffective. What can you say to a person who has lost her baby? How can you, even in the most empathetic part of your imagination, know what it's like for them, feel what they feel? Still, I have to give it a try.

Yesterday was my free day. I forced myself to switch off by reading an entire novel in one sitting. I was unaware until this morning of yesterday's shenanigans until I went to collect the children at seven, when everyone but Sharpie was asleep, or at least quiet in their rooms. The nurse handed the children over to me, instructing me in her stern manner to "take them away," to give them breakfast at my cottage and not to listen to "their nonsense stories." Of course that piqued my curiosity so as soon as we were out of earshot I asked them what they had done yesterday. They regaled me with stories about sailboats and how their pirate friend was teaching them how to sail. And how their mummy was swimming in her nightie and how fun it all was until nasty "Nurse Sharpener," as Lizzie calls her, took their mum away. I had no idea what was fantasy and what was the truth. I'd been so engrossed in my novel I didn't even look out the window all day. Did I miss something? I now regret my actions. I should have been around. But I did so need that time off to catch up with sleep and relax. I still have a bit of jet lag and I needed time off to recharge my batteries. Looking after young kids is harder and more draining than most people realize. Nobody understands how hard stay-at-home mums work, but for a nanny or au pair it's even worse. You have that extra worry of knowing they are not your kids, that if anything bad happens it's all your fault. Mums are allowed to fail here and there, but us lot? We have to be damn near perfect or we'll get fired—or worse, not trusted. There's nothing worse than your employer not trusting you, eyeballing you and watching your every move. And here? Next to an *ocean*, with little ones? It's full-on stress, the kind of creeping stress you aren't even aware of in the moment, but which hits you later when you get a chance to be alone, a chance to wind down from a busy day.

I still haven't actually seen or spoken to Celeste since my brief introduction after my arrival. Every time I go over to the main house, she is "resting," as Sharpie likes to say. But I'm determined to make my way over now to offer my condolences. See if there's anything I can do beyond what I'm being paid to do: look after Lizzie and Liam.

Luckily, I don't cross paths with Sharpie as I enter the house. The door, as usual, is unlocked, just latched. They don't believe in locking doors around here. Everything is open all the time, even at night. The house seems to be empty.

I approach Celeste's room tentatively and peer through the doorway, hovering there. She's in bed, all in white. Everything is white. A gauzy mosquito net is draped over the bed making Celeste seem even more ghostly and pale than she already is. "Celestial," if I'm to play on words. She's thin, I would say scrawny almost, her hair disheveled, crescent moons under her eyes. She looks tired, depleted, and my heart goes out to the poor thing. I stand there awkwardly in the doorway, not knowing what to say. She's worrying her fingers together as if she's knitting or sewing or doing something, staring into space. If I were in her shoes I'd want my kids right there in the bed with me after what happened with the baby.

I'm holding Liam's hand and Lizzie's hand, standing in the middle of my two kids. And that's how I feel about them now: my two kids. It's only been a few days, but they need me so much, and I feel like I'm all they've got right now... because their mum seems too distraught to deal with them, and if it's true about yesterday—her running around on the beach, swimming in her nightclothes—too crazed to be trusted.

I hear voices: Max talking in the other room, seemingly on an important business call. Marjorie, his sister, spots me, but this time she's polite. Hovering around in the corridor, awkwardly, she asks me if I'd like a cool drink, offering to make some fresh lemonade. It's hot outside, and inside too, because this family doesn't believe in air conditioning. It's old-school money: posh, but not wasteful. This place has been in the family for generations, Max told me. Maybe they are what the Americans refer to as a "blue-blood" family. The lot that came over on the *Mayflower*.

Celeste's eyes finally meet mine and she gives me a wan smile. "Jayne, oh look what you've got! Hello, my darlings, come closer to Mommy."

We approach the bed. Celeste's hands fumble through the mosquito net and she clings onto Liam's sweaty little hand. There are tears in her eyes.

"Mommy, Mommy, we've been in the rock pools, we've been paddling."

"Not too deep, you know the rules." But she's smiling with pride and love for her kids.

"It was fun," Lizzie squeals. And she slips under the mosquito net and hugs her mother around the waist, sheets between them, Lizzie pressing her head into her mum's tiny frame. It's amazing Celeste gave birth to a child, she's so thin. Her gauzy nightie, pale pearl, is a paper film between her and her daughter.

She winces. "Be careful, honey, that hurts Mommy. Better go and play now. Jayne, would you mind taking them off for some fun adventure?"

"Of course," I say, trying not to sound sad. "They've had some snacks and I took them for a dip. What should I do now, take them on a walk?"

"How about playing a board game or something?" Her tone sounds a tad sarcastic.

I nod, wishing I hadn't asked even that simple question about what to do with the kids. It was purely to make conversation. It's my job to take the stress away from the parents, to entertain the children.

Celeste sighs. "I don't know, *you* think of something. I'm so tired, my head feels, I can't..." Tears roll down her face.

"It's all right," I tell her, "I've got this." I like that expression, *I've got this*. Or, as they say, *I got this*. It's very American, but it makes me feel like I'm in control and that somehow everything is going to end up all right. I wrench the kids away, telling them in an excited voice that we're going to play I-spy. Lizzie looks bewildered, glancing ruefully at her mum as she leaves the room. She doesn't cry or anything, but I can see her lips are trembling... she wants to cry but doesn't dare, as if grownups have warned her never to cry. Lizzie has so much self-control for such a little girl. When I'm out of Celeste's sight I give both kids a big bear hug.

This whole setup makes me feel like I'm in another era, not this century at all, like it's sixty years ago or more, maybe even before the Second World War, in the days when children were to be seen and not heard and when nannies knew the kids better than the kids' own parents.

I steal a glance behind me before I exit the bedroom.

Celeste is clutching her head, staring into space again, and I think, *Yes she's disturbed, she's not all quite there.* I feel so bad I don't know what to do. I want to help her. I want to reach out and give her a hug, make her feel like everything's going to be all right, but I hardly know her. So all I can manage is what I'm being paid to do: cope with the kids as best I can and try and make them feel loved and that they have a safe haven with me.

All day long while playing with the children, I mull over the Wainwright setup. I can't put my finger on why things seem odd, beyond the loss of baby Violet. Then there's gorgeous Max to factor in (ha! that pun was unintended). It's always odd, isn't it, when you see a couple that seems ill-matched? I gather that Celeste has been struggling with mental illness for a while, even before that terrible car crash. I feel rotten saying this, really crap in fact, but it's what I'm thinking inside: Why did he marry her in the first place? She's distant, standoffish, and he's the one with the money... I shouldn't entertain these thoughts, but I do, I can't help myself.

Envious much?

I know poor Celeste has lost her mind a bit and is suffering from bouts of amnesia, but how can she not be interested in spending more time with her children? It goes deeper than depression and the aftershock from the accident, in my humble, unprofessional opinion. Am I being judgmental? Probably. Most likely I'm being really unfair. Max is such an amazing husband from what I've seen. Brings her meals in bed. Flowers. He reads her the paper every day, sits beside her bed. I mean, he's really attentive and kind and caring. Maybe Celeste has always been like this, sort of broken, and he feels like he can fix her. Men love women they can fix, don't they? I'm already fixed, so, sadly, no man ever gives me that *darling-let-me-do-things-for-you* vibe. Not me. I'm *capable*. Strong. At least, I appear that way to others. Big girls like me never look like they need fixing or helping. *We* are the helpers, the listeners, the sort-the-shitouters. We look like we can handle anything, and I suppose we can. When you get teased in school for years on end, and treated like shit by your own kin, you learn to build up a tough shell. You learn to look after yourself.

"What are you making?" It's Lizzie, catching me in my thoughts, glancing up from her coloring book.

I'm standing in my cottage kitchen. The kids are sprawled out on the rug, loving the casualness of my setup.

I've got Liam coloring too, something he's obviously not used to, since he's letting the crayons stray miles outside the black lines. He's scribbling, but Lizzie, though two years younger, is coloring neatly, carefully choosing each crayon with precision. Funny how something like coloring can give you so many clues about a child's personality. I can tell Liam has problems with concentration, moving on to the next thing before he's finished the last.

"Yeah," Liam chimes in, "what are you making?"

"Toast," I tell them.

Liam's eyes get round. "Cinnamon toast?"

"No, toast with butter and Marmite."

"What's mite?" Lizzie asks, crayon-fingers in her mouth.

"It's a disgusting spread you kids wouldn't like. I'm giving you peanut butter and jam instead."

"Jam?"

"Jelly. Peanut butter and jelly."

"I want mite," Lizzie cries out, insulted.

"No, you don't. It's brown and yucky and salty and nasty. Only the British like Marmite."

"I can be bittish."

"I might like it," Liam shouts.

"Guaranteed you won't," I assure them with a wink, layering on the butter as I watch it melt into the hot, wholemeal toast. I spread the Marmite more thickly than I should and take a bite; the saltiness gives my tastebuds a kick and makes me momentarily homesick. The truth is I don't want to share my Marmite with anyone. I brought it specially in my suitcase from home. It needs to last the summer. "You're getting strawberry jam," I tell Liam firmly. "Jelly, I mean. Homemade strawberry jelly from that nice old lady at the other side of the island."

"Yummy." Lizzie smacks her lips.

It's cozy in my cottage. This way I have more freedom to do what I like with the children without feeling watched. Coloring is great because they can stay peaceful and quiet. There's no TV here. It's against the Wainwrights' principles to let the kids watch television. No iPads or tablets either. We hardly ever have a connection anyway. It's going to be really hard work for me. But that's okay, at least it'll keep me properly focused on the children. And it will stop me checking my Facebook and Instagram every three minutes, or my email, in hope of that elusive message from my ex begging forgiveness and groveling for any crumb of affection from me... *Dream on, Jayne.*

Before I came here I made up my mind I was going to focus on my job, forget my demons from the past, and lose ten pounds. Fat chance. Fat being the operative word. Although we're not supposed to use that word these days, are we? Not very PC. Even if I'm referring to myself. Fat is a bit of an F-word.

I can't do everything at once, I don't have that kind of willpower. I take another bite of toast and let the butter sit on my tongue before it trickles down my throat. It's like religion to me, butter is. I could never give it up, however hard I try. However "wrong" it might be.

"Mommy makes cinnamon toast," Liam yells at me wildly, his arm dashing across his coloring book. He's moving on to felt pens now. Uh-oh. That was a mistake, giving them those.

I was about to say, "I'll look that up," but realize I can't. No internet. "How do you make cinnamon toast?" I ask.

"Cinnamon," he says, like I'm a dunce.

"What else? Sugar? Butter?"

He nods. "I guess. It tastes soooo good!"

"Yummy," Lizzie agrees.

The next round of toast pings out of the toaster, and I spread it with butter and peanut butter and strawberry jam on top. I know what these American kids like, I've done my research. Besides, peanuts have got loads of protein. Even more protein than steak. My ex used to laugh at that. *Bullshit,* he'd say. Look it up, I'd tell him. It's true, peanuts have more protein than steak. That was when I was trying to be vegetarian. I've tried every diet and food combination in the book.

We all sit at the kitchen table and I serve the kids their toast. And orange juice. I'm drinking tea. PG Tips. Another thing I brought with me. I make Liam sit up straight, no slouching under my care. No talking with their mouths full. No interrupting when someone is talking, wait your turn to speak. No ear-piercing squeals. Well, that's turning out to be a challenge. We talk about their favorite books, and I make a note of their passions and what I'll read them at bedtime. Lizzie's into unicorns, Liam dinosaurs. I treat them like little grownups and never do baby talk. I listen to them, really listen, and I know they appreciate that.

"So what's your favorite—"

"Blue!" Lizzie shouts.

"I wasn't going to ask you about your favorite color, I was—"

"Dog!" she interrupts.

I giggle at her wild enthusiasm. "I wasn't going to ask you that either. I was going to ask what your—"

"Vegetable!" she hollers.

"How did you know?"

"I'm smart," she says. "Mommy says I'm super smart. I'm a teacher. I have a school for my dolls and teddies."

"Not as smart as me, smarty pants," Liam cuts in, and grins with a mouthful of toast.

"Who's your favorite parent?" I ask the children with a sidelong glance, trying to make my evil question seem casual, and overlooking Liam's bad table manners. "Your mom or your dad?" My tongue's done its own wayward thing, veering into dangerous waters. I try to rein my awful, nosy words in, so no more wickedness spouts from my mouth.

"Daddy!" Liam blurts out.

"Well, you do look just like him," I say.

Poor Lizzie looks confused. She takes a bite of toast and doesn't answer, suddenly subdued. A wave of guilt whooshes over me.

I know my nanny skills leave a lot to be desired, but children always end up liking me, and I've got great references. I can't resist asking questions here and there to get a foothold, if you like, into the family secrets and dynamics.

I can't help it... it's my curious nature.

I'm dying to ask Lizzie about the accident, but that's going too far. I want to know what she remembers exactly, what happened, but that would be cruel, wouldn't it, to put a little girl in that position? So I keep my mouth shut. Well, not shut—I stuff it with more toast.

Maybe she'll give me a clue at some point, or maybe Liam will. Liam was not in the car, which makes me believe it *was* an accident, after all. Celeste would have either killed the whole lot of them or been on her own. What kind of person would do that? Put her own children at risk when the kids have such a lovely, caring dad who'd be more than happy to give them a perfect life? No money worries, that's for sure. No debts. No work problems, it seems. No third-party love affairs. But then depression doesn't always make sense. There's not a lot of logic behind it, or at least not to outsiders. When you're in it, depression's a dark, unforgiving place. Depression's hands wrap around all of our throats at some point in our lives. The trick is to kick him in the goolies and somehow slip from his grasp before it's too late.

I worry about the kids, about Celeste being so unstable. I wonder what the real story is. I'm certain there's more. I'll get the scoop out of Dr. Stephen, that's the best idea. It feels like everyone's harboring secrets around here, like anything anyone says or does has a double meaning.

Like secrets are festering.

I've such an urge to dig them up.

THE DISAPPEARANCE

Now

It is now several hours since Lizzie was last seen on the island. Nobody can be sure how much time has passed before they spot the rescue helicopter. There are only a few people who hear the noise of the chopper or see its lights. Some are outside in the storm, wondering what to do as the waves crash against their moored boats, panicked the vessels will be swept out to sea. Others are checking for trees smashing down on their roofs. There is confusion. Nobody looks at their watches or checks the time on their phone. Why would they? It is not a wristwatch kind of place, Cliff Island, especially in the summer months. People come here to switch off, to relax, to disengage from their jobs, the relentlessly depressing world news, from social media. This vagueness of the hour of what happened and when, and at what time little Lizzie disappeared is something that will flummox the police in the days to come. There is a ferocious downpour and people fear another hurricane could be brewing, maybe as bad as Hurricane Bob, three decades ago, which the older residents have never forgotten. Nobody can be expected to remember details of the hour of what they saw or when. They are watching this storm, not the time.

As the powerful rain roars ashore, trees perilously swaying with the forceful wind, there are no rescue boats out there, at least not for now. The helicopter circles the raging ocean, its lights dipping in and out between the heavy fog and sheets of rain, before it lands at the other side of the island, out of anyone's view. The coast guard? The police? Even a sturdy helicopter seems dangerous with this unpredictable weather. And then the mist, still lingering in the atmosphere, makes the hunt for whomever must be in peril all the harder. And the wind rushing by people's ears is so loud the sound of the chopper's blade mutes. Somebody must have called the police? Who?

Later—how much time passes nobody can be sure—it is evident that a search and rescue is in full force. It is a miracle, with these poor weather and sea conditions, that the helicopter is here at all. What feels like a century later, the helicopter is back, its high beam lasering down on the water. A helicopter at night means only one thing: somebody has been washed out to sea.

It is serendipity that Detective Adele Alba was already in the air—just finishing up a burglary on the mainland—when they radioed in, and she is able to get to the island, to be on the scene so quickly. A child is missing; there is no time to lose. The first forty-eight hours are critical, before people's memories start to fade about what they have seen or heard. Even the tiniest, seemingly insignificant detail can lead to success. When a child is missing, nothing in the world matters more, not only for the family involved but for Detective Alba personally.

But for now, she does not have the resources to interview each and every islander. The first priority is to find Lizzie Wainwright. The severe weather adds urgency to the tracking mission. The child was last seen in her nightclothes. White cotton pajamas with a pink and yellow unicorn print. The detective has already called for backup and extra resources. Right now, it is only the detective, the pilot, and her partner, Carl. She is hoping Dune, one of Maine State Police's top K-9s, will be dispatched with his handler, George. This smell-sensitive, dual-purpose trailing dog is both a cadaver dog and a tracker, which means he can sniff out human remains, even fifteen feet under water, and track the trail of a victim or a perp. These dual-trained dogs are rare. In the past, Dune has found missing children, lost hikers, and Alzheimer's sufferers.

Alba is also hoping that *Impact*, their thirty-one-foot, high-performance vessel, which can reach speeds of sixty miles per hour, is on its way. Her department needs to throw everything they can into this search and rescue situation. But she and her partner need to get on with the job at hand without waiting for the others. It is a well-known fact the chances of finding a missing child deteriorate tenfold if you're not successful within the first seventy-two hours, so she is working against the clock. They had no luck in the air, no body swept out to sea that they could see from above. Now it's time to search the island itself.

The detective's first stop is the Wainwrights' home. From the GPS on her phone, she locates it pretty quickly. She finds Ms. Sharpe there, flashes the woman her badge, and they briefly introduce themselves to each other. Alex Sharpe explains she is Celeste Wainwright's private nurse, and fills her in on Celeste's recent, near-fatal car crash and how she is suffering from lapses of amnesia, and how Alex's job is to watch her patient, administer her medication, and to make sure she gets plenty of rest. The nurse gives a lowdown of the events of the evening. That Lizzie had been put to bed, and Celeste had read her a bedtime story, and neither of them had heard a peep from her since. When Celeste went to check, later, Lizzie wasn't there. The nurse tells Alba that Celeste is still out in the storm, trying to find her child. That, no, they did not hear anyone enter or leave the house. The door was not locked but latched, the latch too high for a child to reach.

Detective Alba searches the house: every closet, every room. Even the little boy's bedroom, where he is sleeping soundly. She gently opens the door, which brushes against the shush of the wall-to-wall carpet, and she uses her flashlight to look under the bed, careful not to rouse him. He groans but does not wake up. Alba closes the door softly behind her.

She cannot rule out the possibility that the child is right here in the house. Dead or alive. Unless she finds Lizzie herself, there will be no conclusive evidence until the K-9 arrives and the forensic team get here. If nothing comes of her search, the forensic team will dust for fingerprints, take those from anyone living or frequenting this house, search for strange footprints, wheel marks, cigarette butts, candy wrappers—anything and everything that might give them clues to what has happened to Lizzie.

Alex Sharpe waits for her on the upstairs landing. "I told you," she hisses in a whisper, "Lizzie's not here. Shouldn't you be looking outside?"

"That's the next step," the detective says in a calm, even tone. "But you'd be surprised how many children are found right in their homes, in the house itself, fallen asleep in some closet, or in the basement, or... well, just about anywhere. I'm sorry, ma'am, but we have to cover all bases. Is it possible someone came into the house and led Lizzie away?"

"I suppose anything is *possible*, but we didn't hear anything and one of us would have, surely?" The nurse's voice trembles, and she looks as if she feels responsible, guilty for her actions. But that's the way any woman would feel, the detective thinks, about a young child, a child who has gone missing under their nose. In the detective's mind, Ms. Sharpe is already a suspect as well as a witness. And the mother, too. Everyone is guilty until proven innocent. It seems to work that way with missing children, in her mind anyway. She has seen too much. Lived through so much of the shit that humans are capable of, parents and family members included.

Alba asks for a recent photo of Lizzie. "You can send it by text, or email, or airdrop it if you have an iPhone, and I can pass it on to headquarters, share it around with my team." She gives Alex Sharpe her card and points to her phone number, her email address.

The woman hovers midway on the staircase, dumbstruck, a look of hopelessness in her beady brown eyes. "I don't know if I have any photos. I'm just the nurse."

"Take a look, you never know," Alba tells her. Meanwhile, the detective takes a snapshot of a couple of framed photos on the wall, halfway up the stairs, careful to make sure the light of the glass isn't reflecting. In one, Lizzie is smiling, in another, she's staring into the lens, a look of surprise on her face. For now, these will do.

While the nurse is scrolling through her phone, Alba asks, "The parents are together, right? No acrimonious divorce or fight for child custody, or possible parental kidnapping I should know about?"

"Mr. Wainwright's away on business. He would have been back tonight but for the storm."

"The Wainwrights live together?"

"Right here under this roof!"

Alba nods. She was once caught out on that one, a long time ago, when she was a rookie, and it turned out to be more than embarrassing. Her first major blunder in a case. That is why she was reassigned to investigating burglaries and thefts, which her superiors deemed more suitable for her and which is her field of expertise. She is winging it. Missing children are a whole other ball game for her. This feels personal, crucial. Although robberies can mean life or death, they are not the same as this.

She continues, unfazed by Alex Sharpe's frustration at

things not moving along faster. "Have you seen anyone strange hanging around lately, anything unusual in the last few days?"

"No, nothing at all, we know everybody around here. It's so safe. There are hardly any tourists this summer. Only neighbors."

Detective Alba makes a mental note. She noticed a cluster of locals out by the store. "What time did Mrs. Wainwright realize her daughter was missing?"

"She went to turn out Lizzie's nightlight at around ten and Lizzie wasn't there."

"Had her bed been slept in?"

The nurse looks up from scrolling through her photos. "Definitely. Like I said, Mrs. Wainwright read her a story, earlier."

"What time?"

"Like around quarter to nine, nine."

"And what time did Mrs. Wainwright leave Lizzie's room?"

"Around nine thirty, I believe. She likes to lie down with Lizzie till she goes to sleep."

"When she called 9-1-1, she said Lizzie was wearing unicorn print pajamas. Does that sound right to you? Can you remember what Lizzie was wearing?"

"Pretty sure that's correct."

"So you're sure you haven't seen anyone lurking around the house? A stranger, or even someone Lizzie knows?"

"No." The nurse yawns. "Sorry, I'm probably not being very useful, I didn't sleep much last night."

"Insomnia?"

"Mrs. Wainwright, she..." She doesn't finish. "When you have a patient, you know, you need to put them first."

"How long have you been Mrs. Wainwright's nurse?"

"Like I told you earlier, since the car accident, a month ago. I was her nurse at the hospital, at Maine Medical Center and... well, after Mrs. Wainwright was given the all-clear, she and her husband decided it was a good idea to pay for twenty-four-seven care, so here I am."

"So you see a lot of Lizzie in general? And her brother—what's his name again?"

"Liam." The nurse taps her phone. "I've found a few photos that I can text."

"Great. Appreciate it. I'm going to get a search party together while I wait for my team to arrive. They'll also be going door to door. And hopefully we will be able to assign a family liaison officer to take you through all the steps. Meanwhile, can you give me an article of clothing of Lizzie's, or a stuffed animal? Anything not recently washed, if possible, anything with her scent on it."

"Sure, I'll see what I can find in her room. *Please* find Celeste," her nurse pleads. "I can't go out looking myself because I can't leave little Liam alone, but I'm worried she might come to harm. I've tried calling her, but she isn't picking up. She's my responsibility."

They both turn their heads at the sound of the kitchen door slamming, and then footsteps.

"Thank God she's back." Alex races downstairs.

Detective Alba, not waiting for permission, goes to Lizzie's room and finds a suitably worn teddy, dirty enough that it should have Lizzie's scent all over it. She pulls out a clean plastic bag from her workbag, puts on a pair of latex gloves before handling the teddy, and places it inside the bag. Quietly, so as not to disturb Lizzie's brother, she heads back downstairs. She sees a woman in the kitchen, who she assumes is Lizzie's mother—drenched, water dripping from her clothing and her hair, rubber boots turning the floor to puddles.

"I can't find her, I can't find her!" Mrs. Wainwright gasps, out of breath.

"All the more reason to get moving, ASAP," the detective says. She quickly introduces herself to Mrs. Wainwright, who slumps herself onto a rickety kitchen chair, her head in her hands, defeated. She begins to cry. Sobs of exhaustion, of desperation.

The detective asks a few questions again, gently, softly, about how many hours Lizzie has been missing and if Celeste heard anything or suspected anything or saw anything suspicious. But she doesn't have time to get into deeper conversation right now—she'll do that later. She shows her the teddy she is taking.

"You're bringing in *dogs*?" Celeste looks panicked.

"I'm hoping so." Detective Alba turns to the nurse. "Make Mrs. Wainwright a hot drink, and if you have a bathtub here, she could use a hot bath or she might wind up sick. I need to get this show on the road. And please, if anybody calls you demanding anything, or any call from a stranger at all, make sure you call me." She gives Celeste her card, not ruling out the possibility of a kidnapping.

There is no time to lose, even though it is midnight and even though the weather is cruel and unrelenting. She needs to stay calm, and she is; she is used to keeping her cool. With twenty years behind her on the force, she has seen and heard things no regular woman can even imagine. She must stay alert to pick up the tiniest detail. This may be a case of a missing child, or, God forbid, it may be an abduction. If it is a kidnapping, the kidnapper will soon get in touch. Alba always prepares herself for the worst. She's been in this game long enough to know that happy outcomes are sadly few and far between. There are too many weirdos and sickos out there. And perps are canny these days. Television has taught them so much. They cover their tracks. They know a frightening amount about DNA evidence and cleaning up after themselves, and it has made her job a lot harder. She is assuming the worst, of course. Perhaps the little girl has just wandered off on her own. But Detective Alba is paid to be suspicious. She is paid to save lives. And if she can't save a life, she must solve the crime.

She needs to look for a motive. Why does somebody do a particular thing? Even a crazy person has a motive.

What is that person's (or persons') motive in Lizzie's case?

What?

JAYNE

Three days ago

"It's just a formality," Max assures me, handing me the fountain pen.

I wasn't expecting this. Nobody had spoken to me about a non-disclosure agreement before I took the job. What am I supposed to do now? I feel like someone has jumped up behind me and said "boo." This has come as a shock. I suppose signing it doesn't make any difference to me one way or the other, but still, they could've let me know ahead of time. Why didn't the agency warn me? Maybe they hadn't been given the heads-up? Or maybe it's something that's occurred to Max since my arrival. Which means only one thing: he doesn't trust me. It's personal. And it happens to be Sunday, so I can't speak with anyone at the agency.

"I don't understand," I say. "I'm not going to go blabbing about family secrets to anybody."

"Course not, Jayne, no of course not, we trust you completely. We combed through several candidates' résumés and you were the person we chose for the job. We trust you implicitly, but you know… it's a formality." Max's eyes hold mine and I break away. I can feel myself getting red in the face, the neck, because he's so good looking. Obviously he's not flirting with me or anything, God forbid, but his eyes are so intense. Dark brown with flashes of hazel lighting up his irises. Truth is, I can't even look at him, he's making me so self-conscious. I can feel a beetroot flush crawling over my neck, making me hot and bothered like I want to rip off my clothing.

"Where do I sign?"

"Here," he says, pointing near the bottom of the paper. "As I say, it's no big deal… it's for my wife, I need to protect her at all costs. She's very frail. Anything could break her. Any tiny amount of gossip. Her memory, you see, it's broken, I'm—"

"She doesn't recognize me," Marjorie breaks in. "At first I felt… well, insulted. I've known Celeste for years, and she doesn't even recognize who I am, her own sister-in-law."

"Traumatic brain injury… head trauma," Max murmurs. "Her memory comes and goes, even with me. She's not quite herself. Not that you know what she was like before, but I can guarantee she's a different person since the accident. We're hoping she'll get back to being the way she was before."

As this is all taking place I'm having dinner with Max and Marjorie at the dining room table. Marjorie made dinner and, apart from running Celeste's business, that's why she's here, I guess, to help out, to support her brother. I wish they hadn't invited me for a meal though. I'd prefer to be in my cottage, all safe and snug and alone, reading. They've done it to be polite, but I don't want to be here. Dinner was all fancy—three courses—and I wasn't even sure what forks or knives to use. Wine, two different kinds. Not that I drank any. It looks all shabby chic here on the outside, but it's not; there's a lot of money in this man's coffers. I feel so out of my depth. I put on the only elegant dress I brought with me. A maroon, scooped-neck thing. But because of a tatty old bra I packed by mistake—way too small—

it pushes up my cleavage and makes me feel tarty. I've put on even more weight than I thought. How is it possible to put on weight after only three days here? But I have. The fact that they've made me sign an NDA three days after I arrive makes me feel like they think I'm a gossip. I wonder if the children repeated that question I asked them about which parent they loved more? No, I don't think so. Even thinking about it makes me go beetroot.

Max smiles at me. Well, not a real smile, more like a sort of cool, Mr. Darcy twitch of the mouth, which I suppose reads as a smile. My face feels hot again.

Then I blurt out, "Was it an accident or suicide attempt?"

Marjorie and Max shoot a glance at each other.

Then Max says, biting his bottom lip, "Well, now you've signed the agreement, I suppose I might as well tell you." And he lowers his voice to a whisper. "Celeste tried to kill herself, pregnant, and Lizzie too. The impact was..." It looks like there are tears in his filmy eyes and he can't go on. But he croaks out, "The impact of the crash was too much for the baby, obviously. Violet was delivered by C-section and it was a success. We initially thought she was okay, but there had been problems all along, I suppose, and well... Celeste insisted upon leaving the hospital maybe too soon." His eyes shift to the floor. "And the rest is history."

History still unclear to me, I think.

"Poor Max." Marjorie puts a hand on his, in a protective, sisterly way. "He is so, so devastated. We all are. But all we can do now is move forward. Celeste has a history of depression. Right now our biggest priority is to protect the children and help her get better. I trust you understand, Jayne, we don't want this going any further."

I nod. Although we have finished dinner and even coffee (fancy porcelain coffee cups so thin you could snap them, silver teaspoons), we're still sitting here with these papers between us.

My dessert plate is still on the table. I help myself to another sliver of cake, put it on my pretty bone china plate, so delicate I could crack it with a scrape of my utensil. I gently lift my spoon, my silver spoon with fancy initials all over it, and shove the cake into my mouth. I chew, squishing the tasty sponge and chocolate and cherries between my palate and tongue, savoring the liquor melting in my mouth. It's a Black Forest gateau, the brandy—it tastes like kirsch—dances lightly around my tastebuds, and I can't help it, it pulls me down into a rabbit hole of desire, spiraling into a rush of want and need.

I need a drink.

I must have a drink.

No, no, no, no don't go there.

But a little voice cajoles, *Yes, yes, yes, yes go there, you know you want to.*

THE DISAPPEARANCE

Now

It is several hours into the early morning and there is still no sign of Lizzie. Soon word spreads across the island. Celeste's little girl is gone: Lizzie has *disappeared*. Only a parent could understand the agony of such a thing, but there is communal empathy, a sense of solidarity amongst the islanders. People are scared. Nervous. Bewildered. This kind of thing doesn't happen on Cliff Island.

There are still rumbles of thunder. Various islanders—those not fast asleep in bed and oblivious to the drama—are asked to form a search party. The others will be awoken soon enough and interviewed when the team arrive. Those who are awake, those who have come out of their homes to see what is going on, can help.

For now, because the rest of the team on the force hasn't arrived yet, it is a party of five people. The couple at the store, the Oldfields, Dr. Stephen. And of course Detective Alba and her partner, Carl, a young rangy man who hasn't yet seen his twenty-fifth birthday. And then, surprisingly, as they are about to set off, Alex Sharpe arrives to join them, but the detective sends her back to look after Mrs. Wainwright. She does not need two people missing, and Lizzie's mother was in such a state anything could happen to her. It is unwise to leave the poor woman alone. She'll get the teddy to George, to his K-9 Dune, as soon as they get here, *if* he and his dog have been assigned to this case.

Fingers crossed.

It is a great way for Detective Alba to get to know some of the islanders and visitors alike and ask all the questions she can. Although she doesn't have the time to formally interview them, she is able to assess their alibis, find out where they were and what they were doing at the approximate time of Lizzie's disappearance. She quickly assesses them: their character traits, the way they interact with each other. She is trained in sniffing out lies and deceit.

It isn't long before she realizes certain people are probably either lying or have something to hide.

The rain has calmed, and the fog has lifted, the lightning and thunder intermittent, but the wind... the wind has picked up and behaves like a solid sheet raging against the search party, thrusting them backwards as they try to push forward into the dark night, flashlights in hands.

"Keep an eye out for anything that might belong to Lizzie," Detective Alba tells her party. "Any piece of clothing, even a hair tie. Any scrap of evidence that might be relevant. But if you see something, don't touch it—use this whistle and either myself or my partner will bag it for evidence." She hands her group each a whistle to put around their necks. The wind is howling, not as cold as it could be because it is summer, but hard and relentless as if it has a life of its own, as if it is on a personal mission to thwart the search.

The wind in Maine answers to no one.

"We need to check the beaches first to see if any boats have been taken out to sea." She has gleaned, in this short time, that Lizzie has been given sailing lessons. Perhaps the child has tried to take a boat out on her own? Kids do this sort of thing. "Watch for dragging tracks on the sand, and footprints," she tells them. "Especially in sheltered spots that won't have been affected by the wind and rain. If you see anything, stop where you are. And no one's getting off this island tomorrow, even if the weather clears, not until I've interviewed absolutely everybody, is that clear?"

Lizzie's father, and his sister, Marjorie, are on the mainland. This, Alba has also been told. She will double-check this fact, of course. She will check anything and everything, because she knows people lie. Even about stupid things that probably don't matter, people are not candid. Everyone has his or her own agenda, even with the best of intentions, even if only to appear like a good person or a helpful citizen. People, she knows, are prone to deviate from the truth.

Homo sapiens.

It is what it is.

Dr. Stephen is being particularly helpful, letting the detective know that the father of the child and his sister are away. Two people, she thinks, to cross off her list of suspects. This is how she will work, assuming everybody is guilty until proven innocent. Anything anybody says, a scratch of the nose, a jiggle of the foot, a flick of the eye, everything will be locked in her mind and remembered, and also noted verbally, dictated by her, into her phone.

Another thing Detective Alba knows from experience is that the more helpful people are, the more suspicious she is of them. Often the "helpful" ones end up being the perps. She's aware, but not certain of course, that the person guilty of this abduction—if that's what it is—may be in this search group, right now.

The question is, if that is so, where has he or she hidden Lizzie?

JAYNE

Two days ago

Addicts always find a way, we do, we just do. We are clever creatures, our brains working overtime to get what we want. Nothing will stand in our way. No morals or codes or sense of right and wrong can come between us and our desire.

We want what we want when we want and nothing's going to stop us.

It wasn't long before I found the wine cellar. It was perfect. Dust all over the bottles. I knew nobody would miss anything. I didn't go for the antique-looking stuff and things that looked really valuable—that would be too risky. I had noted the wine they drank at dinner that I'd said no to. It was French, so I kept away from the French stuff and the Italian, and grabbed the Californian wine. Napa Valley. Not that I know much about wine, but I reckon wine from the home country would probably be considered less sought after, less flashy, less "haute liqueur," if that's what you can say about wine, which I'm sure it isn't. Nobody saw me. The cellar is next to where the gardening paraphernalia is stored, so I had the perfect excuse. I walked around with a trowel in my hand in case anybody caught me. The cellar part was locked though, in a sort of cage, like a prison. It really gave me the creeps. They could lock someone down here and nobody would find them. Ever, and I mean *never*. We are on an island in the middle of bloody nowhere, with a *cellar*.

Deep at the bottom of a secluded house.

The house is on a tiny island surrounded by rough ocean.

Remote. Not famous. Not touristy. Virtually unheard of.

Pretty freaky.

I found the key after five minutes. It was hidden in an old coffee maker. I took four bottles, shoved them into a shopping bag, hung it over my shoulder and sloped out of the cellar, treading as lightly as possible, trying not to let the bottles clink together.

Now, before you judge me, remember one thing: I don't drink on the job. No, when those kids are in my hands, I will be sober. But what am I supposed to do at night all alone when they're asleep? With all those nice bottles in that cellar begging to be drunk?

I was hoping for a nice quiet moment alone in my cottage, but when I get back, I see a figure sitting in the shadows, waiting for me on my porch.

JAYNE

It's Stephen. He has brought over a couple of beers. He's rocking quietly back and forth on my porch swing, which creaks eerily as it moves to and fro. The bullfrogs are making quite a racket now that dusk is approaching. Stephen stretches out an arm and hands me a Budweiser. I weigh up my options a second before shaking my head, knowing what's in my shopping bag, which I lay down super gently—so nothing clinks—on the deck, next to the door. It annoys me that he has planted himself on my porch without an invitation, but then Americans are renowned for being friendly; it's part of their culture, isn't it? And I feel like an uptight Brit with a rod up my arse being so unwelcoming. Besides, this is what I wanted, wasn't it? To get to know him and find out what's going on around here.

"No thanks," I tell him, "I don't really drink."

"Oh no?" he asks, as if he knows my weaknesses. As if he has already guessed what's in that bag. "What do you mean by don't 'really' drink?"

None of your bloody business. But I answer, "Not on the job."

"But isn't Marjorie looking after the kids right now? I mean, it's your free evening, isn't it?"

How does he know this? I take the beer. "I suppose you have a point." I sit, not next to him—no way—but across from him on a deck chair. I'm about to pop the can and take a sip, but then I change my mind. "I'll get myself some juice, actually."

I stand up. It's beginning to drizzle and the evening light is growing dim. But it's fine since the porch is protected from the rain. A good thing because this place gets chilly at night and we've even had a downpour. Not what I was expecting, being summer.

Stephen looks out at the water, a calm stretch of blue before us. A sailboat in the distance, the sun dipping and casting reflections in pinkish shimmers. It really is beautiful here.

He takes a swig of beer. "I hope I'm not intruding—I thought you might like a bit of company."

"No, it's fine. Give me a second to put something away." Glancing into the bag, my stolen goods lying on their sides, I shudder at my wrongdoing. I notice that one of the bottles is a French wine, after all. A Châteauneuf-du-Pape. How did I miss that? It was dark in the cellar.

I take the key from my bag and unlock my door. It's only the island people here, so nothing to worry about, yet I still like to lock up, to be on the safe side. Not that there's anything here to steal. No TV, just an old-fashioned radio, and my suitcase, which I still haven't unpacked. Nobody's going to want to get their hands on any of my out-of-fashion, cheap clothes, that's for sure. I didn't bring any jewelry. Clients don't usually appreciate that. They want a nice, plain au pair who gets on with the job. Apart from my Marmite, there's nothing here I really care about. I take the shopping bag into the kitchen and decide not to put it on the counter but on the sofa. All open-plan here. I cover the bag with a load of cushions, for good measure. I'm not going to drink beer with Stephen. I can't risk it. I don't know how much he'll talk. Not that anybody has told me not to drink, but still. I pour myself a glass of the kids' orange juice and come back out, wondering if he thinks I'm rude not to have invited him inside.

"I'm sorry, did you want a glass for your beer?"

He shakes his head. "No, I'm good."

"So, how long have you been here?" I ask him.

"A couple weeks. At first I tried the commute to Portland, coming and going on the ferry, but as you know, it's an hour or two each way. It was way too much. Plus I got a bit seasick with those rough waves and didn't really want to be in town anyway. It's rough out there too, right now, isn't it?"

I nod my head in agreement. I think I get what he means by "rough." He's talking about all the on/off, yes, no lockdowns from the last couple of years of Covid, I imagine. The insecurity of not knowing where we stand. It's done all of our heads in, one way or another. Here, it's peaceful at least. I hear there are only fifty-three all-year residents. No hotels anymore, a few Airbnb rentals, although this year, because of the circumstances, it has been spotty, apparently.

"I'm glad to be here, in a way," I agree. "Quite nice, not having any telly. No shitty news, no doom and gloom to listen to that makes you feel like slitting your wrists." Then I realize what I've said. "Joke!" I quickly add. Talking about suicide, even in a jesty way, is not okay after what has happened with Celeste. Sometimes I feel like plugging my mouth: all kinds of rubbish comes out, things I shouldn't say. Like asking the kids who their favorite parent is. *Wrong, wrong, wrong*. "So you're a doctor?" I ask him, changing the subject.

"In a manner of speaking."

"In a manner of speaking?"

"Well, I'm a psychotherapist, so technically I'm not a doctor."

"Oh, because people have been calling you Dr. Stephen."

"I *am* a doctor: a doctor of psychology. I have letters after my name, but I'm not a medical doctor, if that makes sense."

"Oh, I see. So, you think you can help Celeste?"

"I hope so. She needs a sounding board. She needs somebody to talk to, someone she can be open with. Mostly I'm trying to help her piece her memory back together."

"From what I've observed, Max seems to be very patient with her. He must be very in love."

Stephen doesn't reply, and for a second I catch a glint of sadness in his eye and wonder if he's in love with Celeste himself. Weird. No, *ridiculous*. What is it about me that spins these big narratives when the truth is probably so much simpler?

"Max seems to rush around a lot doing stuff for her," I add.

"Yes," Stephen agrees. "He's a very attentive husband."

Did I detect a note of bitterness in his voice, picking out that word "attentive"?

"But his sister Marjorie seems to be a bit superfluous, doesn't she? I mean she's just kind of hanging around, making food. Does she really need to be here?" *Oops, that came out wrong. Superfluous? Where did that come from?* There's something about Marjorie I don't like, so I try to stay clear of her. I'm not sure what it is. Again, me being too sensitive, I suppose, feeling that she doesn't like me and she's judging me and watching me. Yesterday, she took the kids into the bathroom and washed their faces and scrubbed their nails and even their soft little hands vigorously, with a nailbrush. All because of a bit of mud. Lizzie almost cried. It made me feel like I was doing a really rubbish job. But she's my boss's sister, so what could I say?

"So, Celeste tried to kill herself and Lizzie by driving her car into a lake when she was pregnant?" I ask Stephen, trying to get my facts straight.

"Yes, that's pretty much what happened."

"And they gave her a cesarean? After they took her to the hospital?"

"Yes, she had a C-section. The baby was days away from being born when the car crashed. It's lucky they were able to save Violet and lucky they were able to save Celeste."

I frown. "Yet Violet didn't survive in the end, poor lamb." There is a lull in the conversation. I think about that innocent baby, her life taken away so soon. "Is there going to be a funeral?"

Stephen sighs, his shoulders slump. "As far as I can tell, there's going to be a quiet cremation. Look, it's very complicated. Or very simple, depending on how you look at it. Basically, Celeste is suffering from retrograde amnesia. She can't remember things unless they happened a long time ago. She gets flashes of recent happenings then forgets. She seems to have forgotten about the baby, so Max—um, Mr. Wainwright, believes that's the best course to follow. To go with the flow. If Celeste realizes her baby died, it could send her over the edge."

"So they're going to *lie* to her?" I ask in disbelief. "Pretend she didn't have a baby in the first place?"

"We're talking about a suicidal patient here. It could save Celeste's life. The best course is to her get well again and then slowly, carefully break it to her. Introduce the facts—the truth—bit by bit. When she's strong enough to accept it."

"I still don't think it's right," I point out. "It feels so deceptive, so sneaky." It occurs to me that Stephen is discussing a patient with a virtual stranger: me. Isn't that against all patient/doctor codes? Even if he isn't an official doctor?

"We're trying to take one day at a time here," he says. "Look, her condition is not really my field of expertise."

"So why were you hired? I don't get it."

Stephen nibbles his bottom lip, as if deciding how much to tell me. "Max and I went to college together, a long time ago. He remembered I lived in Portland and was... we were friends, way back when, and well, he thought I'd be the right person for the job. Someone he could trust."

"Did they make you sign a non-disclosure agreement?"

"No, they didn't need to. Look, Jayne, I'm only discussing Celeste with you because I know you'll find all this out anyway, and well, *you've* signed an NDA, haven't you." He states this as a fact, not a question. I wonder how he knows. Max must have told him. Or maybe because of what I just said, he guessed?

"It all feels off to me," I grumble, my heart going out to poor Celeste. How can dishonesty be the best policy? Then I think of my filched wine, which is the least of it. And the reason why I'm here, and the big fat secret I'm running away from—I'd be done for if anyone found out about that. I'm the last person to talk about honesty.

"Look, it is what it is." Stephen takes a gulp of beer and stares into the distance.

Maroon clouds are whipping across the sky and it looks like it might rain for real. That's all I need: rain. It's so much nicer when the kids can run around and get loads of exercise, then they're tired and sleepy after a busy day, and it makes my job a whole lot easier. We'll spend tomorrow outdoors whatever the weather. Fresh air is good for them.

"So what about you?" Stephen asks.

"What about me?"

"Where are you from?"

"London."

"Oh, London, that's a great city. I've had some fun times in London."

"Yeah, it's expensive to live there though. It's hard to have fun when you don't have enough money to go out and enjoy all the things a big city like London has to offer. You know, all those mouthwatering restaurants, for starters. I'm lucky if I can afford a curry now and then. Even a pizza in London puts a dent in your wallet, after rent and utility bills."

"Is this your full-time job? Being a nanny?"

"I'm not a nanny but an au pair. It's a means to an end. It doesn't pay well, but it's..." I try to think what to tell him and I can't muster up anything that won't give away my reason for wanting to put as much distance between me and home as possible and leave my past behind.

After an hour or two of chatter, Stephen leaves. I go to bed early but can't sleep. To say I feel spooked is an understatement.

I wake up, the night dark as thick velvet. Creak, squeak, creeeeeak, squeak.

I freeze.

Literally, I'm too scared to even double-check I've locked the front door, although I know I have. I'm pinned to my bed, the sheet drawn up around my shoulders, as if it could protect me from this fearful, spooky sound. At first, I think it's my porch swing. But it's like a kind of rusty groan, as if someone's dragging something heavy, or pulling out a boat from underneath my cottage. A boat stuck in the sand and someone's trying to get it out? *There are ghosts in these waters.* I remember that man, Eric, telling me that on the boat over. I don't believe in ghosts.

The dead still live on.

I don't believe in ghosts! Yet... why is my heart thumping so hard I feel it's going to come out through the other side of my chest? There is something eerie about this island.

Someone is out there...

Waiting.

DR. STEPHEN

I paid a visit to Jayne in her cottage today, a couple of beers in hand, because that's what I thought she wanted: for us to hang out, get to know each other a little. But once I was there I felt awkward, self-conscious, greeted by her shifty gaze. She was a touch unwelcoming.

We talked about the Wainwright family, and it hit me that I said way too much. Never mind, she'll find stuff out sooner or later. Jayne's a nosy type, I've noticed, maybe even a bit of a busybody, only time will tell. She'll find out the score soon enough. When you're living on a postage stamp like Cliff Island, it's inevitable. I can tell by the way Jayne licked her lips and then declined the Bud I offered her, she's a drinker and is in denial. After years on the job I've got a sixth sense for these things. Maybe she's doing the twelve steps? I didn't push her. It would be nice, though, to have someone I could share a beer with in the evenings.

Trying to sort out Celeste has been exhausting. Going round and round in circles, like with an Alzheimer's patient. One minute, things are crystal clear, the next she hardly recognizes me. Same with Marjorie and even Max. I'm not qualified to deal with someone so far gone. Like I say, Celeste should be under watch at a hospital, not at home, so far from real medical care.

I tried to get a handle on Jayne. Strange when someone's from another country, another culture, it's always harder to peg them. Even when we speak the same language. Is Jayne my type? She's very young.

"Why don't we go for a stroll?" I suggested. Something to make us both feel less awkward around each other.

She shuffled in her deckchair. "What, *now*?"

"Yeah, it's dusk, and the horseshoe crabs will be out."

"Are they different from regular crabs?"

"Very different. You want to see? They gather around this time in the evening."

She reluctantly got out of her seat but tumbled back down. I lent her a hand. She took it a bit suspiciously, as if I might harm her. "Thanks," she said, and laughed. "Deck chairs are hard to get out of at the best of times. Like putting a duvet cover on. Surprisingly difficult."

We wandered down to the beach and I took my shoes and socks off, leaving them on a rock. I always like to roll up my pants and wade. The water's warm at this time of year. Well, warm for Maine. She was wearing the kind of dress my mom used to wear. A full skirt, with a big fruit and flower print. Jayne is extremely fair—her flesh looks as though it has never seen the sun. Her calves seem solid compared to her delicate milk-pale feet. She's quite tall, too. Big-boned, I would describe her, like she could punch a man in the face if she needed to. I'm not sure why I took mental notes of her like this, but... she is interesting, unusual and different from the women I usually meet. She has a pretty face. But I can tell by the way she moves that she doesn't feel comfortable in her own skin. Shame, that: her lack of confidence. We walked along the beach, the sun dropping behind the horizon, full and coral-orange.

"If we wait for it to set, we might see a green flash. Have you ever seen a green flash before?"

"No," she said, "I don't know about that. I live in London, you know, we don't get to see regular sunsets very often. Maybe if I go to Hampstead Heath or somewhere quite high up, but the evening sun's always obscured by buildings or clouds."

We came across a group of crabs scurrying around on the sand.

She gasped. "My God, they look like Batman's Batmobile, they really are horseshoe-shaped, and with that spike! What's that spike for?"

"That's its tail," I explained. "Native Americans used those as weapons for spearfishing, once upon a time. But don't worry, despite the ferocious look of the tail, these creatures are not aggressive. They do have spines along the edge of their carapace, though, so it's best not to pick them up."

She laughed. One of her front teeth protruded slightly. It's sexy in a way, that tooth.

"I can assure you I have no intention of manhandling one. Or *wom*an-handling one, more like."

I smiled. "Did you know horseshoe crabs are millions and millions of years old?" I heard my professor voice take over. Jayne's youth, perhaps?

"No, I've never seen them before. We don't have these in England, I don't think."

"They have blue blood."

"What? Did they come on the *Mayflower* or something?"

"Excuse me?"

"Joke."

"No, really," I said, in a serious voice. "The blood is blue because of the copper. Did you know that horseshoe crabs are harvested for their blood?"

"Harvested?"

"The blood is used for vaccines and drips and is crucial in the medical field. There's a whole campaign from activists complaining about cruelty because they've since invented a type of synthetic blood that can be used in its place. These horseshoe crabs are not in danger of extinction exactly, but they are in decline, which is having an impact on ecology. Lots of birds live on their eggs and so on."

Jayne, backing away from the crabs, threw me a look as if I might be teasing her.

My professor voice droned on: "You know that these crabs survived five mass extinction events, even the one two hundred and fifty million years ago? They haven't changed in all this time. Fascinating, isn't it? They predate dinosaurs by more than two hundred million years!"

"I had no idea about any of this. So we humans are acting like vampires, living off their blood?"

"Using their blood, yes," I explained.

"Do you swim a lot?" she asked me. "Even with spiky crabs as company?"

"Yep, every morning. I swim between three and five miles."

"Wow."

"Would you like to come with me one morning?"

She held up her hands, palms facing me in alarm. "Oh, no, no, thank you very much, I don't really do swimming apart from an occasional dip in a swimming pool."

"How come? You don't like the ocean?"

"Oh, no reason. Well, that's not true, but..." She didn't go on.

"You're wary of the ocean?"

She nodded. "Something like that."

"Did something happen to you as a young child?"

"Kind of," she said, but it was clear she didn't want to tell me what.

There's a vulnerability to this girl, but she guards herself with a tough exterior, a shell not unlike a horseshoe crab. It makes me think there's so much more to Jayne than meets the eye. I think we could be friends.

"You wear a wetsuit when you go swimming because the water's so cold?" she asked.

"No, not because of that. I once got stung by a box jellyfish —a Portuguese man-of-war. They're everywhere these days, even in waters where they don't belong. Since then, I guess it's become habit, even though it's summer and I don't really need one." I nodded in the direction of her cottage. "You planning to take out your rowboat?"

"Maybe," she said.

"I can show you how to row, if you like."

"That's okay. My brother was a rower and he gave me some tips, though I haven't done it for ages. Are there dangerous currents round here?"

"You'll be fine, just don't go too far. But then again, if you don't swim..."

"Who said I didn't swim?"

"Oh, I'm sorry, I—"

"I don't get out to the seaside very often. Wish I did. That's why I like being an au pair, I get to go to different places. But lately..." She didn't finish her sentence. Again I had the sense she was hiding some crucial piece of information about herself that she didn't want to share.

"It's getting dark, I think I should be heading back to my cottage," she said.

"Sure, I'll walk with you."

"That's okay, I'm fine. See you around, Dr. Stephen, and thanks for the horseshoe crab lesson, it was absolutely fascinating."

Is she teasing me? I wondered. *Yep, she thinks I'm a jerk.*

The story of my life with attractive women.

"Call me Stephen," I told her, piqued by the rejection. "Just Stephen."

But she was already gone.

THE DISAPPEARANCE

Now

Lizzie has been missing all night. The search party has combed all the beaches on the island. No sign of her. No sign of any boat being taken out to sea this night. It is now early morning, and the backup team has arrived. The search party has grown to twenty-five people. Soon the professional divers will arrive and scour the seabed. Meanwhile, Detective Alba and her team will interview everyone on the island.

It has occurred to her and her boss, Scully, that this could be a kidnapping; if so, they will hear something soon. Alba hopes so, anyway. Then they could hand this case over to the FBI. Missing children are way out of her comfort zone. She is flying by the seat of her pants.

Praying she won't screw up—she has to get this right.

She is not particularly religious, never goes to church, but a Catholic childhood got into her veins. *Once a Catholic always a Catholic*. It's at times like this it sneaks up on her.

She and Scully are in contact by phone. He will be the one checking the databases, investigating her leads. Why? Because he is her boss, he is the one calling the shots. Meanwhile, Alba is here in the midst of the mayhem, relying on her gut feeling and her instinct, two things in her many years of experience that have served her pretty well. She is not always good at following rules and protocol, not when she feels they are a hindrance.

For instance, right now. When Dr. Stephen tells her that he is exhausted and is going back to his cottage to get some sleep, she decides to accompany him. She instructs her partner, Carl, to stick close to the other islanders. She wants to take a look at Dr. Stephen's cottage. Something about him puts her on edge, but she can't pinpoint what. Perhaps it's the way he was demonstrating out there how eager he was to find the child? This made her suspicious. He seemed a bit too nice. Too helpful.

On his porch, she notices a wetsuit laid out on the wooden railings.

"You're a diver?" she inquires in a casual tone.

"Not a diver, no," Dr. Stephen answers, scratching his ear. "But I swim every day."

"A wetsuit, in summer?"

He smiles. A gratuitous smile that has nothing to do with this conversation. His teeth are even, small and white. A man who looks after his appearance, she decides. But the small teeth unnerve her. She estimates he must be about... thirty-nine? She will find out more about him. If he's married. Past employment. That is, if they don't find Lizzie. If they do, she couldn't care less about this man and he will be of no concern to her whatsoever.

"I got stung by a jellyfish once, the wetsuit's a precaution, I guess."

"No bottles? No speargun? No gear?"

"No, no. I'm not into snorkeling or diving or spearfishing, just... swimming." He shifts his body weight onto his other leg. He is still grinning at her. Desperate to seem friendly. She nods. Out in the field, while they were searching for Lizzie, Dr.

Stephen was super eager to be useful. He gave her the rundown on Mrs. Wainwright, although he referred to her as Celeste. How distraught she is, how she has lost her memory after the car crash—although it comes and goes.

They are hovering on his cottage porch awkwardly. "Would you mind if I come in and do a quick search around your property?"

The therapist's smile drops, his face blanches. "Sure. Come in."

He unlocks the front door and they walk inside. The cottage is all wood, very simple, open-plan, a kitchen and living room all in one. It is one-story, no upstairs, a door leading to a bedroom, which she notices because it is ajar. There are newspapers in piles. Books. Unwashed cups and plates in the kitchen sink. For some reason the mess doesn't match this man's neat appearance: the thought he has put into his careful personal grooming, as if he is two personae in one.

Interesting.

"Would you mind if I make a quick trip to the bathroom?" he asks. "I felt too ashamed pissing in front of the others. I can't hold it in any longer." He laughs nervously and offers up a rictus smile.

"Go ahead."

While he is in the bathroom, she scans the room. Peers into the bedroom. Looks in the closet, under the bed, checks the window, which is locked tight. She searches under the disarrayed comforter on the bed to check for a child's toy, a bobby pin, anything that might not belong to him. She finds nothing incriminating. She walks back into the main room and presses her ear against the bathroom door. No sound except the flush of the toilet, a gush of water from the taps. She pulls back before Dr. Stephen opens the door.

"I'd like to ask a couple quick questions and I'll get out of your hair," she tells him. She makes a quick visit to the bathroom, looks behind the shower curtain, checks the window, looks in the medicine cabinet. Valium, Xanax, vitamin pills. She comes out and gives him a minuscule smile of encouragement. She doesn't want to be too curt in case he clams up. Wants him on her side. "How long have you been Mrs. Wainwright's therapist?"

That ingratiating, good-guy smile again. "Since the accident."

"The car accident you told me about?"

He nods.

"And was it Mrs. Wainwright who hired you or was it her husband?"

"It was Max, I think. I can't even remember now. We're... we go back a ways, Max and I. College friends."

"I see. You say you go swimming in the mornings?"

"Yes, every morning."

"Did you swim yesterday afternoon? Yesterday evening?"

"I don't usually go out in the evenings"—he shakes his head vehemently—"I mean, never..."

She nods. "Well, thank you, Dr. Stephen, that will be all until tomorrow. Hope you manage to get a little shuteye. Thanks so much for your cooperation."

"No problem."

On the way out she sticks her finger on the neoprene wetsuit, draws the droplets of water to her lips, and licks them. Not wet from only the rain, but salty. The water seems fresher than if it had been in the sea yesterday morning. She quietly steps behind the cottage to where the bathroom window is, wanting to be sure. She shines her flashlight on the ground, checking for a child's footprints. Nothing. She checks the backyard. There are no garden sheds.

Her next stop is the main house. To pay a visit to Lizzie's mother again. It's 5:30 in the morning but this is not the time to be worrying about waking people up or being polite. If she were a parent with a missing child she would be awake, and if not she would want to be roused from sleep. Seeing a light on in the kitchen, she knocks on the back door. She hears the sound of a radio but no reply, so she gingerly pushes the door open. It is not locked.

There is Lizzie's mother nursing a coffee—she can smell the aroma—looking disheveled, distraught, staring into a void. The detective stands by the door, coughs loudly.

Mrs. Wainwright looks blank, but jumps up. "Did you find her? Did you find Lizzie?"

"No, I'm afraid not."

Celeste turns off the radio. "Been listening, in case. There's an amber alert out. I've been trying to phone my husband. He's not answering. He's off the island. With his sister. I don't know where they are."

"You may have gathered from the radio the storm didn't only hit here, Mrs. Wainwright. Things are looking pretty bad on the mainland as well. Chances are—"

"I'm so worried about him. He should have been home today."

Alba nods. "I'm sure he's fine. Things are in turmoil right now. When did he leave?"

"Yesterday, I can't remember what time. With his sister. We have a house in Portland. It feels like everything is caving in on me. Poor Lizzie. We *have* to find her! Please, Detective."

"We're doing everything in our power, I promise. We won't leave any stone unturned. May I sit down?"

Celeste nods and noncommittally motions Alba to a spare chair.

The detective sits, steeples her fingers—an unwitting habit of hers—and fixes her gaze on Celeste. "I hope you don't mind me asking, but do you and your husband have a stable relationship?"

Celeste's mouth parts as if surprised. "Oh, very. He's a *wonderful* husband."

"And father?"

"God, yes. If you think Max had anything to do—"

"Just asking, please don't take offense. But he's away quite a bit?"

"His work means he has to travel, yes. And he's often in Portland or Boston. It's hard to run things from here. He has meetings with clients and, well, he has a lot on his plate right now. Especially with me being ill. It's been even harder on him in some ways. He's been amazing, really supportive. I'm so lucky."

Alba reaches out and touches Celeste's hand very gently. "Your therapist told me that you have lapses in memory since your accident and you sometimes suffer from fragmentary blackouts?"

Celeste regards the detective blankly.

"Your car accident?" Alba clarifies.

Celeste looks down at her hands as if ashamed by her condition. "Yes, it comes and goes."

"Right now, for instance, can you remember what happened that day of the car crash?"

"Well, I remember getting into my car and I remember strapping Lizzie into the back seat. In the child seat, you know? I remember I was heavily..." She breaks down into sobs.

"But Liam wasn't in the car, right?"

"No, thank God. He never even knew about the accident. He's sleeping now. Thank goodness he seems to have slept through this whole thing."

"So when was it you last saw Lizzie? Do you remember the time?" The detective is asking this question for the second time. She needs to be sure.

"Yes, of course. I tucked her into bed around eight thirty, quarter to nine. I read her a bedtime story."

"Just her, or your little boy, too?"

"No, I read to them separately because they're both into different things and they don't like the same books. Because Lizzie's younger, she gets the first story and then I go into Liam's room and read *his* story. He's into dinosaurs, Lizzie's into more magical things at the moment. Unicorns and fairies and goblins, things Liam thinks are stupid. He tells her they're not real, only imaginary."

"The two kids get on? Do they fight at all?"

"Oh, they get on, apart from occasional silly squabbles, like all kids."

"I noticed your kitchen door was unlocked. Had you left your house unlocked earlier, around the time she went missing?"

"We leave it secured by the latch—it's up high so the children can't reach—but locked, locked, no. In case one of us goes for a walk and needs to get in. People don't go round locking up, not on this island, nobody locks up here. The neighbors are so trustworthy."

"What about when tourists come in summer? Or when unknown people are around?"

"Well, sometimes we have day trippers, but if anybody does come they're usually renting an Airbnb or something and they're so nice and friendly and there are never any robberies and nothing bad happens on this island, ever. Apart from a few ghost stories, nobody's frightened of anything. It's inconceivable what has happened. Of course, in hindsight I feel stupid about not bolting the door. The latch was on but..."

"Up until I first saw you, you were out all night searching for Lizzie?"

"Of course. The second I realized she wasn't in her room I searched the house, and when I didn't find her anywhere I went out into the storm. I hunted everywhere—I was out for hours—but couldn't find her."

"Hours? But you called me to report her missing from the house, from the landline."

"I mean it *felt* like hours... the weather, the storm."

"Does Lizzie sometimes go wandering around on her own?"

"No. I mean it has happened once or twice, but no. And we have an au pair who keeps an eye on the children. A British girl who arrived last week. Of course, technically, she's off duty right now so..."

"Tell me more about your au pair." It is vital that Detective Alba speaks to this woman immediately and she wonders why they didn't mention her before. How come Dr. Stephen didn't mention her? "Where is she now?"

"She lives in one of our cottages, half a mile away from here. All the staff or people who come to help us, we give them their own cottage as it's so much nicer for them, and for us too. It means we're not on top of each other."

"Can you tell me more about her?"

"Shoot, I can't remember her last name, I've got a mental blank, but I've got it written down somewhere in emails... I'm sorry, things come and go."

"Don't worry, that's not important for now. How long has she been working for you?"

"Jayne has only been here just over a week, poor thing." Tears fill Celeste's eyes; her breath catches as she talks.

The detective stores everything she is being told in her mental notebook. Clocking away this information, this vital information. She will dictate all this info into her phone as soon as she is out the door.

"So if Jayne is meant to be looking after the children, why is she in a different location, even if it's only half a mile away? No judgment, I'm just curious."

Tears roll down Celeste's cheeks. "Well, I'm here, and my nurse, and my sister-in-law, and Max... though they're not here right now, of course."

"So if you are..." The detective wants to be delicate here as she can see this woman is suffering not only from bouts of amnesia but with frayed nerves. "If you are sick, how can you look after the—"

"Nurse Sharpe," Celeste interrupts. "My nurse has been helping out with the kids."

"Where is she now, by the way?"

"Sleeping. She's been hired to look after me. You know, with my memory relapses I need constant care."

"Yes, we talked already. Does she have a close relationship with Lizzie?"

"No, no, she... she's looking after *me*."

"But you said she's been helping you out with the children?"

"Occasionally, if I can't manage myself but, oh, God"—she claps her hands to her ears as if she can't bear to listen to her own thoughts—"I feel like I've been such a terrible mother... you must think me so remiss, so—"

"No, the only thing I'm thinking, Mrs. Wainwright, is that we need to find Lizzie as soon as we can. I'm not here to judge anyone, least of all you, I'm here to find your missing child."

Celeste sighs and gulps down the dregs of her coffee.

The detective continues in a softer tone, "Is there anybody we should be interviewing that you can think of that might know something?" It is in this instant that Alba hears light footsteps coming down the stairs. She turns her head and half a minute later a little boy appears in the doorway, dressed in pajamas, bedhead hair, sleep in his eyes.

"Mommy, what's up?"

Celeste opens out her arms. "Come here, my darling."

He pads softly over to his mother, in bare feet. His eyes flip down to the gun on the detective's lower waist. He gasps, then smiles. "Cool."

"I'm Detective Alba. I'm here to talk to your mother. And to you."

"He doesn't know anything," Celeste whispers.

"Mommy? Why is there a police person in our kitchen?" You can tell by the solemn atmosphere that this is not a fun visit; this is not like the visit they had at Liam's school when a policeman and a policewoman came in to talk to the children about crossing the road the right way and what to do in emergency situations.

His mouth begins to tremble, seeing the tears in his mother's eyes. "Mommy?"

The detective turns to him and says sweetly, "Did you see your sister after you went to bed?"

He shakes his head. "Mommy? Where's Lizzie?"

The detective gets up to go.

Celeste realizes her manners. "Sorry, you must be exhausted, would you like a coffee?"

"No, that's fine, I've taken up enough of your time, Mrs. Wainwright, I need to get going now. If you could just tell me where the au pair lives?" She rummages in the back pocket of her pants. "Here's my card, call me if you need me or if you think of anything relevant at all. This is my direct line." This is the second time she's given Celeste her card.

"Thank you," Celeste says, eyes staring at her in shock.

"Mommy, Mommy?" Liam begins to cry. Celeste folds him in her arms.

"It's the pale blue cottage, the first one you get to heading north. It's the one by the little beach."

"The first beach you come to?"

"Yes." Celeste nods. "That's the one. It's got a sign outside: Blue Cottage. Not very original."

The detective is halfway out of the door when she turns. "Thank you, Mrs. Wainwright. I'll be seeing you later today. You should get some rest."

JAYNE

One day ago

I find Celeste, as usual, in her bedroom. She and Max don't seem to share a room. I suppose that's normal, considering her condition. Up at odd hours, and Sharpie always there. Not so romantic. I peer through the open door. Slip in as quietly as I can. I know I'm taking liberties but I can't let it rest knowing she's suffering so with no friend to confide in, or so it seems. Max and his sister have some kind of business to attend to in Portland. Poor Celeste has been left alone with that frosty nurse. Hardly good company. Who, right now, is hanging up the washing outside, in the garden. Strange... this family's choice for help, for staff. They could employ more people: a cleaning lady, for starters. A cook. But Sharpie has been doing quite a bit of cooking, as if she doesn't trust anyone to do a better job than her. She's very possessive of Celeste, never straying far from her side. Marjorie, when she's around, always seems to be on her laptop, working on the luxury linens website, I suppose. The two never seem to converse. I steer clear of them both.

All I can think about is how Celeste has lost her *baby*. It's heartbreaking. I need to know if she's aware of this, if she needs a shoulder to cry on. I'm gobsmacked they're all lying to her. I almost feel like calling the police and letting them know what's going on in this household, but last I heard, lying wasn't a crime, especially when it's supposedly for the patient's good. But what kind of patient is Celeste? Stephen is a quack, by all accounts. I mean, fine, he's a therapist, but she needs so much more than that. She needs a psychiatrist, surely? Who prescribed her medication? Which professionals green-lighted Celeste's dosage? My eyes land on her bedside table. No vials of pills. I'd like to rummage around in the drawer and find out what she's taking, if anything. Is she asleep? Awake? Celeste is motionless, although the rise and fall of her breath is evident—barely—from a stirring of the sheets wrapped in a tangle around her frail body. Her nightie is bright white. All is white. Everything seems serene, but I know it's anything but.

"Jayne," she calls out weakly. How does she know it's me? She hasn't even looked up. Are my footsteps *that* clumsy? "What are you doing here?"

"I thought you might like the company," I answer in a whisper.

Celeste turns her body and lets out a groan. The broken ribs must still hurt like hell. Nothing you can do except let time heal broken ribs, apparently.

"Have you had a doctor's visit recently?" I ask.

"Dr. Stephen," she replies in a reedy voice.

"You don't think you need a second opinion? Someone specialized?"

"He was recommended." She coughs into her sheet.

I take another step closer. "He told me he was hired for the job because he used to know Max and went to college with him. Is that true? Is that the only reason he has this job? Don't you think you need somebody much more qualified? A real top-notch psychiatrist?"

She sits up in bed, startled. The mosquito net has been drawn back and I can make out her features clearly now. She looks more attractive than before, the bone structure of her face chiseled but less angular. Her soft dark hair has been brushed, creating a sort of halo around her face. Despite the bags under her eyes, she is so much prettier than I took her for. She still looks exhausted though, mentally drained.

She rasps, "How did you even get in here?"

I sit on the edge of her bed. "I thought you might need something. A cup of tea or water or something. Are you thirsty? Your throat dry?"

"I thought the door was locked." She isn't angry or snappish, merely stating a fact. She yawns, and it strikes me she's younger than I thought. Something about her pearly teeth, her little heart-shaped face, make me warm to her all the more.

"You're locking your door?" I ask. "I don't think that's a good idea. People need to see you, to talk to you. You can't lock yourself away in here."

"*I'm* not locking myself in here, *they* are."

My jaw drops. "Who's 'they'? Stephen? Your nurse?"

"They're worried about me, they're..." But she doesn't finish.

"What are they worried about? And who... who's doing this?"

She shakes her head as if to rid it of nonsense, as if she'd just made this up. "Nobody." She rakes her hands through her hair, agitated. "Would you mind, Jayne, getting me a glass of water? I don't know where my nurse is, she hasn't been around today, nobody's been around today, nobody's been here looking after me!" Her voice is trembling.

I'm glad I've come. This woman needs twenty-four-seven care. It's unusual for Sharpie not to be glued by her side. "Would you like to talk to me about anything? Get things off your chest? I can help."

"The doctor says I need to rest."

"Your therapist, you mean? Stephen?" I sidle closer to the bed so as not to startle her, not to spook her.

"Yes, my doctor."

"Mrs. Wain— I mean, Celeste, you know he's not a real doctor, don't you? I mean, he is a doctor," I relent, "but only a doctor because he's got some letters after his name. But he's a therapist, not a *medical* doctor. Have you also got a proper doctor who's been visiting you? A psychiatrist who's qualified to prescribe medication?"

"My wedding photos have disappeared," she tells me in a conspiratorial tone, as if someone might be listening.

I'm startled by the change of subject. "Framed ones?"

She shakes her head wearily.

"What, do you have a photo album or something?"

"Yes, a white leather-bound album. I need those photos, *please* find them for me, Jayne!"

I feel chuffed she knows who I am. Silly, but it feels as if that's a step closer to being friends. "Is there anything in particular you're looking for?"

"Yes," she answers. "Proof."

"Proof? Proof of what?"

She scrunches her eyes closed as if in pain. Mental or physical, I can't tell.

"Proof that you married Max?" I ask her. "You did. Before I accepted the job I looked you up on Google. You're a couple, you're real, you did marry each other, I promise. There's a picture of you both at a fundraiser at the Metropolitan Museum in New York. 'Mr. and Mrs. Wainwright, newlyweds,' it said." I feel so bad for her. Imagine not remembering your wedding, poor thing.

"It's something else I want to find out," she says in a hoarse whisper.

"What on earth is going on around here?" The door flies

open and Sharpie breezes into the room with a pile of clean linen in her arms. The sheets smell of sunshine. She's like a whirlwind; I can actually feel the cool air rushing by her side... she chills the room, she really does. She turns her pointed face at me like an arrow, her eyes bulging, her nostrils flaring with wrath as she clocks me sitting on the edge of the bed. *What cheek!* her expression says.

"What are you doing in *here*?" she seethes, not even addressing me by name.

"Mrs. Wainwright needed a glass of water." There's something about this woman that makes me feel like I'm back at school and about to get detention.

"You have no business bothering Mrs. Wainwright. I have everything under control, thank you very much for your consideration. Now would you please leave the room." It's a command, not a question.

"Maybe she needs some water for her medication?" I throw out, wondering if Celeste has been given anything for the pain in her ribs. "What's she taking?"

"As if it's any of your business." Sharpie gives me a fake smile. "I need to get on with things and, quite frankly, you're in the way."

I get up, but lift my chin. "*Quite frankly*, I don't appreciate you talking to me that way." My voice quakes, my hands shake. It's taken me my whole life to feel this brave and I'm not going to cower down to bullies now.

Meanwhile, my eyes circumnavigate the bedroom, scanning the bookshelves for a wedding album. All I see is a handful of paperbacks. Some romance novels and bestseller, thriller-type books. I don't see an album anywhere among the knickknacks. Sharpie and the rail-thin angles of her legs dart around the bed, fluffing up pillows and straightening the covers.

I still haven't left the room, although I'm standing in the doorway. "I'm more than willing to help," I offer. "To make

Celeste a nice lunch, read her a story, or just keep her company. She's imprisoned in this room all day long, she must be getting bored, this can't be good for her."

Sharpie stops what she's doing. "I am her *nurse* and I think I'm the one best qualified to see what is good for her. Please leave, er..."

"My name is Jayne."

"Jayne, please leave. You have your own cottage and you're here to look after the children, not to meddle with Mrs. Wainwright's health or well-being."

"The children are having their nap, and I have a couple of hours to kill," I retort thick-skinnedly.

"Then I strongly suggest you go 'kill' your hours elsewhere," she snaps, emphasizing the word "kill."

Meanwhile Celeste says nothing as she twiddles her hands together. That thing she does like she's knitting. It makes me wonder what she was like before the accident. Surely, that nervous tic is not a result of the car crash? This whole setup is beyond bizarre, and I want to get to the bottom of it.

"Remember, she wanted some water," I fire out as I swish out of the room. Or at least I try to swish, though in truth it turns out to be more of a "galumph" out of the room, as I trip and end up bashing my leg into a chair in the corridor, sending it flying.

Before I leave the main house, I sneak into the living room and look around to see if I can find the wedding album. No luck. It does make sense that there should be a wedding album. It's obviously really important to Celeste, and I can understand if you're losing your memory how you'd want to get your hands on that. You'd want to claim a piece of your past, lay truth to maybe the happiest day of your life.

Photos would make her feel safe, loved, and help her remember.

JAYNE

It's interesting. Having pinched the wine bottles from that cellar, I've yet to touch them. Well, I have *touched* them but I haven't opened the bottles, haven't taken one sip. Sometimes you need something close to hand to be able to deny yourself. I know I shouldn't be thinking of it this way; I'm not "denying" myself anything, I'm giving myself a gift by not succumbing to temptation. Having the bottles there is enough. I've hidden them along the back crease of the sofa behind the cushions, laid out one by one in single file. They're there, but I don't need them. I can even sit on the sofa knowing that I have the strength to not touch a drop.

It's been a long day. The children have had their nap and I'm sitting on a rock on the beach, watching them and their mini sailboats, which are perilously far out to sea. Seems extreme to me that you can start learning to sail so young. Their sailing teacher is with them, obviously. A man, but the sun's glaring in my eyes so all I can make out is a silhouette against the light. The kids don't know I'm watching them as their lesson started during my hours off, but after missing the drama last time with Celeste wading into the water in her nightie, I wanted to be around, just in case. I tell myself it's for the safety of the children, though it's more than that. But the water's calm, like a mirror, the blue a sheen of peace and tranquility. It's freaky how it can change so quickly. It's like a different world today than the choppy ocean of last week. It's mad, it feels like months have already passed.

I can't believe that little Lizzie is only four years old and is managing to sail a dinghy herself—with the instructor in the boat with her, but still. I make out her little figure, her red life-jacket on. She's not exactly going very fast, but there she is, managing to steer. And Liam is in his own boat, also sailing. It's the most adorable thing I've ever seen.

I'm about to go to the shore and wave to them—even though my shift doesn't begin for another hour—but Sharpie (appearing from nowhere), is suddenly right here on the beach, glaring down, lording it over me. At first I don't recognize her because she's not wearing her white Crocs and nurse's uniform and her hair's down. She's in shorts and a T-shirt. Skinny but surprisingly toned legs. She looks quite carefree like this. But her cutting voice with its authoritative, cocky tone lets me know for sure it's her.

"Jayne," she barks, standing right in my light, my sun, her looming shadow casting me into instant shade, "I'm going to take the children inside to clean up. A quick shower and a visit to their mom and then they'll be all yours."

"It's fine," I tell her. "I'm here, I'm available. I'm very happy to—"

"If you know what's best for you, you should go back to your cottage."

I can't believe she has the gall to talk to me this way. "Actually I'm enjoying the sun," I counter. "I'm quite happy where I am."

She raises an eyebrow. "You'll burn. The sun's a lot stronger than you think. My advice is... go back to your cottage."

"Um, last I heard this was a free country. I'd rather stay here, thank you very much." I give her a big smile.

"Suit yourself. But don't say I didn't warn you." She stalks off toward the sea. I want to follow, but of course that would look ridiculous, so I stay where I am. As the sailing coach draws the dinghies up onto the beach, I observe Sharpie shouting at him, waving her arms around. I can't hear what she's saying but they're in discussion, the two of them, as if there's been some huge mistake and he shouldn't be giving them this lesson. I'm dying to jump up and go eavesdrop on the conversation, but I resist the urge. I don't need her as my enemy; things are already bad enough. I had specifically set myself back a bit on the sand because it was too wet closer to the shore. Here it's dryer, but I am too far off to have a clear view of what's going on. The coach is wearing a baseball cap pulled down over his eyes. I can't see the color of his hair or make out whether I recognize him or not. But one thing I have noticed: he only seems to come on the days that Max is off the island. I wonder if it's a coincidence?

JAYNE

Max lent me Celeste's bicycle yesterday.

"But I thought it was your gift to her," I protested when he handed the shiny new bike to me. It was as blue as the sky. I would have given anything for a bike like this as a child. Or at any age.

"She refuses to use it." We were standing at the back of his house, although he didn't invite me in. He held a spanner in his hand, his features so disarming suddenly, and Heathcliff-like, with an angry scowl on his rugged face, where I noted a smear of oil, and his heavy black brows so intense, and with his eyes drilling into mine, I felt myself blush. But he wasn't flirting. Quite the opposite.

"Just take the damn thing," he snapped. "Sorry, I mean, it's upsetting, that's all. My wife is scared of anything with wheels now, you know, after her attempted—" He broke off mid-sentence.

I jumped on the bike and pedaled away, mortified by his sharp tongue. Up until then he'd been nothing but charming. The bite in his voice, the anger. I could feel the smoke sizzle off him like dry ice.

The bike has turned out to be a godsend, allowing me to explore the island and get some exercise, and take the kids along too. Liam has his own bike and mine has a child seat at the back for Lizzie. I found some protective gear for all three of us, although the roads are devoid of vehicles apart from a stray car once in a while, or other bikes, or golf carts. Liam and Lizzie absolutely loved our excursion. I can remember myself the first time I had wheels—a secondhand number I found at a charity shop—it made me feel invincible and free, like I could do anything, be anything. No way, though, would I ride around London on a bicycle these days, not with so much traffic. Riding around here is like being reborn.

I packed a picnic with stuff that the kids like, which was okayed by Celeste. I brought extra water, too, which I stowed into the front basket, and we set off to the other side of the island to Rocky Beach, a place marked on an old map I found in my cottage.

There was a group of boys in the beach scrub, somewhere between the ages of eleven and thirteen, with nets and buckets in their hands.

"Where you goin'?" Liam called over.

"We left our lobster trap over there," one shouted back. "Watch out for the rockweed, it's slippery." It looked like they were heading to the promontory, and Liam gazed at them longingly, hoping they invite him along. The boys looked wild and weathered, shoeless and shirtless, their skin tanned nut-brown. and I was relieved when they picked their way over the algae-laden beach like agile hermit crabs and left us alone.

"Those boys are mean," Lizzie told me, crumpling her nose.

"Why?"

"They go frogging when it's dark."

"What's frogging?"

"They eat frogs," Liam explained. "They hunt 'em and eat 'em."

"Ew," Lizzie yelled out in the direction of the boys, "that's mean and gross and cruel!"

"Shut up!" Liam shouted at her. "They'll think you're a sissy."

"I don't care," she sang. "I don't like those mean boys and they know it!"

"You're a baby," Liam taunted his sister. "A little baby *girl*."

Lizzie flung her arms around my legs and squeezed me tight. I hugged her back. I noticed little pinch marks or tiny bruises on her arms, and when I took a closer look, there were some on her legs. I mean, I bump into furniture all the time: bedposts, corners, corners of tables. I always seem to have bruises on my thighs, being so clumsy, but Lizzie? It made me nervous, it made me wonder.

But it wasn't till after we'd eaten that I found out what the problem was.

Lizzie was full of questions. Nothing passes her by.

"When the sun goes to sleep, where does she live?"

Oh, God, I thought. I could hardly say, "I'll look that up." So I told her, "Good question, Lizzie, you're a clever thing, aren't you? Well, she doesn't really sleep, she's always awake somewhere. Her going to sleep is only an illusion."

"Who's Anna Looshan?"

I laughed. "The sun's busy shining somewhere else in the world." I loved the way Lizzie personified the sun as "she."

"Doesn't she go to sleep? Ever?"

"Wow! Look at these shiny pebbles!" I said, distracting her because her questions were getting too complicated and I didn't want to tell her rubbish. I bent down and picked up a couple of pretty stones. "To add to your collection."

Lizzie, I find, always has something interesting to say. Her mother's right: she *is* smart. A savvy little thing, and she picks up the most fascinating tidbits of information and retains them. Not like Liam. Liam is simple and solid in his ways.

Or so I thought at first.

"I'm going to make a garden like an octopus," Lizzie announced, arranging shells and pebbles in a snail pattern on the sand and then rising to her feet to admire her handiwork. She plopped down the stones I had handed her as the centerpiece for whatever she was creating. It made my heart swell. *She is so adorable*, I thought in that moment. *The perfect child with the perfect amount of sass and sweetness*. The realization that I was only there for what remained of the summer and that I'd have to say goodbye to Lizzie at the end of this job suddenly filled me with a heavy sadness. *Will I ever have a child like Lizzie of my own?* She felt so *mine* that day. So part of me. So meant to be.

"Have you seen an octopus?" I asked. "An octopus here in the water?"

"I seen a movie," she shouted out, with her hands on her hips like the bossy little madam she is, "and I know all about octopussies now. They make gardens and they're very, very smart. They can change color too!"

"She saw that dumb movie *My Octopus Teacher*," Liam broke in, kicking the sand right by Lizzie's creation.

I kept my eye on him. "Oh, I hear that's a beautiful film. Be careful of Lizzie's garden, sweetie."

"She's dumb," Liam bellowed, picking up a pebble and throwing it at his sister.

I grabbed him by the wrist and prized another stone out of his hand. "Hey! No, no, no, no! We don't do that kind of thing, Liam. Never hurt anybody else, ever, ever, *ever*, and you never touch a girl—you know that, right? You might be stronger than Lizzie but that doesn't give you the right to hurt her. Never. Okay?" I smacked his hand. Not hard, just a little tap to get the point across.

Liam howled, screaming, "I'm gonna tell my dad on you!"

Oh God, I thought. I could picture myself back on the ferry, suitcase packed, the minute Max returned from Portland and heard about this little "go with the flow" scene.

"I'm gonna tell my dad you hit me!"

I stood there in shock, not knowing what to say. There was not a mark on him, of course there wasn't. All I'd done was tap his hand for effect, but I know what parents are like these days. Even touching a child is practically a sackable offense.

"Well, do you know what?" I chanted back. "I'm going to tell on you, *too*."

He pouted. "I done nothing."

I didn't bother correcting his grammar, just said in a calm voice, "Yes you did. You threw a stone at Lizzie."

"He does it all the time," Lizzie said, carrying on drawing in the sand as if it didn't bother her one bit.

"I do not."

"You do too!"

"Shush, children. Liam, seriously, you must never ever hurt another person, do you understand?"

"She started it."

"No she did not. I have been here the whole time and Lizzie has not done anything to you. She's been a good girl."

"Good girl," Lizzie repeated.

"She's a brat," Liam burst out.

"Where did you learn that word?" I said, thinking maybe it came from Sharpie.

Liam, his little mouth turned down, didn't answer.

"I *was* going to make cinnamon toast, but now I'm not so sure," I said in retaliation.

"You don't know *how* to make cinnamon toast," Liam sneered.

"Oh, don't I?"

He eyed me suspiciously, frowning, looking disconcertingly like his father.

"I was going to make some delicious cinnamon toast, but I don't give cinnamon toast to boys who hit girls."

"I didn't hit her."

"You threw a stone—that's just as bad, maybe worse."

The rest of the day was dampened by a niggling panic festering in my mind about Liam telling on me, and worry about poor Lizzie and her bruises. Liam, of course, swore it wasn't him, and Lizzie seemed perplexed when I asked about them. Was she too scared to tell the truth? Was somebody abusing her? Or were they everyday bruises from her sailing lessons and bumping into things?

I vowed I'd keep an eagle eye not only on Liam but everybody around Lizzie. Parents, the therapist, the nurse, the sailboat instructor... oh yes, and the aunt.

Someone was guilty.

And I was determined to find out who.

THE DISAPPEARANCE

Now

Lizzie Wainwright has been missing for approximately eight hours. The rain and wind have almost subsided, but not quite. Dawn is breaking and begins to light up the sky and ocean. The sun will soon show its face. There is still a crescent of moon and some stars gradually fading. The smell of the ocean wafts on a gentle summer breeze. Salt, sand, rockweed, granite. The subtle aromas of the coast.

Detective Alba loves this time of the morning between night and day when it's on the pre-dawn cusp like this. Apart from the sodden ground and branches whipped off the trees by the wind, it is eerily calm as if there was no storm at all last night, no thunder, no lightning. Now the misty light leaches the last of the dark from the sky and air, and the morning breaks every second more into day.

Alba makes her way toward the blue cottage, still finding it strange that the family would house their au pair in a separate building from the children. Surely the whole point is to have someone there at all times? But then an au pair is different from a full-time nanny. Au pairs are paid a lot less and are usually young, often foreign, maybe somebody learning English. But no, that's right, the girl is British.

The detective fills her lungs with the salty air, releases a great yawn, wishing she'd accepted that coffee. She purposefully didn't ask for too many details about this au pair. She wants to form her own first impression unbiased by others' perceptions of the woman, reel in her own impressions of what Jayne is really like. It irks her that Jayne was not part of the search party last night. Lizzie's mother was out in the storm before Alba even arrived, so why wasn't the au pair helping? She must have heard the commotion? Why didn't she at least come out to see what was going on? Strange, that.

She locates the cottage a good half a mile away from the main house. It's cuter than the cottage where Dr. Stephen is staying. There are flowers in front. And some kind of creeper growing up one side. It faces the sea head-on. It's less run-down than the other cottage. She walks up a couple of steps, onto the porch, and tentatively knocks on the door, but there is no answer. She tries the handle. Locked. *Well, at least somebody locks their door around here,* she thinks. She tries again, this time a hard bang. Still no answer. And then she peers into the shut window. It has the same kind of layout as the other cottage, except in reverse. An open-plan kitchen and living room. The detective notices several wine bottles on the coffee table, empty as far as she can see. Maybe Jayne conked out last night, drunk? That would explain a lot.

Alba walks down the steps and around the side of the cottage, looks through the bedroom window. Trying to interview someone with a hangover may not sound like a great idea but interviewing this au pair ASAP is paramount. The blind is drawn. She directs her flashlight into every corner and up at the window itself, but there is no response even when she knocks on the glass. She cannot break in without a warrant. In a normal situation she would secure the premises and wait until another member of her team arrives, but right now she is a one-woman show. The only alternative is to come back in a short while, hopefully when the K-9 arrives. Either this woman Jayne is not here, or she is nursing one hell of a headache, judging by the amount of empty wine bottles.

The detective is about to leave, but before she does, she notices something. On the porch there is one of those wooden chair swings and resting on the arm is a little cardigan. Coral pink. It looks like it would fit a four-year-old perfectly. She takes out her phone and snaps a few shots. In a perfect world Forensics would be called in, the cottage surrounded by tape, but she doesn't have the resources to do things by the book right now. So she draws out a plastic bag from her workbag. Goes through the same routine as before, slipping on latex gloves to avoid contaminating evidence. The cardigan is heavy for its size. Wet. She brings it to her nose and smells the unmistakable odor of brine, of the ocean. And what she suspects might be a straggle of kelp hanging from a button. She stashes the cardigan in the bag. It's nothing conclusive. This woman is Lizzie's au pair, after all. Still, Detective Alba will be back within the hour. She wants to look into Jayne's eyes and see her reaction when she asks her about the cardigan.

THE DISAPPEARANCE

Detective Alba is grateful for being united with her team. Her partner, Carl, has a coffee waiting for her: black, two sugars, the way she likes it. He pours out a cup from the Thermos.

"Any luck?" she asks.

"No, not so far."

"Is George with his dog?"

"Up at the north side of the island, that's where the scent was leading them. What there was of it. *Is* of it. It's faint as hell."

"Strange."

Carl heaves a sigh. "You think this is an abduction, don't you?"

"Hard to say. Looks like it, maybe. Or maybe not. Could be a drowning. Or something worse. Breaks my heart. This is a shitty job sometimes."

Carl nods. "The coast guards are on the way. I guess the best we can expect is a dead body. Being realistic. But at least it'll give the parents closure. Heartbreaking, isn't it? She's only four years old. If it's an abduction why would someone do this? Why?"

Alba draws in a long breath, then exhales slowly. "Beats me. There are so many people who have screwed-up reasons for doing things that make no sense to you or me. I know... it's tough to accept, isn't it?"

"Sure is."

"I'm going to call George now and see what he's got. I need him to take Dune to the au pair's cottage."

"Good idea. I'll be with the others if you need me."

Detective Alba calls the dog handler and he picks up on the fifth ring.

"Yep, George here."

"Alba. What do you have?"

"Circles. Dune's going round and round in circles. Something happened up here, but I have no idea what. There's no real lead, it kind of fizzles out. It's like he's sniffing the air, but with all that rain last night whatever it was has been washed away. Truth be told, I don't think we're onto anything here. I think it's a bogus lead."

It dawns on Detective Alba, in that second, that the little girl would've probably been carried by somebody. Four years old, not too heavy. No wonder the dog couldn't pick up any distinctive trail scent on the ground.

"I'm going back to the au pair's cottage. Near the beach, not far from the dock. Can you get there ASAP? I'd like Dune to check her place out."

"Sure thing."

As Alba is approaching the girl's cottage, Jayne is walking out the door, locking it behind her. When Jayne sees her, she takes a step back as if startled.

"Oh my God, you scared me," she yelps in an accent that is not that familiar to Alba. She would've pegged it as Australian, but they told her Jayne was British.

"Morning. Sorry, I know it's early, I'm Detective Adele Alba with the Maine State Police." She flashes her badge.

"Can I help you?" the girl asks, her tone surprised. If this woman does know something about Lizzie's disappearance, she is doing a good job of pretending she doesn't.

Alba walks up the steps of the cottage toward the stoop. "I came earlier, but there was no reply. Were you out? I knocked pretty hard."

"No, I was here all night."

"You stayed home the *whole* of last night?" Alba checks.

"Yeah. Is something wrong? Is everything okay? That was a horrible storm we had, but the truth is I was out of it pretty much the whole night. Slept through most of it." Jayne has a look of alarm on her face as she glances around her, to the left, to the right. "Sorry, is something wrong? Did something terrible happen to someone?"

"Why would you say that?" Alba doesn't mean for it to come out that way, but her mouth utters the words before she can stop herself. She sounds antagonistic, even aggressive, and this is the last thing she wants. Not sleeping the whole night and not eating has done her no favors. She would kill for a donut right now. *Why did they not bring donuts with the coffee?*

"Actually," she concedes, "something bad *has* happened. Lizzie Wainwright went missing last night. She's still missing."

"You're joking." Jayne's eyes mist over.

"No, I'm not. We have search teams out trying to locate her. Do you have any idea where she might be?"

"No, it was my night off last night. This is awful! Are you sure she's not at home? Playing hide and seek somewhere? Did you look in Liam's room? Her brother... did you—"

"Yes," the detective interjects, "we've searched thoroughly. My team are on it, going door to door interviewing everyone on the island."

"Sorry." Jayne takes a step back. "Would you like to come

in? I was about to head off to the main house... to get Lizzie and Liam, but if—"

"Thank you, yes, I'd love to take a quick look around."

Jayne unlocks the door and they step inside.

Alba surveys the open-plan kitchen. There are coloring books, crayons, paints, children's story books here. She notes their titles. Some toys. What is she expecting? Hoping? Other than seeing Lizzie there in the flesh, nothing is conclusive. Lizzie's DNA will be all over the place. Still, she looks through the cottage until she has satisfied her curiosity. Checks all the closets, the bathroom, under beds, in every nook and cranny a child could be. The place is in disarray but nothing seems out of the ordinary.

"When did you last see Lizzie?" Alba asks.

Jayne wipes away a tear. "When I took her to her house yesterday evening, around seven o'clock, I think."

"You're not sure?"

"Well, I know it was before sunset, and sunset's around eight o'clock so, yeah, I took her home around then. They had dinner ready for her, and after that she usually has a bath and a bedtime story before going to sleep."

"And this is not something you do, being the au pair?"

"Well, sometimes, yeah. Depending."

"Depending on what?"

"Well, when Max is around—that's Mr. Wainwright—or his sister Marjorie, sometimes while Celeste's in bed I might bathe the children then read to them. Or sometimes I'll read to Lizzie while Max does Liam's story."

"You're on first names with Mr. and Mrs. Wainwright?"

"Yeah, they don't like formalities."

It strikes the detective as strange that when the father is around, the au pair is also around. Surely it should work the other way? More hands on deck, less need for the nanny? "Celeste Wainwright's a little bit frail right now and needs your help?" This is a dumb question. But she wants to see what the au pair has to say.

"She's out of sorts, yeah, but it depends on the day. Sometimes she's very lucid and likes to bathe Lizzie and Liam herself. Other days she's in bed and can't remember what day of the week it is. It really depends. Her memory comes and goes... she had a terrible car accident and that's why they hired me."

"Well, thank you for letting me look around." Alba steps back out onto the porch and calls George to make sure he is on his way. He tells her he'll be there in five, and she relays this to Jayne and asks her to stay here until the dog has swept the area.

The au pair looks panic-stricken at the mention of a dog. "But Lizzie hangs out here all the time—her scent will be everywhere!" Her lips tremble when she speaks.

Alba notices a bicycle leaning up against the cottage that she didn't see earlier. She can't be sure if she missed it, and she is now kicking herself for not taking a photo, a longshot of the cottage. The bike leaning against the cottage looks very picturesque. In a photo it might look like something a blogger would post on Instagram. The perfect postcard cottage. Flower beds and a pretty blue bike.

"Nice bicycle," she remarks.

"Oh, it's not mine, it was lent to me by Celeste. Well, not Celeste, actually, but Max. He bought it for her but she never uses it."

"It's got a child seat—useful, that."

"Yeah, it means I can take Lizzie on the back."

"And the little boy?"

Jayne wipes her nose with the back of her hand. "Oh, he has his own bike."

Something occurs to the detective.

The bicycle.

If Lizzie was sitting on the back seat there would be a less distinctive scent trail. With no footsteps on the ground, the sniffer dog would have to rely on air scent. Not easy after a storm, with all that rain washing away clues. K-9 Dune is a Belgian Malinois mix and has had great success in the past. Some K-9 search and rescue dogs are trackers, and the ones that sniff the air are known as scouters. Is Dune also a scouter as well as a tracker and cadaver dog? She knows that some abductors have gone as far as using cayenne pepper to confuse a dog, or even cause permanent damage to the canine.

Maybe it's the way Alba is focusing on the bike, or maybe the expression on her face that makes Jayne start talking quickly, as if to fill the silence.

Jayne cuts into her rumination about the K-9, the different ways Lizzie could have been taken. "I can't *believe* Lizzie's missing! I mean, I'm going to go searching for her myself. There must be some explanation."

Detective Alba notes how Jayne is as jumpy as she is distraught. Alba prays that the little girl is still alive. "Any reason you didn't wake up last night? There was quite a lot of commotion outside."

"I... er... I took a sleeping pill. I've got terrible jet lag and have been having a shit time of it, trying to get to sleep. Jet lag can last for ages, you know. The therapist... I don't know if you know him, Dr. Stephen? He's Celeste's therapist. Well, he gave me some kind of sleeping pill, I'm not sure what exactly, but wow, it really knocked me out. You Americans really know your stuff when it comes to sleeping pills, I guess." She titters nervously in an attempt to hide her faux pas. "Sorry, that sounded a bit rude, I didn't mean that, but yeah, I'm not used to taking sleeping pills, that's all."

"Is there any reason you can think of why somebody might have taken Lizzie somewhere?"

"God, no!"

"Seen any strange people around or anything unusual?"

"No, nothing, nobody weird. I think I'm in shock actually.

I'm sorry, I'm still a bit groggy from last night, but shit... I can't believe she's missing. What if she went... I don't know... down to the sea? Oh, God!" She covers her face with her hands.

"Do you think she might do something like that?"

A sob escapes Jayne's throat. It takes a while for her to answer through her sniffles. "Well, she does know how to swim, and she's been having a lot of sailing lessons recently."

"Sailing?"

"Yeah, believe it or not, sailing lessons, even at her age."

The detective shifts her weight. Her legs are tired. She hasn't sat down all morning. She is not about to sit on that swing and contaminate possible evidence. "Can you tell me about these sailing lessons?"

"Well, Lizzie and Liam have been out a couple of times with the sailing instructor."

"Do you know the name of this person?"

"No. I know he's a man, but I've never met him. I observed him from a distance, but Nurse Sharpe knows who he is." She grabs a roll of paper kitchen towel and blows her nose.

"And you know this, how?"

"I saw them having a heated discussion yesterday. The kids had gone out for a lesson and the nurse was very pissed off about it."

"Okay, thank you for the information, I'll be sure to ask her mother. I have one more question." She leaves that to hang in the air a beat and notices the alarm on Jayne's face. "Earlier this morning when I was here there was a cardigan on that swing chair on your porch."

"A cardigan?"

"Yes, a child's cardigan, coral pink. I'm assuming it belongs to Lizzie. Do you know anything about this?"

Jayne shakes her head, frowning. "No. Are you sure?"

"Yes, I bagged it as evidence. It was wet, like it had been in the ocean. I have a snapshot of it on my phone." The detective gets her phone out and scrolls through the photos. She holds out the phone for Jayne to see.

Jayne takes a look. "No, that's not Lizzie's cardigan, or if it is I don't recognize it."

"You're positive?"

"Well, I haven't seen that cardigan around, but you might want to ask her mother?"

"So the last time you saw Lizzie was... sorry, I've pulled an all-nighter, I'm a little hazy." She remembers Jayne's answer, all right, but she's asking again to see if the story changes.

"Like I said, I dropped her off at her mum's house at around seven last night. Then I came back here, had a shower, read my novel, and then the next thing, with that sleeping pill, I was out for the count."

"Did you have a drink? A glass of wine or anything?"

Jayne steps back, offended. "No I didn't, although I'm not sure what it has to do with Lizzie's disappearance, whether I had a drink of wine or not. Detective... are you accusing me of something?"

"Absolutely not. Just covering all the bases." Alba spots Dune and his handler approaching and lets out a breath of relief.

If Lizzie is in or around this cottage, dead or alive, Dune will find her.

CELESTE

Lizzie has been gone for twelve hours. And Violet, six days. I am standing by Violet's vacant crib, holding her little yellow blanket to my nose, breathing in the remnants of her scent. My tears plop on the cotton crochet and I use it to dab my damp cheeks, my eyes. Every hour without my girls is a particular brand of mental torture. The emptiness slips into the crevices of my mind like fungus, settling into my gray matter, spreading its spores. Growing. Multiplying. Not letting me forget.

I haven't gotten rid of this crib and have no intention of doing so. It lives here in the attic, in a secret room that you get to through an old-fashioned wardrobe, where my grandmother's vintage fur coats from the 1930s also live, smelling of mothballs and age. It was when I was a child, obsessed with Narnia, that Papa made this space for me. The small room, only a few feet by a few feet, is painted like it's all pure snow. Even Max and my children do not know about this room. Here I put my treasures, and it is here I have housed Violet's crib.

When the police searched the house they did not find this room and I wasn't about to enlighten them. Obviously not.

I sink into my memories. How I'd hold my beautiful baby in

my arms and rock her, sing to her in a hushed voice near the pearl of her ear, kiss her soft, paper-thin head that felt so delicate it could be crushed by the smallest pressure. As I hold her yellow baby blanket over my eyes, my nose, I really can smell her still: her sweetness, her warm skin, and that unmistakable baby scent I'd inhale till it reached the back of my throat, all the while Violet making tiny noises of pleasure after her feed. Tears are flowing uncontrollably down my cheeks, trickling down my neck in sticky wet tracks. For a second I feel as if Violet is still here with me.

I think of Lizzie as a baby, too. Different from Violet in so many ways, but my baby girl just the same, my special divine little girl growing into a whole amazing being, bubbling with questions and curiosity and laughter. I could make her laugh even when I pulled a monster face.

Am I a monster?

Perhaps.

Perhaps I am.

My girls, I think. *Oh, my beautiful girls, I am so, so sorry, please forgive me. I tried my best.*

JAYNE

Lizzie has disappeared? I can't believe it. I feel physically sick. There's no way she would've gone out into the water alone, she's too smart for that. Then I remember how Liam threw a stone at her, and wonder if he... no way, he was in bed, he would've been in bed. But with Max and Marjorie away... who knows what's been going on in that household? I know sometimes Celeste is completely out of it and that bitch Sharpie doesn't seem to even notice the kids, she's so wrapped up in Celeste's well-being. Though it is her job to look after Celeste, to be fair.

That cop must've been spying on me through the window, looking through and seeing the empty wine bottles. How else would she have known to say something like that? To ask me if I'd had a drink? I'm wondering how she knew... how she knew to push my buttons. The fact is I opened each wine bottle with a corkscrew, one by one, laid them out in a row as if they were to be executed by a firing squad. I sat in front of them for over half an hour, not letting myself pour, not even one glass, not letting my finger even touch the necks. I poured the wine down the sink, listening to the *glug, glug, glug* with satisfaction, each bottle, one by one.

No more of a waste down the sink than in my gullet, is it?

It gave me a feeling of power... that I could manage my addiction, that I could be strong.

So what the hell was that detective talking about, the cardigan on the swing chair? I did *not* leave a cardigan there, and I've never seen that bloody cardigan she showed me on her phone, never in my life! I'm wondering if she planted it there to see what my reaction would be. Isn't that the kind of thing these people do, to try and catch you out?

Who knows.

This island is really getting to me now and I want to leave. But then I feel too much for Lizzie. I can't abandon her when she needs me more than ever. Even in the short space of time I've been here, she's won my heart.

I *need* to find her.

I run over to the main house as fast as I can, and it's not long before I'm hopelessly out of breath. I need to lose weight, my health is on the line, my knees feel the pound—and the pounds —every time my trainers hit the ground.

I finally reach the house, gasping, feeling sick, and wish I hadn't had that sleeping pill last night. "Groggy" is an understatement. I had a cup of coffee earlier but didn't eat and now I need something to fill my stomach. There is crime scene tape around the kitchen door. I hover there, realizing the seriousness of this situation. Lizzie is *missing* and the police are treating it not as a missing child but as a *crime*.

"Never mind about the tape, you can come in," Celeste cries out through the open window. "They've done what they had to do, the police."

"Are you sure?" I ask, not convinced. If so, why is the tape still up? Don't these things take time? Don't they want to brush everything down for evidence? What does this mean? They must think that Lizzie has been abducted, they must think it wasn't an accident... why do they think this?

Then it dawns on me. There is a murderer in our midst! And the terrifying thing is I'm one of the suspects! At least, as far as... what was her name? Detective Adele Alba is concerned.

I push the kitchen door open to find Celeste and Sharpie making breakfast, talking as if nothing has happened. The second they see me they stand to attention, changing their demeanor, rearranging the expressions on their faces into ones of worried concern. But I swear I didn't hear that a few seconds ago. I heard two women calmly making breakfast.

"Is it true that Lizzie's missing?" I blurt out, without saying good morning.

"Yes." Celeste hangs her head. "There's been a search party. I hunted for her myself last night, but I can't find her anywhere."

Something beyond weird is going on around here. I'm sorry, but it does not make sense that two of Celeste's kids have either died or gone missing within the space of a week. I'm beginning to wonder about Celeste, if she's the ditzy person she portrays herself to be. I see her in a new light now. She frightens me. Chills run down my spine. For a second I see a murderous woman who has killed her kids, one of them for sure, and maybe another. A bit of a coincidence, isn't it, that she was out last night, in the rain? Maybe she took Lizzie out there herself, dumped her in the ocean. Drowned her in that coral-pink cardigan and then left it on my porch when I was passed out asleep?

"Has anybody found anything?" I ask.

Celeste shakes her head, her eyes all puppy-dog sad. "No, not really. The detective asked me earlier this morning about a coral-colored cardigan. But I honestly can't remember. I can't remember if Lizzie owns a coral-colored cardigan. I took a look at it and it didn't ring a bell, but then who knows?"

Very convenient, I think. Very bloody convenient how Celeste has suddenly "forgotten" everything, because she "loses her memory" all the time.

There do exist women who kill their kids. It seems extraordinary, but it's true, it does happen and it doesn't necessarily have anything to do with wealth or poverty. Like domestic violence, it cuts across every level of society, rich and poor, privileged and desperate, in different countries, in all walks of life. Could it be possible that Celeste is a child murderer?

I can't trust her, and I don't know who she is anymore. Not that I ever did know who she was, but this, this is...

"Would you like some breakfast?" Sharpie asks, breaking into my thoughts. Her tone is friendlier than usual. I want to say "yes" because I'm starving, and I can smell sizzling bacon and farm-fresh eggs, but I shake my head.

"No thank you, I'm not feeling hungry," I lie. "Would you mind if I went into Lizzie's room?"

"What for?" Celeste looks put out.

"I feel like I want to search the house for her."

"You think we haven't already done that?" Celeste sniffs, showing how sad she is by wiping her eyes. *It's an act.* I don't believe this woman, not for a second.

"I don't know, I just want to look in every closet, in every nook and cranny. I need to look for her, it'll make me feel better." *Or worse.* "I mean... at least I'll give it a try, you never know, she might have—"

"They've been here *three* times, I've gone through everything." Sharpie shrugs her bony shoulders. "There's nothing we can do except—"

"What the fuck's going on?" It's Max, storming into the kitchen with Marjorie on his tail. "What the hell has happened? I bumped into one of the coast guards. I came by private boat because the ferry's been canceled. Nobody allowed on the island today. I heard... I'm so sorry, I didn't pick up your message, honey. But Liam's okay, right?" His voice is desperate.

Celeste and he embrace. Quivering, she can hardly get the words out. "He's upstairs in his room playing with his trains. I was so worried about you, Max, I was beside myself!"

"Christ!" he barks. "Whose fault is this? Who was looking after Lizzie?" His eyes land on me.

"It was my..." I can't get the words out.

"It was after we put Lizzie and Liam to bed," Celeste breaks in. "We hadn't bolted the back door, but we had latched it where the children can't reach. I don't know how she wandered off."

I summon up my voice. "Could she have stood on a chair?"

Max retorts, "That's not what the police seem to be thinking. They seem to be thinking somebody abducted her!"

Celeste holds Max by the wrist. "They've been here, they've searched for fingerprints, footprints and they found nothing. It's nonsense—of course she wasn't abducted."

He breaks free from Celeste and paces around the room. "Where is she, then?"

Celeste looks struck with panic all of a sudden. She shouts —and this is the first time I've heard her raise her voice—"I need something to *eat* and then I'm going to go to every single place on this island to find her... maybe... maybe she wandered off and ended up in somebody's house or something."

"Is there anything I can do to help?" Marjorie pipes up.

"I'd better be going," I say, edging my way out through the throng, rushing to the door. I can't bring myself to be in that house a moment longer with these people. All of them disgust me.

I scramble home, not as fast as I came because I haven't got the energy and because I have a killer stitch stabbing my stomach, slowing me down. When I get back, I make a cup of tea and binge on toast, butter, Marmite and some Cadburys I find in my suitcase, all melted. I can't prove it but I have this horrible feeling that Celeste has done the worst thing imaginable.

Has she killed both her little girls?

Between drinking my tea and shoveling toast in my mouth, I burst out crying, heaving with sobs, nearly choking myself to death in the process.

If they find out about my dodgy past, they'll blame me.

THE DISAPPEARANCE

Max Wainwright rakes his hand through his dark wet hair, droplets of rain plopping onto the polished walnut table. He has been out searching for his daughter. An Aquascutum raincoat is flung across the back of this chair, dripping onto the herring-bone parquet floor.

His eyes lock with Alba's as if challenging her. They are in the parlor, not the kitchen. Max's sister, Marjorie, brings in a pot of coffee on a tray, with porcelain cups and saucers to match. There is a plate of fancy, gourmet cookies, almost as if Mr. Wainwright has been expecting guests in this rather formal setting. Alba has asked him to talk to her alone, without his wife. After interviewing him she is set to speak to Marjorie as well. Both have alibis. Still, she needs these interviews. It would be great to do them at the station, back in Portland, but the logistics of that, along with the journey, would be a waste of precious time.

"It makes no *sense*!" Max Wainwright is staring her down.

Alba wonders what it must be like for Celeste to be married to this dominant man. From Celeste and Alba's conversations earlier, it seems Celeste sees her husband with rose-tinted shades. Or is Celeste in denial? His voice is deep, almost gruff. His lips are a thin line of angst. He is as angry as he is upset by his daughter's disappearance. The sort of man, it seems, who must always be in control and cannot accept failure. This is something he had not anticipated, clearly.

He pours them both some coffee. "I searched the whole damn island. So has your team. Where the hell could Lizzie be? And don't tell me she drowned because, no, that little thing knows how to swim and she knows not to swim alone, she knows that. There's no way she would've gone in that water, at night, in a storm, on her own."

Alba takes a sip of coffee, "But she's only four, do you think she might've set out for an adventure, got lost somehow?"

He shakes his head. His eyes are watering. From the weather or tears? "You've been door to door, right? Is there anyone you haven't talked to? You've searched in sheds, under people's boats in their gardens, right? I mean, your guys are on it, yes?"

Alba nods. "We are interviewing every single person. Is there anyone who lives on this island who, you know, behaves weirdly with kids? We're checking out each and every resident, obviously, but sometimes people can slip under our radar. Any clue might help."

"There are no pervs or weirdos on Cliff Island, thank God. At least, not that I know of. Did you interview the Lansings? Bill Hawkins? They know everyone."

"We did. Lizzie doesn't have a cell phone by any chance?" Alba has already asked Celeste this, but it never hurts to double-check.

"She's only four, no way. Kids' brains are developing at that age."

A beat goes by.

"You have a boat, Mr. Wainwright?"

His eyes flash cold like two shiny pebbles. "As a matter of

fact, I do. A Boston Whaler, which I take out on sunny days. And no, before you get any ideas, I did not whip over from Portland in my Whaler at midnight, throw my daughter into the ocean, power back to the mainland, all in record time, battling the raging seas under thunder and lightning, and then hire a private boat and spend two hours in the rain pretending to search for Lizzie before I came home and found you, and am now faking being upset because my child has disappeared!"

Alba keeps her cool. A desperate father's aggression is understandable. "You had business in Portland?"

"A business dinner, yes. You can check it out if you like. Dinner at Fore Street with two colleagues, Mike Draper and Danny Fielding. We were at the restaurant till pretty late. Ten thirty, I'd say."

"And your sister, Marjorie?"

"She was planning to get the afternoon ferry back here but missed it, so she stayed home—at my house in Portland—and from what I gather, she and our neighbor, Selina, binged on Netflix all evening while I was out. You'd have to ask her for details."

"Thanks, I will."

"But if you think she'd be able to make it here in a storm, go back to Portland—"

"I don't think anything, Mr. Wainwright, I'm—"

"Sorry, that was rude, I'm upset." He takes a deep breath and claws his large hands through his thick head of hair again. He swallows. His Adam's apple bobs in his throat.

"The nurse, Ms. Sharpe, told me you had planned to be home last night, yet you had dinner at a restaurant already booked?"

"My plans changed. I did call my wife and let her know but, well, you know she has problems with her memory since her car accident last month. She forgets all sorts of things, gets very confused."

"I'm so sorry about that. It must be tough for you both. Do you think it's possible that—"

"No."

"I haven't finished my sentence."

"You want to know if it's possible my wife harmed her own daughter? Or, better put, if she's responsible for Lizzie's disappearance?" He gives Alba that cold stare again, but then his gaze flickers with softness and something in his expression melts. "No. Celeste is all over the place right now, emotionally speaking, but..." He looks at the wall, into middle space, as if something has just occurred to him.

"You were saying?"

"Nothing. I mean, no, she wouldn't hurt her own daughter. This makes no sense at all. Have you interviewed Jayne, the au pair?"

"Yes. And our K-9 checked out her cottage. How well do you know Jayne?"

"Hardly at all. I mean, she seems harmless enough, good with the children, but still... why would... I guess it happens all the time, right? People who work with kids and old people abuse them?"

Alba frowns. "You think that's possible? That Jayne is capable of hurting Lizzie? Did you see any signs, did she give you any clues—"

"If she'd given any clues, I would've fired her on the spot."

"Is there anyone you can think of who might want to harm Lizzie?"

He swigs the last of his coffee. There is something incongruous about the delicate rosebud china touching this man's gruff lips and brushing against his five o'clock shadow. "No."

"Nobody who might think of kidnapping her?"

He scoffs. "Wouldn't they have gotten in touch by now?"

"Would you be willing to give us access to your cell phone data?"

"Course, that goes without saying."

"Thank you. I think a statement to the media is our next step. Would you and your wife be prepared to talk on live television?"

"We'll do whatever it takes."

Marjorie is timid, her voice gentle. Alba asks her about last night, and Marjorie confirms everything that Max has said. He is out of the room now. Alba can hear him in the kitchen, his voice booming. It sounds as if he is talking to various neighbors on the phone, grilling them.

"When did you last see Lizzie?" Alba begins.

"Yesterday. The kids waved us off at the dock as the ferry left for Portland on the morning boat."

"Did you notice anyone or anything suspicious, out of the ordinary? Any strangers?"

"No. But then I'm not from the island so I don't really know a lot of people here. I mean, how would I know?"

"You think Lizzie might've gone off last night alone and managed to get out by herself?"

Marjorie scrunches her face in thought. "Those kids are pretty wild. They kind of do what they want. Pretty spoiled, you know?" She smiles. "In a nice way, not an obnoxious way. They're very free."

"What movie did you watch last night?" Alba asks. She pops this question out of nowhere.

Marjorie replies smoothly though, without even reflecting. "A couple of episodes of *The Missing*." She gulps in a nervous breath. "But then I changed my mind and watched *Emily in Paris*. It's a silly show but feel-good, you know?"

"You been feeling down lately?"

"No, not at all. It's a girlie show. I was in the mood for something light. Fun. But then there was a power outage, with the storm."

"Were you alone?"

"No. I was hanging out with Max and Celeste's next-door neighbor, Selina. Her husband was away so I invited her in for a drink and she ended up staying for hours. Until the power went out."

"What time did she leave?"

"Guess it must've been around ten thirty. Not long before Max came home."

"How long have you been in Maine, Mrs. or Ms....? Sorry, I don't even know your last name?"

"Wallace."

"Married?"

"When I was twenty, for a New York minute."

"Divorced, then?"

"Oh, yeah, a long time ago."

"Kids?"

"No kids."

"You live in California, right?"

"I was living there, yes."

"When did you get to Maine?"

"A couple weeks ago. Max asked me to help out after Celeste's accident. It was clear he couldn't manage alone."

"Is this a permanent arrangement?"

"Not really."

"Not 'really'?"

"I split up with someone recently. We were living together—it was her home, my girlfriend's, not mine—so, you know, I'm thinking about moving to Portland for good, at least for a while anyway. Be closer to family."

Alba lets this information sink in. "Are you and Celeste close?"

"Yes, I would say so."

After a pause, Alba asks, "Are you close to Lizzie?"

Marjorie's mouth drops in surprise, her gaze watery; she is holding in a well of tears. "Sure. I mean, yeah, I'm getting to know her, or *was* till this happened. You think you'll find Lizzie? I'm so worried she drowned or..."

"Or?"

"I don't know. What if some whacko took her? They are so many crazies out there."

True, Alba thinks. *So many crazies*.

Crazy is her line of work.

Crazy is her job.

CELESTE

Max wants to do a press conference, for us to make a statement on live television on the news. So far there has been no evidence whatsoever found of an intruder breaking into our home and taking Lizzie. No fingerprints, no tracks or marks or anything unusual that can't be explained. Max wants to appeal to the public. Beg them, if anyone knows something to please come forward.

"We have to," he says. "The sooner the better."

I stare into a void, not knowing what to say, what to do. I'm not good at speeches. It's all right for Max. He's so attractive, his eyes glitter with warmth, his face is friendly, open. When he makes speeches he is so articulate, he never stumbles or has to read from a script. He could have been an actor, a politician if he'd wanted. People always root for him, warm to him, trust him. Of course they do, he is charm personified, but because he has such presence, a sense of himself, they respect him too. But me?

"I can't," I tell him. "I'd feel so—"

"Of course you can, we have to, we have to do this."

He snaps up the detective's card from the kitchen table and

dials her number. They offered for us to have a liaison officer here to be with us at all times, but I declined. I don't *want* some stranger in our house. Max and Detective Alba discuss talking to the press, and I feel as if I'm about to faint.

After he ends the call, I say, "They always accuse the parents, don't they?"

JAYNE

A realization rushes over me in a sudden wave. It's when I burp, after I've eaten so much toast, that I can taste wine in my throat.

But that's impossible. *No, no, no,* I didn't go there last night, I didn't!

But maybe I did.

And then the reality of who I am and what I am capable of crawls back on its dirty hands and knees.

I didn't pour those four bottles of wine down the sink, did I? I poured *some* of it down the sink, yeah, maybe two bottles, maybe two and a half, maybe... I can't remember. It was my wish, it was my *desire* to be free of the wine, but I have a horrible, horrible suspicion that I did drink at least a bottle, maybe two. Worse, I can't even remember if I took that pill or not.

I can't remember.

And now I have some hazy, fuzzy memory of Stephen being here in this cottage with me last night.

All while Lizzie went missing. *Please tell me I played no part in that?*

My God, I don't even know... *shit, shit, shit!* What did I

take? Stephen gave me a pill from his vial. He said it was a sleeping pill. It could've been anything.

I'm shoving the last piece of toast into my mouth when there's a knock at my door.

It's Stephen, smiling through the screen door. I'm not in the mood for a smile and there's something about the look in his face which makes me remember for sure. He *was* here. But everything is a blur.

He opens the door and says in a jolly voice, "How are you feeling this morning? Last night was pretty heavy, right? I'm sorry to have left you that way."

"Lizzie," I say. "What happened?"

"I went looking for her with the search party after I left here."

"You were here?" I check, still willing my memory, and his memory, to be wrong.

"You can't remember?"

I say nothing, racking my brains for a coherent picture of how the evening unraveled. Nothing comes to me, just snapshots of Stephen, of us hanging out together. Laughing. *Ugh*, the thought makes me sick. *What did I do?* Little did we know Lizzie was out there wandering around, alone. Or worse, being abducted by some pervert. Or *even* worse, being drowned by her mother.

"How long were you out looking for her?" I ask him. "Why didn't you come get me?"

He throws his hands in the air as if to show me what a lost cause I was. "I tried, Jayne, but you were so freaking drunk."

"What?" I deny, in disbelief. "I didn't drink a drop last night."

Please say I didn't.

"That's a good one," he says, smiling. Stephen is a master at smiling and talking at the same time.

"Wait, what are you saying? You're saying you came round

here last night?" I know this is true but I am still praying that, no, he simply popped by for a few minutes, that he was not here for long.

"Don't tell me you've forgotten everything?"

I have forgotten everything. Pretty much everything.

"I emptied these bottles of wine, most of them at any rate, down the sink," I tell him.

Stephen chuckles. "Oh yeah, you're gonna waste good French wine, just like that?" He picks up one of the bottles and reads the label: "Châteauneuf-du-Pape 2005. Really? And this 2016 Reserve, an expensive Cabernet Sauvignon from Napa Valley. You know that high-end Napa Valley wines are scarcer than Bordeaux wines? You gonna throw that great stuff down the sink? I don't think so," he says in a sing-song voice, and laughs. He puts his hand on my shoulder, and the way he touches me makes me slink out from under him, my head screaming, *What happened, what happened? What did I do? No, please don't say it's true, no!*

"'You're quite a goer,' that's what you said to me last night," he says.

"You're taking the piss," I throw at him. "I had an early night last night. I was still suffering from jet lag and went to sleep early. I do remember you giving me some sleeping pill, something mild. That's right, it was an Ambien. I remember reading the bottle... that's what you gave me, and I took one."

"Oh Jayne, oh Jayne, what am I gonna do with you?"

"Please, Stephen, don't talk like that, I'm not in the mood for this."

"Hey, sorry, I didn't mean to offend you, but we had a *great* time last night."

"No we didn't!" I plead. "We *did not* have a good time. I had an early night. I remember, I took Lizzie to the house around seven, then I came back here at... it must've been eightish, I had a light dinner, made myself some beans on toast then..."

"You texted me, remember? Sorry if I took it as an invitation, but I'm a guy. It was night, I mean, hey, what would you think if someone texted you at night?"

I shake my head.

"Check your phone," Stephen urges. "Go on."

I check my messages, and oh my God, there it is.

Dr. Stephen do you have any sleeping pills? I need to knock this jet lag on the head. Nothing too heavy. In my cottage.

Sure. I'll be right on over give me 10 mins.

A rush of nausea: Marmite and tea come up my throat. I swallow.

No, I swore to myself I wouldn't do this again. Yeah, I've had flings in the past, yes, I have used men to make myself feel better. That feeling of a hug, a kiss, hot sex, it can make you feel wanted. And I saw the way Stephen looked at me on the beach when we were looking at those freaky crabs with blue blood, I knew he desired me and it was what I needed, but I didn't... I wouldn't, not here, not... not while I'm working, not while I'm an au pair, I wouldn't do it, not here. I made myself promise.

"No." My *no* is emphatic. "We just hung out, had a few sips of wine."

"You don't remember? I asked you if Max had given you that Châteauneuf-du-Pape and all that fancy Napa Valley wine, and you went bright red and told me that yes, he had. And I knew you were lying because Max never gives his wine to anybody. And I said, 'I'll tell you what, Jayne, I know you're fibbing, but hey, if you open the bottle I'll keep this a secret between us.'"

"You blackmailed me?"

"Don't be silly, that's not blackmail, that's having fun. You were lonely, I could tell. I'm lonely here, too. We're in the middle of nowhere on this godforsaken island, trying to help a woman who is completely out of her mind. We needed each other, that's all. We had some fun together last night, what's the big deal?"

"And then what happened?" I ask tentatively, wanting to know and yet not wanting to know.

"I opened the first bottle... we let it breathe, for, I don't know, a good ten minutes, you need to let a good wine breathe, of course, and I got out some glasses. Look, there they are." He nods his head.

"Where?"

"One's over by the bookshelf, over there, see? The other..."

My gaze runs over the room. He's right, there's a wine glass sitting on top of an Agatha Christie, and then following his gaze, I spot another. This one's on the floor by the sofa. I don't know why I hadn't noticed the wine-stained glasses before.

"We shot the breeze for a while. You told me all about your family."

"My family?"

"You got pretty wasted and then I advised you not to take the pill because it wasn't a good idea to mix wine with medication, but you'd already taken it from me and put it somewhere, so I didn't know where it was or if you'd swallowed it already."

I feel sick at the thought of what I let out about myself. *What did I tell Stephen?* I have no alternative but to ask him now. "What did we talk about?"

"We talked about your troubled childhood. We spoke about your foster parents... your various foster parents along the way, and how your little sister Wendy had died when she was only five years old, and how you felt responsible for her."

Fuck.

"So, after what has gone down with Lizzie, I thought you might wanna talk about it today. That's why I came over. I thought it would've brought all those memories back."

After what has gone down with Lizzie. I let those words sink in, wondering if I am responsible in some way. *No, impossible. Impossible!* Why is it all such a blur? "What else did I say about my sister?"

"That you were only ten years old and your mom was—this is of course before you ended up in the first foster family—your mother was not there for you, she was absent, she was using, had a drug problem, and how you had to look after your sister as if she was your child, and how... well... you told me about that fateful day."

Oh, God. "What did I say?"

"That you'd taken her for a bike ride to have a picnic by the river and, well, that you went to take a pee in the bushes and then she was gone and... and how... how she drowned."

Oh no. I can feel the waterworks spouting from my eyes, remembering what happened to Wendy. How my life after that moment was never the same again. How my life was destroyed, not only because of how I felt about it—totally devastated—but because of my guilt and the way other people saw me. My mother blamed me, everybody blamed me, and from then on I was tarred as a *bad* girl. I was the "bad girl"—and then I made that prophecy come true.

Stephen goes on in an even voice: "You told me about the difficulties you had with your various foster families. What a nightmare it was. You used that word, 'nightmare.' There was one you liked, with the little boy who you felt was like a brother, but then he was sent off to boarding school and the mother felt she couldn't handle you alone as you were a very 'bumptious, boisterous kid,' and then you got 'fobbed off' on another foster family somewhere along the line, where the dad was... I'm so sorry, Jayne, but I'm sure it's really good to talk about this, and I do feel bad that we ended up discussing it last night over so many drinks. I shouldn't have mixed business with pleasure."

"What do you mean by 'business'?"

"You know, I consider one-to-one talks pretty much my job, even on my days off or hours off. We shouldn't've been drinking wine and discussing your intimate past in this way. I apologize. I really apologize."

I am gobsmacked, I don't know what to say. He's trying to be nice and I can't believe I told this man I hardly know intimate secrets about my life, about my family, about Wendy. I never tell *anybody*.

"What... what else did I say?" I stumble, my brain doing mental gymnastics. *Please don't tell me I told him the worst of it.*

"Oh that's about it. But don't ask me to repeat everything word for word because, you know, I drank a lot too."

"Why do I remember pouring the bottles down the sink?"

"Dream on, Jayne, there's no way you did that. We got through... well, I don't know, maybe you poured a few dregs down the sink at the end of the evening, but we both drank a lot, put it that way. That wine was *good*, it was too delicious to waste! I would've killed you if you'd poured that good stuff down the sink."

"Please don't tell Max."

"Of course I won't tell Max."

"But you're friends."

"Yeah, well, we're not really 'friends,' that was a long, long time ago. Max and I live in different worlds. Look at him, he's loaded. He has the big house here and all these cottages, a huge house in Portland, you know, these people have money. I don't have money like them. I'm like the poor relative, without being related. So you stole a couple of bottles of wine, so what?"

"*Four* bottles."

"Four bottles, what's the big deal? By the time he notices, you'll be long gone. You're only here for the summer, right?"

The whole time he's speaking, I notice something. He's hardly mentioned Lizzie. She's missing, but he doesn't seem to care. Like it hasn't affected him in any way.

"I don't know what to do," I tell him.

"About the wine?"

"No, for fuck's sake, the wine's nothing. Whether I drank the wine or not is so unimportant right now. What's important is finding Lizzie." And then this ominous voice whispers in my ear like it's accusing me, taunting me, when I know it's nonsense and total rubbish: *What have you done with Lizzie?*

Stephen asks, "Do they know anything?"

The way he says this makes me suspicious about him, too. I feel suspicious of everybody because nobody seems to give a damn.

But the worst thing of all? I'm suspicious about myself.

"What time did you leave here last night?" I ask.

"Shit, I don't know."

"What happened last night?"

"We had a good time."

"I need to know more detail. What happened exactly?"

He gives me the Matt Damon Ripley smile. "What do you want to have happened between us?"

"That's not an answer, Stephen. Did we... did we..."

"No, we didn't. I'm not one for taking advantage of women when they've had too much to drink. Hey, maybe we fooled around a bit, maybe a kiss."

Please don't let me have slept with this man. The idea I had sex with someone without remembering any details creeps me out.

Because... if I can't remember that, what else can't I remember?

I look into his eyes, picturing the coral-colored cardigan. "Stephen, do you know anything about a pink, coral-colored cardigan belonging to Lizzie? Somebody left it here last night, on the swing porch, the swing outside." *It wasn't me it wasn't me!*

He shakes his head. "No, I know nothing about that."

I try to read his face to tell if he's lying or not, but I don't know him well enough to know what that expression would look like. He appears guileless, innocent. Maybe too innocent.

"That was some storm we had last night, I mean crazy," he says. "A real raging storm, and after you conked out... you know, I made sure you were in bed, shoes off—"

I narrow my eyes. "My clothes were *all* off when I woke up this morning."

"Well, I'm sorry, I took the liberty of—"

"You *undressed* me?"

"I thought... look, calm down, nothing happened between us, I swear."

Again, I don't know if he's lying or not.

"I put you to bed and that's when I left. I heard a commotion outside. A helicopter. And the rain and wind, man, it was crazy and amazing you slept through it all. Anyway, I went to see what was going on. A bunch of people were out there, lots of folks wondering what was happening, and then I joined a search party... the police came, the detective woman... everything was happening all at once."

"But you were drunk, surely?" I ask with suspicion.

"Well, not as drunk as you."

"You made out like we were both having a ball and we were both drunk and it turns out *I* was the drunk one? I was the only inebriated one?"

"I can hold my liquor pretty well."

"Charming," I say. And then, after a very uncomfortable gap in the conversation, I add, "I think it would be better if you leave now, Stephen. I need to think this through, need to get my head round all this."

"Hey, there's no need to get offended or upset, I didn't do

anything wrong! I promise I'll keep everything you told me between us: the wine, your past. I'm *great* at keeping secrets."

At this point, I don't even care about any of this. I just want Lizzie to be alive. "I want to find Lizzie. I need to find her! I'm going outside right now to search this whole bloody island until I do."

And then that nasty inner voice comes back and hisses in my ear, *That's right, Jayne, find Lizzie. Because if you did something...*

DR. STEPHEN

As I leave Jayne's cottage I'm aware of one thing: I lied to her about what time I left last night. What was I supposed to say?

There was a good hour between my leaving and the helicopter arriving. How could I explain that to Jayne? It's easier if we can give each other an alibi, if it comes to that. It probably will, with Detective Alba sniffing around. Course, I had no idea that Jayne would black out that way. She must've taken that pill. I wasn't thinking... I wasn't thinking things through. I doubt she's going to want to admit to getting wasted last night, blacking out, not remembering a thing. She'll feel too embarrassed—at least, that's what I'm hoping.

It sounds like she had one fucked-up childhood. You can always tell, can't you, when someone is... I wouldn't even say "vulnerable" because yes, she's vulnerable, but she's also tough as nails, that woman. I can see it in her eyes. People like her never really recover, however hard they try, however many therapy sessions you give them. And I consider myself in that same bracket of misfits, FYI. I shouldn't be saying this—I mean, hell, it's my job, this is the last thing I should be saying—but it's true. Once damaged goods, always damaged goods, there's no going back. There's no wiping away the past and all the hurt... not from childhood, it runs too deep. But it's what keeps people like me in business so I can't rail against it.

I keep this close to my chest, of course, these fateful, negative thoughts of how people like me and Jayne are rotten inside.

Oh, Lizzie, Lizzie, Lizzie, what a mess. What am I going to say? What am I going to say that won't incriminate me?

I'll have to keep my mouth shut.

Shut tight.

DR. STEPHEN

A couple of days go by with the detective and her team milling around. Their numbers are shrinking with each passing day, yet they're still here. The sniffer dog is still prowling round and round the island. It got all excited about Lizzie's sailboat, but that's to be expected, isn't it? Her scent must be all over it.

Detective Adele Alba, I think. I can't help myself... I am fascinated by her. Cool, calm, her feathers never ruffled, her short dark hair cropped into a sort of pixie cut, her long neck elegant, belying her strong, athletic figure. Either she wears mascara or she has naturally dark, thick, long lashes. Natural, definitely, I decide. She's not the type to fuss over her appearance. Twenty years ago, if you switched on the TV and saw such an attractive policewoman in a cop show or movie, you'd think it was Central Casting—no way were there such sexy police officers in real life. I mean, none I had come across on the streets in those days. But now beautiful women are everywhere. Being interviewed on TV. Rocket scientists, physicists, economists, even politicians sometimes. Beautiful women with serious, kick-ass jobs. I suppose it's not politically correct to notice this, but I do. Detail is something I don't take for granted. It's my job, after all. I want to know what is going on in the minds of everyone, particularly professional women. And Detective Alba in particular. I can tell she is judging me. Watching my every move. The fact that she is beautiful not only unnerves me but excites me.

Russian roulette.

Apart from the mayhem, things sort of carry on as normal. Jayne is still here, threatening to leave but then breaking down in tears every so often about Lizzie. She feels she can't leave with things up in the air the way they are. I feel bad for her. I do. We haven't spoken since *the morning after the night before*. I know she feels ashamed, caught out. I keep urging her to talk to me as a therapist, a shoulder to kind of cry on, free of charge, but she won't. She's been avoiding me. Every time we cross paths she shuttles away as if I'm the last person in the world she wants to see. Hurtful? I can't deny that, yes, it hurts a little, it stings. *Same old, same old*. I'm not sure why I have this effect on women. But then again, Jayne wasn't quite herself during that wild night... neither of us were. We both went on "a bit of a bender," to use her expression.

I find Celeste in her bedroom again, surrounded by scented candles. Kind of strange, a tad gothic, but I suppose that's her line of business: these candles, these high-end sheets and bedlinen. Or rather, it *was* her business before the accident—Marjorie seems to be running things very smoothly now.

"Celeste," I say, peering around the door, "are you ready for a chat?" She's watching TV. This is a new addition: the TV in the bedroom. Alex Sharpe put it here. She's quite handy, that nurse. A modern, self-sufficient woman. She can do stuff like unblock drains, fix the internet when it's down; she's good with a screwdriver, I've noticed. She'd be attractive, too, if she didn't always wear her hair scraped back, if she took off her glasses.

The nurse's uniform is kind of sexy though in a kitsch kind of way. But Alex is not here right now. Just Celeste, alone.

Celeste sits up. "Stephen, come in."

Well, at least she recognizes me today, knows my name.

"Any updates about Lizzie?" I ask her, knowing there aren't. Knowing from what the islanders say there have been no leads, no new developments, no body has washed up; it's as if Lizzie has vanished. After Celeste and Max made that statement on TV, things have been a little crazy on the island. Reporters camping out, trying to get another statement from one of the parents. People are fascinated with this case, half of them believing the parents are to blame. They suspect Celeste might be guilty of wrongdoing. Others are sympathetic, and there is an outpouring of love and kindness. Some have even brought gifts of teddy bears, which they leave with bunches of flowers wrapped in cellophane at the front door. All that plastic, as if the island needs it. Who was the genius who decided to wrap flowers in cellophane anyway? And as if Celeste would want a freaking teddy bear, reminding her...

No wonder she's been holed up here in her room and hasn't ventured out the door.

"You know I can't talk about Lizzie," she says in a solemn tone. "Please don't try and make me, I can't, I just can't."

"I thought you might know—"

"Stephen, I don't want to talk about her, *please*."

"Okay, I'm sorry. By the way, have you been writing your diary lately?"

She shrugs. "My diary has disappeared."

"You're kidding me?"

"No, I'm not."

"Why would anybody want your diary?"

"I can think of a hundred reasons why somebody might want my diary."

I let out a chuckle. "Well, don't look at me, I didn't take it."

"I'm not accusing you, Stephen, course not, but somebody got their hands on it."

"Who do you think it is?"

She smiles. "I have a pretty good idea."

"And?"

"I think you can guess."

She's playing the enigmatic game. Celeste loves to tease. "Well, if you don't feel like letting me in on your secret..."

"It doesn't take a genius to guess."

I wait to see if she says more. She doesn't. "Where is Max, by the way?"

"On the mainland. Since they opened up the ferry again... I wish they hadn't done that. I suppose they've done all they can, really, the police."

"I guess so."

"Max says he's doing his own investigation, whatever that means. That dog's still sniffling around here. Nothing so far."

"That dog... yes, that dog has combed every inch of the island."

We sit for a while and I can see Celeste isn't in the mood for therapy. Still, I push on.

"How about today we talk about your childhood," I suggest.

"Seriously?" She makes a face. "You've heard it all before. My overbearing father, my hysterical mom who popped too many pills, my ugly duckling childhood and sheltered upbringing."

"Well, if you're not in the mood to talk about Lizzie or your missing diary—"

She smiles. "All right, all right, have it your way."

We talk about her childhood, but it's nothing I don't already know.

"Do you remember the last thing you wrote in your diary?" I ask, bringing the conversation back around to the thing I really want to ask about.

"I do. I wrote about Marjorie."

"Oh yes? What did you say?"

"I said that she really is an amazing sister-in-law and so kind and so helpful and how I'm beyond grateful that she's taken over the business, because the truth is the business was beginning to stress me out. I don't think I was cut out to be a businesswoman."

"But you did so well. You started up a little empire, and you made quite a bit of money, didn't you? You *were* a businesswoman. You could be, still."

"It did make money... it does very, very well. Even though the sheets and what have you are so crazy-expensive, people still spend money on the most ridiculous things. People need luxuries in their lives and I suppose sheets, compared to real estate or boats or cars, are actually very cheap. A cheap way to feel special about yourself. A scented candle, a soft, plush towel."

"You had a good idea and you marketed it well. So why do you think you told Max you didn't recognize Marjorie last week?"

"I don't know, I wasn't thinking. I think on some level I was jealous. Jealous of the close relationship they have. I wrote about that in the diary, of course, how a sibling relationship is something that can't be broken, it's a bond so close that not even matrimony can match it. That is assuming the siblings are close. Not all are. I wrote in my diary that perhaps these lapses of memory were actually to do with denial, of not wanting to remember, of not wanting to admit the truth. It's easy to shut your brain off if you want to, isn't it? You know all about that, don't you, Stephen, from your experience... from all the patients, clients you've had sessions with?"

I pause and reflect on what she has said. "That can happen, yes, I guess it does happen a lot. People lie to themselves or are in denial in order to shut out emotions, to save themselves from feeling hurt. So, tell me, who do you think took your diary?"

She shares her suspicions with me and I nod. She tells me a lot of things, some I already know. We discuss her big secret. I like that we share this. And of course I would never tell. I'd never spill the beans on Celeste.

I made an oath as a doctor, as a therapist, and I will keep that oath at all costs. Patient–doctor confidentiality is sacred.

You can say whatever you like about me. But I do know how to keep a secret.

JAYNE

Liam has been taken off the island for a couple of days by Max and Marjorie—or that's what Celeste told me. They decided it would be a good idea for him to get away from the terrifying situation of Lizzie being missing and the press and the rubbernecking visitors roaming around. I can see how frightened they must be, especially for Liam's sake, perhaps not trusting anyone, even those close to them? I wonder if Max has a secret suspicion about his wife? He seems to forgive her for everything and is endlessly patient with her, has shown no signs whatsoever of mistrust. But how could he not? I simply don't believe Violet suffered from a cot death, from SIDS. For some reason that particular story hasn't been picked up by the media. I'm assuming Max has managed to keep it hush-hush.

Mentally, I'm knackered, I can hardly think straight. And the truth is I'm delighted to be able to have a couple of days off without having to look after Liam. Not only for the break it offers me, but also after what happened with him and Lizzie... Liam throwing that stone at her and shouting. I can't say I've warmed to Liam. I know he's only a little boy and it's normal, and I know all that stuff about sibling rivalry, but the stone-throwing business turned me off him.

It makes me think about Wendy. I've been having nightmares, dreaming about her, dreaming about the river. Of course with memories you're never sure if they're real or your imagination or from things people told you, over and over again. *"It's your fault, Jayne, it's your fault. It was because of you. Because of what you did."*

How do I even know that? I can't remember what happened! I would never have hurt Wendy. Never! I loved my sister, I loved her with all my heart. I remember overhearing them discussing me, talking about what they were going to do with me, hearing whispers. They thought I was jealous of her, that she was so much prettier than me—and she was. Like Lizzie, she was blond, slim, delicate, with big blue eyes. Nothing like me, with my cow-brown eyes and ungainly body.

Is it possible? Is it possible I was jealous of my sister?

No. *No way.*

But then again, I can't be sure of anything anymore.

Anyway, Liam is off the island for a couple of days with his dad and aunt. Apparently they're going to go on a submarine ride in Boston, visit some museums. I can't imagine Liam being interested in museums. Lizzie, yeah, she loved that kind of stuff, it fascinated her, she would've had a million tricky questions I couldn't answer.

And then I gasp. *Correction*: not "loved" but "loves." Lizzie *loves* that kind of stuff. Why am I talking about Lizzie in the past tense?

I find the main house eerily quiet. Celeste is in her bedroom, as per usual. I can hear the television. Some trashy game show. I don't know where Sharpie is, but I'm relieved she's not around. I've noticed when Max isn't here she's less on Celeste's case. Maybe she's trying to prove to him what a great job she's doing? That he's getting his money's worth.

I silently trudge up the stairs to Liam's bedroom. I don't know what I'm expecting to find—nothing in particular. I feel like having a rootle around to see if I come up with something. It's absurd, my thought process. He's only six years old, it's not as if he could have had anything to do with his sister's disappearance. Still, I can't help myself, my curiosity is driving me crazy.

I slip into his room. Nothing unusual. Posters on the wall, a few items of clothing strewn about, his trains, his cars, his toy gun (which if I were a mother I wouldn't let him have, but never mind). I spend about twenty minutes in his room, sitting there on the bottom part of his bunk bed. Occasionally he has friends over, apparently, and they sleep on the top.

I don't know what I'm looking for but feel at peace sitting here for some reason. Away from everybody else. And then something catches my eye. There's a pile of drawings on top of his chest of drawers. I flip through them. Done with crayons. He doesn't have Lizzie's artistic touch. Some are airplanes, some boats, but there's a picture of a mum and a dad and a little boy, and a girl, standing to one side. The girl has long yellow hair. But the interesting thing is, the girl has been scribbled out, quite violently, in black crayon.

THE DISAPPEARANCE

Lizzie has been missing for almost seventy-two hours. The clock is a ticking time bomb. Detective Alba has been living on sandwiches from the local café, coffee, and their homemade ice cream, for three days straight. She has circled the island more times than she can count, back and forth, both on her own, with her partner, and with George and K-9 Dune. No leads, no clue that has led anywhere conclusive. She's interviewed every household on the island, gone door to door, had a few misleading tips, such as somebody hearing his dog bark at a certain hour, or a phone call with the caller hanging up. Nothing conclusive, nothing that helps the case whatsoever. She has scheduled another face-to-face interview with Max Wainwright and his sister, Marjorie, back at the station, recorded this time. Alba will talk to them separately, of course. Although neither one of them was on the island the night of Lizzie's disappearance, she needs to garner clues, wants to find out more about his marriage and see what part of the puzzle, if any, is missing. There is only one person of interest whom she has not interviewed, and that is Eric Lawson—the sailing coach. Thing is, when she finally tracks down his whereabouts, he has an airtight alibi. He wasn't on the island that night but in Portland. It all checked out perfectly: phone calls he had made getting a pizza delivered to the apartment where he was staying with his sister. With her as witness and cell phone records, plus GPS tracking of his movements, showing how Eric hadn't been anywhere near the island that night, or even that day. Still, she wants to interview him anyway. Looking into someone's eyes when you ask questions can unlock so many clues.

All the young boys and teenagers on the island, the wilder ones, the ones that hang out on the beaches with their lobster traps and who hunt for frogs, all their alibis check out.

Adele Alba is beginning to think that she's gotten it all wrong, that this was no abduction, this was a child wandering out into the night in the middle of a storm and drowning. There are sharks in these waters. What if Lizzie stumbled, knocked her head on a rock or something and got swept out to sea? It's possible she was already dead before she ended up in the water. Or perhaps she drowned and her little body got pulled under by currents and entangled in seaweed or kelp, and later eaten by sharks. It doesn't bear thinking about.

But Alba *does* have to think about it. It's her job. These are the cases that keep you up at night: the ones with no answers, the ones with no closure. She can't imagine what the parents must be going through. She has talked to Mrs. Wainwright a couple of times, but there is nothing she can tell her. Adele Alba is not the kind of person who is good at holding people's hands and saying the perfect thing, in the perfect moment. She does the best she can do, considering what her job is. She is straight and honest with people, but not a huggy kind of person. She isn't going to win any medals for being Mrs. Nice. She offered the Wainwrights a liaison officer, but they didn't want a stranger in the house, so it is up to her to keep them abreast of the latest developments, of which there are few. All Alba can do is her job to the best of her ability and try to find answers for the family, for herself, for Lizzie, and for every little girl or child out there.

She is trained to not take it personally, not get emotionally involved with her cases, but she can't help it; she is not cut from granite. People think it is like on TV, solving cases, one after another, getting the bad guy in the end, seeing justice, but it isn't like that. She feels like shit, not having answers. Over the last few years she has been used to going home to an empty apartment at night after an interminable day, eating crap food, drinking too many sodas. She is forty-three years old and feels like a failure on days like this. The enthusiasm from when she joined the force at twenty-three is now somewhere on a scale of three out of ten. Her family life is non-existent since the breakup of her marriage, and she regrets she didn't go ahead and have that baby when she was nineteen. It seemed inconceivable at the time; she was so young, she thought she had all the time in the world. Nobody gives you the memo about how, in the force, no time is the right time to start a family; nobody warns you how sexist it is, how women don't get the respect and opportunities men take in their stride, the support to build a family and have a career at the same time, which in her line of work is like juggling with three balls while trying to cross the road in heavy traffic. Nobody sits you down and tells you that in the end, a career means very little when you have nobody special to share your success with. Or your failures.

Her ex has moved on. Has a baby with a woman in her early thirties. A woman who leads a "normal" life, with a job that doesn't suck the very soul out of her. Sam—that's his name—is now sitting behind a desk, so he can hang out with his family more, do barbeques on the weekend, be a dad, everything he swore he had no use for, in the early days, anyway.

Would Alba change the course of events? Would she trade her life for this *would've-could've* one?

No.

How nuts is that?

It's with these dead-end thoughts that she ambles to the water's edge to catch the ferry back to Portland, mentally preparing the questions she has for Max Wainwright, some of which she has asked before. *Do you think it's possible your wife could have hurt Lizzie? Are you happily married? Any money problems or debts? Do you have any questionable business partners or anyone you owe money to? Is it possible someone kidnapped Lizzie? Why are you not at home with your wife presently?* She mulls this over. He was taking Liam away from the island for a few days, away from the media, the commotion, but he never okayed it with Alba. Not that she could have stopped him... Still, it would have seemed like a logical thing, for him to fly it by her first. And surely supporting his wife and staying home is equally important? Perhaps more so.

Now Alba needs to gauge the expression on Max's face, watch for clues, for telltale signs. There are always tells. A flicker of an eye. A crossed leg. A tic in a jaw muscle.

Something is off. This formal interview will give her a lead. It has to.

She waits by the dock for the boat. She arrived in a helicopter and is leaving like a civilian, taking the public boat, head down, the feeling of futility engulfing her, how she has failed this mission. This case will be one of those open-ended questions: *What the hell happened... where is Lizzie?* There are flyers everywhere, Lizzie's face is splashed all over the news, her big blue eyes staring into the camera, a half smile on her face, long blond hair blowing in the wind, with her chubby baby-grown-into-little-girl cheeks, rosy and pink. There is even a video clip of her on her last birthday. A cute little girl gone, disappeared, vanished.

Vanished.

How is that possible?

Alba fears what might be coming next. Scully, her boss, has

called her in for a meeting. What if he pulls her off the case, assigns her to something new? It was, after all, pure chance that she was given this case in the first place. Missing children are handled by another department. She got called in because she was already in the helicopter after finishing up a robbery when the SOS call came in about Lizzie. Adele Alba was in the right place at the right time.

Or *the wrong place*, as it turns out.

Perhaps a different detective would have found something crucial, would have had success by now. Even found Lizzie alive. This is something Adele will always have to live with: this sense of failure, a new notch in her mental prison sentence of the things in life she hasn't gotten right, she hasn't achieved.

"Hey, Adele, wait up!"

She turns around and sees George, Deputy George Finn, with his dog, Dune, looking quite the part in his brand new, bullet-proof harness. These harnesses were donated by a dog-loving entrepreneur because for some reason the force doesn't have the budget to protect their canines. POLICE K-9, it reads.

"Is he working still or is he off duty?" she asks.

George smiles. One of those smiles that's all wonky. "I think he deserves a break, don't you? He's worked his ass off, or should I say, worked his hind legs off."

She takes a step forward. "Can I pet him?"

"Sure. He's super docile if he knows you're my friend. Go ahead, get as close as you like, he won't bite. Not if I give the okay."

"And you're giving the okay now?"

He laughs. "Yep, the silent okay. Dune can sense my approval. He's super smart, super tuned into me, to what I'm thinking or feeling."

She bends down to the dog's level. Dune, excited for the attention, approaches her, tail wagging, and nuzzles his long nose in her face. "Hey, buddy." She lets her head sink into his neck, breathes him in, and something about his soft fur, the warmth of him, makes her want to cry. Dune reminds her of a dog she had as a child, when they lived on the farm. When she ran free and wild and when she didn't have a problem beyond deciding where she was going to build her camp, what candy to buy with her pocket money, and that they were having liver for lunch, which she hated. "You're a very good boy," she whispers in his pointy ear. "You've worked so hard. It's not your fault we haven't found Lizzie. The rain made it so..." She can't go on, there's a lump in her throat.

"You want to give him a treat?"

She nods, still crouching on the ground. George hands her some little biscuits which she feeds to Dune, one by one, letting him lick her fingers. She can actually feel her heart expanding, tight against her chest. She quickly wipes her eyes with the back of her wrist, she can't—she won't—let anybody see her like this. She's in a public place. Being weak—even over a dog—is not something she wants to add to her résumé.

"He likes you," George comments.

"I like him too."

"You catching the ferry back home like me?"

"Yep. Kind of lame, catching the ferry like everybody else, huh? I had visions of us bringing the Wainwrights' child back to them safely, carrying her in my arms, alive, and here we are going back to Portland with nothing to show for all our labor."

"The nature of the beast," George replies.

"Yeah, the worst part of this shit-ass job."

"You love it though."

"Not today, I don't," she admits.

George is cute. With a slim, athletic build, like a welter-weight, if he were a boxer, and he does have a bit of a boxer look about him, with a slightly crooked nose, a small chip in his tooth. Maybe he broke it once or twice. The nose. She's not going to ask him that now though. She feels like she could go to bed with this young man, not even to have sex necessarily, but to spoon, to sleep, to be held for a while. To cozy up next to him, flesh on flesh, feel the warmth of his breath on her neck. To wipe her mind clear of the last few days. But she's not about to act on her desires. No, she's done that before and it's a bad idea. *Don't mix work with colleagues, with what you need.*

"It's all so strange," George says. "You know, at the beginning I felt like Dune really, really had a lead, like he was so excited, loud snorting, tail up, ears perked up, wagging pretty good, sniffing the ground, sniffing the air and then suddenly the trail stopped." He swats a fly away. "Jeez, it's hot." He moves himself and his dog into the shade. The midday sun is pounding down. The air thick with humidity, the afternoon torrid and unforgiving. Adele follows them, and the trio wait for the boat, under the arch where it says CLIFF ISLAND.

"I'm hungry," she tells him. "Been eating like a lazy teenager for the last few days."

George nods. His eyes crinkle. "Me too. When we get to Portland, you wanna go get lunch?"

She smiles, and despite her previous misgivings, and all the ramifications that might come with this invitation, she says, "I was wondering if you'd ask."

THE DISAPPEARANCE

Adele Alba, George Finn, and Dune are about to board the ferry when her phone buzzes. It's Scully. Maybe he doesn't even want her to come in for the meeting after all, maybe he's going to tell it to her straight, issue a cool dismissal by phone. She's lost her touch and he needs her to take a desk job. She's not like her ex, who prefers it cushy and safe. If she's not in motion, she can't function. She would rather jump off a cliff than sit behind a desk. She's thinking about lunch with George, and maybe this evening—after she's done with interviewing Max and Marjorie —a glass of wine or beer. She takes the call.

"Alba," Scully barks.

"Speaking."

"If you're about to board that boat, don't. Stay put."

She watches as day trippers pile off the ferry, brought here, no doubt, by the media frenzy. She can imagine what they are thinking and saying to each other, about what a crap-ass job the police are doing. How the police have come up empty in the search for Lizzie, not even a body for the parents to bury and mourn with closure. In fact, she sees a young mother eyeballing her now, clutching her little boy's hand as if Alba's ineffectiveness might be contagious in some way, as if to say, *And this is what I pay taxes for?*

Alba left her earbuds behind, so talks into her phone, turning her back on the woman. "What's up, sir?"

"I need you to stay there, something's come in," the gruff voice instructs her.

"Important?" She thinks again about that meal with her name on it, and maybe hanging out with George and Dune later that evening, back in Portland. She'd forgotten how nice it is to be with a dog. The small things in life... these are what count.

"Dr. Stephen Stephens," he begins.

She can't help but let out a small laugh. "Did his mother really call him Stephen Stephens?"

"It's not his real name."

"What?"

"What do you call it, a nom de plume? No, that's for authors. He actually changed his name legally, five years back."

"Why would he do that?"

"Because he was convicted for sexually assaulting a minor. Our prime suspect, now I've found this out. I need you to follow him. I need you to keep your eyes on him, I'm betting he's our man."

"Jesus."

"Yep."

"What have you got on him?"

"A criminal record."

"So how come we didn't know about this up till now?"

"Some people slither under our radar."

"Sir, the boat's about to leave and I have a question."

"Which is?"

"Do we need Deputy Finn and Dune to stay on the island too?"

"No, they can come home."

Damn. "But don't we need the dog?"

"If the dog hasn't come up with anything so far then there's nothing more we can do."

"But, sir..." And she starts to disembark, shaking her head at George and pointing to her phone as if to say, *This is out of my control, catch you later*. She lowers her voice and cups her mouth to hide it from any potential lipreaders. A habit from one time she got caught out, years back. People can lipread more often than you think. "What if he's buried her somewhere? We'll need the dog to sniff her out."

"You don't think we need the K-9 for other cases? Cliff Island is small, if there was anything to find he would have come up with something by now."

"But this is priority, this is—"

"I've made up my mind," her boss says.

"I was also scheduled to interview Max Wainwright, and his sister, Marjorie."

"They have alibis. And you spoke to them already."

"That was before we knew what we know now. They might still give us some leads."

"Carl's here, he can do it. I need you to stay on Cliff Island, Alba."

Normally she and Carl work as a pair, but because of "resources" and the lack of accommodation on the island, Alba is now here alone. She has been lodging in a room above the café, paying them nightly, although the owners didn't want to take any money. She gave it to them anyway, left it in an envelope in her room. But the idea of going back there now, alone, fills her with a sad, defeated dread. Coming up empty, she'll find it hard to look them in the eye.

But she's disembarked the ferry and is heading toward the café. "So tell me more about Dr. Stephen Stephens. What's his real name?"

"Stephen Knox."

"Knox with a K?"

"Yep."

"So how the hell did he get this job as Mrs. Wainwright's therapist if he has a criminal record?"

"Beats me, but I'm assuming they don't know either, or they wouldn't've hired him. Especially considering they have kids."

"What exactly was he convicted for? Who was the minor?"

"His student."

"He was a teacher?"

"Yeah, some kind of professor, some sort of psychology professor at an all-girls school in Delaware."

"How old was the girl?"

"Sixteen."

"And it's eighteen in Delaware, right, the age of consent?"

"Yep, eighteen."

"And how old was he at the time?"

"Like, thirty-four."

"That's a big age difference when you're only sixteen years old."

"Exactly."

"So what happened? Was it statutory rape he was done for, or did he actually rape her?" She feels bad differentiating this way, but she needs cold facts.

"It was a long-term 'affair,' Stephen Knox told the court. The girl claimed to be in love with him. It was her parents who brought charges. Still, she was under age and he should've known better."

"Look, what he did was wrong, but there is a difference between a sixteen-year-old and a four-year-old."

"I still need you on his case, Alba. I need proof. I need a smoking gun. Watch him, see where he goes, what he does, keep an eye on him. Anyone who's capable of having sex with a sixteen-year-old schoolgirl is capable of anything."

This is personal, she thinks. Scully happens to be the father of a sixteen-year-old daughter, Ali. She's his pride and joy, Alba knows this, how he dotes on her and how protective he feels. His views of women have changed over the years, she has noticed, mostly due to him having a daughter. There are no more sexist jokes tolerated from the guys on his team. Alba had a raise recently. He values women a whole lot more than most of his colleagues do. One of the main reasons she has stuck this gig out. He treats her well. Besides, what else could she do for a living? She doesn't know another life. Another adult life, anyway.

Alba arrives back at her digs at the café and finds the nice couple who run the place, who gave her the room. She asks if it's all right if she stays on a few nights more.

"Truth be told," the owner says, "we were shocked you were leaving so soon. Freaked us out, what happened to Lizzie. You really think it could've been an abduction?"

"We don't know, Mrs. Oldfield, we just don't know, but I'm doing everything I can to try and find out."

The detective is itching to talk to Dr. Stephen or, as it turns out, Stephen Knox, but she knows that's not what she's been asked to do; she's been asked to spy on him. She'd love to hear his side of the story, because even with sex offenders you can find out something new, and she wonders what exactly went down with this schoolgirl. She'd like to talk to the young woman's parents, too, but that's not what she's been asked to do. Her brief is to stay on the island and keep her ear close to the ground.

But someone she *is* going to talk to is Jayne.

JAYNE

I watch the ferry move off from the comfort of my cottage and heave out a huge sigh of relief. Having the detective here made me feel constantly stressed out. I wanted to be helpful but I felt like that woman was breathing down my neck. What does she know about me?

I do some laundry; there's a washing machine in the kitchen and I can hang my clothes up outside to dry, no need to go to the main house, thank God. I'm pottering around, getting a few things organized when there's a knock at my door. My stomach lurches; it'll be Stephen. I wish he'd leave me alone. The looks he's been giving me, like we have something in common, like we have this great big bond. I don't want a bond with Stephen, thank you very much.

I drag my feet to the door, and peering at me through the screen is that bloody detective.

"I thought you'd gone," I say, hearing a snap in my voice, which I really would have rather hidden because it will only make her more suspicious.

"I was leaving but... well, there's been a change of plans."

"What plans? Did you find Lizzie?" My voice rises to a squeak.

"No. Sadly we have not found Lizzie. May I come in?"

"Course." I motion her in and pull her out a chair.

The place is a mess. I'm not the tidiest of people. Detective Alba looks around the room surveying everything, her mind tick-tocking away, sizing stuff up, judging, no doubt. That's how their brains work, isn't it, these people? Everything gets filed away to use against you later. My eyes follow hers, frantically searching for clues as to what she might say, what's going through her mind. What does she know? I'm so confused, so upside down with my emotions, I can't see straight, I can't think straight.

"I wanted to talk to you about Stephen. Dr. Stephen."

"Okay. What about him?"

"How well do you know this man?"

"Well, I know he's Celeste's therapist and I talk to him once in a while."

"You told me the other day that you were both here during the time of Lizzie's disappearance?"

"Yeah, that's right."

"What time did he leave?"

"I can't say for definite, but... well, he told me that he left when he heard the police helicopter, when he heard all that commotion."

"Can you verify this?"

"No, sorry, I can't."

"You told me, when I first asked you if you'd been drinking, that you'd spent the night alone and you had an early night and took a sleeping pill, but then when it came to the issue of the alibis, you changed your story, told me you spent the evening with Dr. Stephen. Why did you lie?"

I can hear myself groan. "Because when I said that, I'd honestly forgotten. Look, I was plastered, I was out of my head.

God knows how many bottles of wine I drank—at least two, and I took a pill, I think, maybe, probably definitely. I must've done because that pill wasn't around the next day."

"Do you know for sure what pill you took?"

"A sleeping pill he gave me. Ambien?"

"How do you know it was a sleeping pill?"

Ugh. I'd been through that possibility in my mind before and shut it out. Spending an evening with him, inebriated, being naked when I woke up in the morning. And now she's putting it into words—the possibility of the worst, a reality—it makes me sick. Would Stephen really be capable of doing that?

I look her in the eye. "Why? Why are you asking me this?"

"Do you think there's any way that pill could've been a date rape drug?"

"I don't think so. I mean, it was me who asked him for a sleeping pill, so why would he have a date rape drug? After all, he's a therapist, right? Why would he—"

"Did you remember what happened the next day? You told me that you'd forgotten."

"Not really. Little bits and pieces have come back to me, but most of it, most of the evening is a complete blur. I know I drank a lot, and he told me various things we discussed and talked about which I had completely forgotten. I mean, I swear I couldn't remember telling him personal stuff but, well, I must've told him because he knew stuff that he wouldn't know in a million years."

"What did you tell him?"

"Oh, you know, trivial things about my life. Ex-boyfriends, school, that kind of stuff, nothing important. But he remembered every single word... so."

The detective nods but says nothing. I've noticed this about her. Her silences are intended to get me talking when I should keep my mouth shut. *What* is on her mind? She's really beginning to bug me... clearly she knows something I don't.

"Look, why are you asking me about Stephen? Do you suspect him of killing Lizzie?"

Her eyes take me in but she doesn't respond.

"Lizzie is missing and she's been gone for over three days and no body has been found. Someone did something, right?" Tears run down my face. I swipe them away with my sleeve. "It wasn't me, if that's what you're thinking. I would *never* do something horrible to a child."

"You're denying something nobody is accusing you of."

"Of course I bloody am, because you don't think people aren't looking at me too? The au pair? The new girl in town? Of course people are looking at me suspiciously, it's human nature. But I love that little girl. Look, it could be anybody, it could be Celeste *herself*, have you thought of that? Have you considered the mother doing something to her children? I mean, you know all about Violet, right? You think it's normal, a baby dies and six days later, oh what a coincidence, her other child goes missing, maybe dead? Don't you think that's a bit fishy? Don't you think it's awfully convenient the way her memory 'comes and goes'? Why don't you go and grill her instead of me!" I can feel the indignity rising inside me, bubbling up. I'm hurt, quite honestly, that Detective Alba suspects me of murder! *Me!* I feel like shaking her so she sees sense. Why is she so calm? This detective shows no emotion.

There is a pause. The detective is silent; something I have said is ticking away in her brain. Max had given me specific instructions to keep quiet, to not offer extra information. I know I've said too much. Too bad. I'm not shutting my mouth. They might blame *me* otherwise.

I tone my voice down several notches, try to sound less wound up, but continue, "Look, Celeste was raving around outside in the storm that night. How do you know she didn't have Lizzie in her arms, how do you know she didn't take Lizzie down to the beach, dump her in the water and drown her? Who knows, maybe she tied her up with the stone around her to make her sink and that's why nobody's found her body. Maybe she even took a boat out. You know Celeste is a good sailor, right?"

Her response is measured, unperturbed by my theory. She merely nods.

"Yeah, innocent Celeste who's forgotten everything, butter wouldn't melt in her bloody mouth. And Nurse Sharpe—have you checked her out? You know what? I wouldn't be surprised if the two of them are lovers... Sharpie's all over her like a rash. A serial killer duo, working as a team!" Tears are streaming down my face. It's finally got to me... Lizzie is actually, truly *missing*, maybe dead. Sweet little Lizzie who wouldn't hurt a soul. I can't take it anymore, I am gutted.

"Look," I stutter through sobs. "If you think I'm guilty, arrest me. But you're barking up the wrong bloody tree."

Alba holds my gaze, as if considering what I've said about arresting me. I have no idea what is going through this cop's mind, but I'm scared.

What does she know about me?

DR. STEPHEN

I hear the clumping footsteps first, like the way you hear the rumble of an earthquake before it happens. I remember that from California, one time, when there was an earthquake and all the alarms in the city went off: car alarms, house alarms, and all the dogs in the city seemed to bark in unison, and the growl of the breaking ground beneath my feet... all this happened before I realized there was an earthquake.

And this is how I feel when I hear her clunking footsteps pounding on my porch. An omen of something bigger yet to come? Maybe this is just the beginning...

"What did you do to me?"

It's Jayne. I suspected she might be the type to be highly strung, and here it is in full force. She's sobbing, banging at my screen door, pretty much incoherently. Bleating at me about how untrustworthy and sneaky and cruel I am.

I open the door with decorum, with composure. One thing I'm good at is keeping my calm. "Jayne, come in. Would you like—"

"No, I wouldn't 'like,' you bastard!"

I'm not sure if she's found something, some kind of evidence against me, or she's referring to the other night. Either way, this is not looking good. I invite her in again, in case anyone overhears. There were people milling on the beach earlier. I close the door behind me, and the windows, to keep the sound in. There's no AC here but I turn on the ceiling fan.

"Does it feel good to have sex with a corpse?" she hiccups through tears.

"What on earth are you talking about?" Is she accusing me of murdering Lizzie and then sexually molesting her?

"I was lying there, obviously out for the count, and you had sex with me?"

I blow out a sigh. "I already told you, I did not touch you. Yes, I undressed you, for your own comfort, but I did not do anything... maybe a hug, maybe a little kiss or something like that, but no big deal."

"Oh, it's no big deal to you, but how do you think I feel? What was that pill you gave me? It was a date rape drug, wasn't it? What's it called, that one beginning with R? WHAT DID YOU GIVE ME?"

She elbows me out of her way and stomps into the bathroom, slamming the door behind her then bolting it.

I pummel on the door. "There's nothing there that you need to know about." I can hear her shaking bottles, rummaging through the medicine cabinet.

Then there's silence.

"Jayne, what are you doing in there?"

"I'm trying to bloody well get a connection so I can look up some of these drugs online. I want to know what you gave me."

"I can tell you, if you'd listen to me for a second."

"No, I don't trust you. I know you had sex with me the other night, I know you did."

And now she's got me thinking. Your brain does weird things, doesn't it, when somebody accuses you of something, when they're so convinced, it almost convinces you too. *I didn't,*

I didn't, I didn't! But then I'm thinking maybe I did? If she's so convinced I did?

No, she's got it wrong.

"Jayne, I swear... it's not sexy, not my thing to have sex with somebody who... who is out of it like you were the other night, it's not my style."

"Oh, we're talking about style now, are we? Forgive me for saying so, Stephen, but I think you score a three out of ten for style!"

Her words sting, what she said hits below the belt. A strategic kick where it hurts. "There's no need to insult me."

"And just so you're aware, that detective's back and she thinks you did it and maybe she's right. You're hiding something, aren't you, Stephen?"

I feel that *sinking sinking* feeling, like I want the earth to swallow me up. All of it coming right back again: that hole of despair. I can't go there again, I can't. What does the detective know? Why isn't she confronting me? I need to get away from this. I need to shut Jayne up. I need to get out to the ocean. To be free of this.

I need my underwater cave.

JAYNE

Finally I get a connection and look up various different pills. I sit on the toilet seat lid and spend a good ten to fifteen minutes reading everything on various doctor websites and Reddit. Then it dawns on me that Stephen has stopped banging on the bathroom door.

There is no sound whatsoever coming from the room. I gingerly unlock the door, feeling ashamed for my outburst. Is it possible he's completely innocent and didn't do anything? None of the pills I found in his cabinet resembled anything like a date rape drug.

There's nobody here.

"Stephen?" I call out.

Nothing. No sound beyond the whirring of the ceiling fan. "Stephen, you here?" I look around. His bedroom door is closed. I bang on it. I try the handle. Locked. He's locked himself in his bedroom in a sulk? *Bang bang bang.* I thump my closed fists hard against the wooden door.

"Stephen, I'm sorry, look, I didn't mean to insult you so much, I swear I didn't mean it." Then I panic. *Oh my God, he's not the type of person to go to slit his wrists, is he?* "Stephen, come out! Look, I haven't found anything weird with your pills. I'm sorry, but you can understand why I'm a bit paranoid, can't you? With what happened to Lizzie."

Truth is, I don't think it's Stephen who's abducted Lizzie. I'm still convinced it's Celeste. She just doesn't feel like a "natural" mother to me. I mean, sometimes, yeah, she's really sweet with her children. But she's so cut off, so detached, absent in a way. I think that crash did something to her brain, and I do, I do think she killed her kids. Even if she is unaware herself, even if she practically did it sleepwalking. She had a mental breakdown, after all. Women have been known to do terrible things when suffering from postnatal depression. Or maybe Violet's death was a real SIDS cot death and it sent her over the edge? And that's what made her kill Lizzie?

"Stephen, what are you doing in there?"

Absolute silence.

I walk out of the cottage and go around the back. I have to stand on tiptoes to see into the bedroom window even though I'm tall. No blinds drawn, which is lucky. I peer in through the dirty glass. He's not there. So why did he lock his room? I trundle back inside the house and, yeah, it has a regular lock and key on the bedroom door so he must've locked it before leaving. What a weird thing to do, to leave his house open with me in it and him outside.

This is beginning to give me the chills. Where is he?

What kind of head game is he up to?

I don't like it. I don't like it one bloody bit.

THE DISAPPEARANCE

Adele Alba, stunned by what Jayne has revealed about baby Violet and her SIDS death, calls Scully. The coincidence is too great. Two children in the same family in less than a week? *This is not normal.* Knowing there must have been a death scene investigation and an autopsy taking into account the clinal or medical history of the baby, she is flabbergasted that this has not been on their radar.

"There was a baby," she tells her boss. "Named Violet. Why were we not aware of this? Nobody mentioned a baby when we interviewed them."

"Interesting. What else do you know?"

"Well, apparently Celeste's baby passed away from SIDS. You know, one of those mysterious crib deaths? There's mention in one of the local papers about Celeste surviving the car crash and how she and her unborn baby were in critical condition, but I can't find anything else online about a birth, and certainly not a subsequent death after Celeste was released from the hospital."

"Let me look into it."

"Call the coroners ASAP and find out who the chief medical examiner was. These Wainwrights are proving to be pretty cagey. Neither the nurse, nor Dr. Stephen, nor even Mr. Wainwright mentioned a baby. As for Celeste herself, well, she's very unreliable, her memory really does seem shot. The au pair let it slip and by the look on Jayne's face afterward seems like she'd been told to keep her mouth shut."

"Okay, I'll look into it."

Alba glances at her watch. "How did Carl get on with the Max Wainwright interview?"

"Funny you should ask."

"Why?"

"Wainwright didn't come in and isn't answering his calls."

"Did you try calling his sister?"

"Yep. Same thing."

"You think they forgot?"

"Search me." He sighs down the line. "Don't worry, kiddo. You concentrate on Stephen Knox, I'll find Max Wainwright."

Alba ends the call. At first Alba hated it when Scully called her kiddo. Then she grew accustomed to it. It made her feel like she had a fatherly figure in her life, something she missed after the death of her real dad. But now this endearment feels way off base to her once again, disgustingly patronizing. She is a child who needs guidance, at her age? With her experience and career successes under her belt? He would never call one of her male colleagues "kiddo."

The kiddo remark is surging in Alba's gut and rising up her throat like acid reflux. Everything feels like it's weighing down on her all at once: both parents dead, Alba single, childless, working *under* somebody for years on end who is "nice" to her and treats her with "respect" but only in his own paternal, patriarchal way.

It sucks.

If she had a female boss, things would be different, she's pretty damn sure. Or better, if she were her own boss.

She calls her partner, Carl, at the station. Tells him to find out more about the deceased baby and who the medical examiner was, track down the coroner's report for Violet Wainwright. She knows Scully can be slow about things that in his opinion are not urgent.

Logging into databases is too unreliable with this island's spotty connection, but Alba has found the blog of the girl who convicted Stephen Knox for statutory rape. Madison Cardman. Except she is no longer a girl. Five years have elapsed between then and now. She is twenty-one years old.

At the time, I didn't relate to any other "victims." I refused to "join the bandwagon" to "come forward." I did not want my personal life to be an open book. He and I had something special, why would I want to tarnish our bond, our love? I refused to get involved with other women—or girls—who felt they were in the same boat as myself. I hated, loathed my parents for ruining my life, for turning the man I loved against me, for destroying his life.

They had trashed something beautiful. It was as if I had been run over by a car and my father was at the wheel.

I locked myself away for two years, blaming them. Angry, bitter. I hardly ate. In fact, I developed the beginnings of anorexia because it made me feel I had some modicum of control over what I put in my mouth—at least they could not take that control away from me.

He saw me. He loved me. He saw me as an intelligent woman, not as a little girl.

He defined me.

And now I was being defined—and defiled—by something ugly. I was the poster child for "rape," for "women's rights." It made me sick to my stomach.

"You've ruined my life," I told my mom as she came to my room for the millionth time with a bowl of hot soup and some crackers on the side. I couldn't chew anymore because I didn't have the energy, I couldn't pass real food between my dry lips because it made me want to choke.

"No, Madison, he *ruined your life."*

What is the truth? The reality?

What do you do when you are a vulnerable sixteen-year-old and a man who seems to have all the answers, a smart man, tells you that looking into your eyes is like "seeing the ocean," like "twinkling sapphires in the mist"?

Detective Alba stops reading. *Seriously? She fell for the sapphire line?* But then she checks herself. *Of course she did, she was sixteen.* And Alba remembers one of the striking things about Lizzie: her blue, blue eyes.

She scans the blog for different posts and then finds a more recent one.

And now it is seeping in, all these years later. How it affected me. How he stole my childhood, that delicate space between being a child and a woman, a period in your life that you can never get back. He stole it, really, without asking, because I was too young, too naive to say no, to understand that the "love" he gave me wasn't his decision to give... because that's what I now know... it was a decision that I believed I was making of my own free will, from my sixteen-year-old, hormonal curiosity concerning desire, yet he was in control of my emotions, not I, not me. It split my persona in two, like I had a choice to make: to be a woman before I was ready.

Did I get to choose? Was I old enough to make that choice?

So, the question that begs to be asked—aside from what the law dictates—is:

Was it consensual?

Yes, technically it was.
Morally?
I leave that for you to decide.

That's what laws are for, Alba thinks. To protect people.

Not only to protect you from others, but to protect you from yourself.

THE DISAPPEARANCE

"These Wainwrights must be really dumb or have a hard-on for hiring people with criminal records." It's Scully on the line.

Alba is chomping at the bit to find out what Scully has on baby Violet's death, because when she spoke to the coroner's office they informed her that her usual contact was on vacation. The person replacing her seemed clueless and could find nothing. Alba pressed to speak to another of her contacts, but he too was on vacation. *This is what happens in August*, she growls to herself. People are away, and those who are working feel like they *should* be on vacation. There should be a Lost and Found for the amount of information misplaced or lost in August.

Scully, however, is not perturbed; he is more preoccupied with Stephen and Jayne anyway. Alba listens to his latest hypothesis about Jayne as she downs a black coffee, planning her next step. She has spent the afternoon on a hike, watching Stephen as he swam, clad in his wetsuit. It was hard to keep tabs on him because he was hugging the rocky coastline, in a vertical drop from where she stood. Below, from her bird's-eye view from the clifftop, she observed the neon orange buoy-float bobbing above the water, right near the edge of the cliff, attached, no doubt, by a cord to Stephen's waist. The small colored buoy is designed to avert accidents, let people know someone is there. *There must be some pretty interesting fish down there*, she pondered, *why else would he stay in the same place for a couple of hours*.

But then with a jolt she'd remembered something Stephen had said: "I'm not into snorkeling or diving or spearfishing, just... just swimming."

What's there that is so interesting?

Alba would have liked to go into the water herself, but swimming has been a problem for her ever since a bullet from a shotgun nearly blew her head off. She has a hearing problem in her left ear and is prone to infections. While standing on the cliff, she made a call to a team member with diving experience. Fearful the professional divers missed something the first time around, she sent GPS coordinates for Stephen's position, in case Lizzie's body was down there, weighted by some rock.

It is well known that perpetrators can't help themselves, they can't resist going back to the scene of the crime. *Is that what he's doing?*

Or perhaps the floating buoy was not attached to his waist at all, but a decoy? He suspected he was being watched, perhaps? Alba has a nasty feeling she's been duped.

"What have you got?" she asks her boss, her phone on speaker as she finishes her coffee.

"At fourteen, Jayne was put in a juvenile detention center. Seems to have gotten her act together around seventeen. Worked as an assistant in a clothing store for a couple years—had dropped out of school, didn't go to college. Looked like things were going okay but then she got arrested for shoplifting. This time, as an adult. She was tried and sent to jail. Six months, out early with good behavior."

"So Jayne has a criminal record for shoplifting. That doesn't make her dangerous to children."

"But it does prove she's a liar, and wait... there's more..." He lets that float for a moment.

"What?"

"After she got out of prison she went to work as a cleaner... get this, at a daycare center."

"And she moved on to au pair work from there?"

"Who'd want to hire an au pair with a criminal record? And I can't see any jobs listed with kids anywhere before the Wainwrights. Beats me how she got the job."

Alba had already checked out the email correspondence between the Wainwrights and Jayne and what the agency's requirements were. They provided a J-1 visa sponsorship for UK citizens working in the States. The agency was one of those modern, online-only businesses that also functions with an app. Still, Jayne had to provide references, plus a recent DBS certificate (turns out the DBS is a public body which carries out background checks on British citizens for prospective employers). If Jayne had a criminal record, she would not have passed screening. Yet now Scully is telling her Jayne *does* have a criminal record? How did she get the job?

"Ballsy," Alba remarks. "She must have a great skillset when it comes to forgery."

"Like I said, these Wainwrights must have a thing for criminals. Subconsciously choosing deadbeats? Or purposefully? This is the question."

"Why would anyone purposefully hire anyone who might jeopardize the safety of their kids? Even be an active danger to them?"

"Great question. This is what we need to find out."

"So we can't believe Jayne when she said she dropped Lizzie off at around seven p.m. that evening?"

"Nope."

Alba is not sure she agrees with her boss. "But the time was confirmed by Ms. Sharpe and Mrs. Wainwright."

Scully clears his throat. "Allegedly, true. But my point is, Jayne has gone from being a regular witness to an extremely unreliable witness with a criminal record, who is in all likelihood not qualified for the job she's doing. She's a liar and a schemer, with balls of steel. You realize foreigners with a criminal record are not allowed to work in this country? Aside from deportation, she could face prison. What she did is a felony, on both sides of the pond."

"So what do we do now?"

"If we let on we know, it could disrupt the investigation. The last thing we need is her being deported back to the UK at this point in time. For now, we sit tight. The little boy isn't in her care anyway, he's with his dad. So if she is guilty of murder, at least he's out of harm's way."

Alba wonders if there was a reason for the Wainwrights' actions. Is it possible they could be so clueless? She can't believe they would do this on purpose... but then again, she's seen some pretty crazy shit over the years. Even people with severe mental illness and psychopaths who wind up being perpetrators have reasons for what they do. Nothing seems to make sense. Still, Jayne's criminal record for shoplifting and her apparent skillset with forging paperwork does not mean she'd abduct or harm a child.

"Sir, not to detract from what you've come up with concerning Jayne, but there's something else I wanted to discuss with you."

"Any development with Stephen Knox? You think the divers missed something first time around, don't you? It's possible. After a heavy storms, things can move, things can shift position. I think you're right to get divers down there again."

Alba swallows, her throat is parched. It's hot, she needs a

drink. "Actually, it's not only *that* I'm thinking of. Any news on Max Wainwright and his sister's whereabouts?"

"Nope."

"Shouldn't we be worried? This speaks volumes to me."

It isn't the first time it has occurred to Alba and Scully that this could be a kidnapping. The Wainwrights have money. But if someone has Lizzie and wants to make a trade, why have they not heard from them yet? Unless the kidnapper is biding his (or her) time, upping the stakes. This theory doesn't really make sense to Alba, because the family is very low-key. They are not flashy, not ostentatious with their wealth.

She has checked out both Wainwrights' social media accounts. They seem to have abandoned them over the last few years. Many people, she notes, have weaned themselves off Facebook lately, probably because of the privacy problems. Celeste hasn't posted anything for over a year and a half, and when Alba goes through old posts, she does not see any signs of obvious wealth that might attract outside attention. Celeste has applied privacy settings, Alba notes. Hardly any photos of the kids, either.

Most people would not know that the Wainwrights own a chunk of this island, with all these private cottages. It would have to be somebody who had rented from them in the past, who is in the know, but still, this theory is unlikely. Surely a kidnapper would have come forward by now?

Money is usually the motivating factor when it comes to crime. They say money makes the world go round, but in Alba's experience money often makes people's lives grind to a halt. The love of money or the fear of losing it can be toxic.

Scully clears his throat. "You think Max Wainwright's hiding something? Like someone's kidnapped Lizzie and has made a demand and he's not sharing the info with his wife, some shit like that?"

"No, I don't think so, although..."

"What?" His voice is gruff.

"Well, it seemed to me that although he was upset about Lizzie, he was much more concerned with his son Liam."

"With the press there, I would be too."

"Yeah, guess that makes sense," Alba agrees. "But where the hell are they now? The three of them? It makes me nervous."

When Alba had spoken to both Max and his sister at the house, neither had given her any useful information. But the fact they're now AWOL has put a new spin on things. She wants to discuss Celeste with Max and find out what kind of marriage they have, discover whether there are any money problems causing rifts in the relationship. Business debts, money owed to third parties. Plus, there's Violet. When she spoke to him before, at the house, Violet was not part of the conversation because, at that point, Alba did not even know of the baby's existence. She is also itching to interview Marjorie again. The woman has absolutely no digital footprint whatsoever, which makes Alba suspicious.

"Any development on baby Violet?" she asks Scully. She thinks back to how Stephen was so "helpful" yet one thing he never mentioned was the baby's death. *Why? What is he hiding? Who is Stephen protecting?*

"Got the birth certificate," Scully replies. "Violet Wainwright was born, all right. Checking out the rest—nobody can find anything so far, not even a death certificate—but let's concentrate on one thing at a time, Alba."

"Sir," she says, a thousand things swirling through her mind: the coroner's report for baby Violet's death being at the top of the list. "Could you please locate Max Wainwright ASAP? I need to talk to him again. I want to find out more about Marjorie too." It is not easy for Alba, with limited internet, to access the data she needs. Her boss is methodical but too slow for her liking. She is counting on him to scour the police databases, something she cannot do from her phone. Both Max and his sister have alibis and were off the island when Lizzie disappeared, but that doesn't let them completely off the hook. *Where are they now? Why didn't they come in for that interview?*

"We need to think outside the box, sir. Consider the people who were not on the island the day Lizzie disappeared. I need to talk to Eric Lawson, face to face." His alibi checks out, but that doesn't mean she can't learn something.

Scully's cough booms down the line. "Eric Lawson is already taken care of. He's coming in for an interview tomorrow."

"Great, that's great. What time?"

"Carl and I are going to interview him."

"But, sir, I want to be there too, I—"

"You stay put," Scully interrupts. "I need you there, Alba. We got this covered. So, you think Max is hiding something?"

"It's a possibility. I want to know if they have any money problems. Have you pulled their bank records?"

"Somewhat."

"Somewhat?" She rolls her eyes.

"I've tried, but it's not so easy with offshore accounts. It looks like they must have their 'real' money in shell holdings abroad. What I can see from here, in the US, is that there are no debts, but no big savings either. The surprising thing is, there's no separate business account for Max. His and his wife's accounts seem to be joint. And there's something else that piques the hell out of my interest." He pauses as if for effect, waiting for a reaction from her.

She pictures Scully in her mind's eye, in his office at the station. She bets he is leaning back in a swivel chair, his belly a few pounds heavier than last year, his face shiny and red. Alba wonders if he's been drinking lately. This case is turning out to be all smoke and mirrors. As if someone is playing a big joke on them all. Or maybe it's because she has completely dropped the ball. She's tired, needs a vacation. Yet, at the rate she's going she doesn't *deserve* a vacation.

"So... what have you found?" she asks.

"When we pulled up the Wainwrights' bank records, we discovered something else interesting going on with this family."

"What?" The constant pauses for effect are starting to get to her.

"Max Wainwright is not his real name. The Wainwrights—Celeste's family—well, you may have guessed by now that they're the ones with the money, they're the ones with the land. In fact, not just here in Maine, but all over Canada, Europe, America."

Why does this not surprise Alba? She replies coolly, "What was Max's name before?"

"Dickman."

Alba wants to laugh but doesn't: this is too serious. "Well, I guess he wanted a nicer name. Bet he got teased at school."

"You're probably right."

"So Max doesn't have his own money?"

"Nope, doesn't look like he had much before marrying Celeste."

"Interesting."

"But guess what's *really* interesting?"

Get on with it, she thinks, as he lets another pause sit between them.

A beat goes by. She taps her foot.

He finally comes out with it. "It's one of those families where they pass the money down by skipping a generation. You know, they do that sometimes to keep the money in the family so the spoiled child doesn't go AWOL taking private jets and, you know, spending all the inheritance in one go."

"So who inherits?"

"Not Celeste Wainwright. The money will all go to the kids."

"Seriously?"

"It's in trust, of course. The kids get the whole shebang when they turn twenty-one."

"And who benefits if the children die?"

"Their mother."

THE DISAPPEARANCE

Despite the last conversation between Scully and Alba, everything has been put on hold now that this lead on Stephen Knox is proving so fruitful. Scully, as usual, is jumping the gun. The divers have been working tirelessly, concentrating on the rocks below the cliff, and when they find a little pink plastic shoe belonging to a child, wedged between two rocks near where Stephen had been snorkeling, Scully's excitement is palpable. K-9 Dune is brought back from the mainland. He sits in a Zodiac above the water where they have found the shoe.

Nothing. No reaction from the dog.

But then again, how is Dune supposed to be able to sniff through water? Even though he has been successful in the past, finding human remains in water, too many days have passed since Lizzie's disappearance, and the storm would have washed away much of the evidence.

The afternoon is drawing to an end, the heat no longer pounds the air, and the water glistens with reflections from the setting sun and diamonds twinkle across the great expanse of blue when the divers finally discover the opening to an underwater cave, carved out of the hard granite by longshore currents and centuries, maybe millennia, of smashing waves.

The excitement ripples through the very water, the divers cannot believe their luck.

This is where Stephen has hidden the child, no doubt about it. As far as Scully is concerned, anyway.

It is Detective Alba's luck that she's on her way back to Portland to check new evidence, and hopefully to interview Max Wainwright—assuming he shows up now that she's put out an APB on him—when the discovery about Stephen is made. But it looks as though, even if Max and Marjorie are located, she won't be interviewing them after all.

Scully's excitement zaps through the telephone, so loudly she has to hold it away from her good ear. "Now that we have this lead on Knox, we don't want to waste time," he enthuses.

Before Alba knows it, she is being sent back to the island. This chain of command is something she finds hard to accept. Though he claims to respect her as a detective, Scully still gets to call the shots. He is stubborn. He tends to jump to conclusions, hook onto something at the expense of other leads. She can tell his mind is now channeled into Stephen and nothing else matters. All other leads, interviews, are on the back burner. This is the part of her job she finds tough.

Two police officers escort Stephen into the Zodiac, and motor over to the sea cave. To get inside the cave is a complicated maneuver, considering they have to dive way down and then through a four-foot, horizontal tunnel. In the boat, they offer Stephen diving gear, but he declines. He has no idea how to use it: the bottles, the breathing equipment. All of it makes him feel claustrophobic. He's been going down there armed only with a waterproof flashlight. His beautiful private sea cave is being soiled, desecrated by strangers who see it as a means to an end. As far as he is concerned, these people are incapable of appreciating its sheer beauty and magnificence, its magic. Its geological history.

Stephen does not deny knowing about the cave, does not pretend he hasn't been here before, does not deny anything at all; it's almost as if his behavior is fatalistic. The diving team takes lights and equipment inside dry-bags and sets them up in the higher, waterless part of the cave. It is the size of a large church, majestic with stalactites and strange rock formations that look like icicles, pointed and crude and cold to the touch, fresh water clinging to them dripping from above. This place is centuries... no, millenniums old.

The divers are excited, forgetting for a moment they are here with a suspect criminal, probably a pedophile, a man who is being accused of murdering a child. Unless he is keeping Lizzie Wainwright inside this cave, alive, and bringing her food and water.

Anything is possible. They need to find the girl, dead or alive.

"What do you *want* from me?" Stephen shouts into the void. He is sitting in the shadows, genuinely bewildered, looking around the sea cave in awe at the way it is all lit up, because he has never been able to achieve such a thing himself with his small flashlight. The chamber echoes with his words ricocheting around the great space.

He is shivering. They had not let him go back to his cottage to get his own wetsuit and he did not want to use one of theirs. It is obvious he is not used to this and feels sorry for himself, miserable, as if he is a victim, as if there is no dead child, no missing child at all.

One of the officers, Detective Greene, a thin man with long lean muscles from hours in the gym since his divorce, crouches down next to him.

He lowers his voice so it won't echo. Humiliating Stephen

Knox is unlikely to move things along. "Tell us where you're hiding her. Show us where Lizzie is."

"I know what you're thinking, and it's crazy," Stephen answers.

"We're not going anywhere until you tell us... *show* us, where the child is."

"I have no idea... I swear, I don't know what you're talking about."

"It would make everybody's life so much easier if you fessed up. You know we're going to search this place, you know we're going to find her, don't you? Why not tell us right now, you'll be doing yourself, and all of us, a whole lot of favors. Not to mention her poor family. Her mother must be out of her mind with grief, with worry, have you thought of that?"

"I swear, I don't have Lizzie, I don't know where she is."

"How do you explain the little pink shoe right outside the cave?"

"I have no idea, things get washed up, how do you even know it's Lizzie's?"

"Because we called her mother. Sent her a photo of the shoe, and she has confirmed that, yes, it belongs to her daughter."

"She said that to you?" He lets out a sarcastic laugh. And then under his breath he says, "*Bitch!*"

"What was that?" the detective asks.

"Nothing," Stephen says, shaking his head, raking his hands through his wet hair. "Look, I can't give you what you want. You have to believe me! You'll find out soon enough. Go ahead, search this place, bring that dog in, if you want."

Well, *that* is the problem. How the hell can they bring the dog in here? They can hardly put the dog in a dry-bag, swim with him underwater and bring him up the other side. This is not like a Mexican cenote where you can get in from above. The only entryway is by the underwater tunnel. This sea cave is completely sealed in; the only opening is through the channel that reaches ten feet under the ocean's surface.

They can't believe this cave exists and that this man managed to discover it. Does anybody else know that it is here? If so, they have kept quiet about it. Not even a tiny opening, no chink of light to show there is a way in from above where the cliffs meet the ocean.

Greene whispers in Stephen's ear. "If you don't cooperate, it's going to look really really bad for you."

"I can't help that," Stephen replies. "I can't invent a truth that doesn't exist!"

"What does that even mean?" The detective wants to laugh. This man is some kind of intellectual? "You're so full of it, man. You killed that girl, why deny it?"

Stephen purses his lips and says nothing. He crouches, his hands cradling his knees in an upright fetal position. This goes on for an hour until Stephen is blue, shivering. Finally, with the lights still set up in the cave, one of the detectives ushers him back to the boat.

"You're one hell of a lucky son of a bitch that dog couldn't get in the cave. He would've sniffed her out in seconds and then..."

Stephen says nothing. The detective wants to punch him. There is no form of life lower than child molesters, child murderers. They're the lowest of the low.

DR. STEPHEN

I don't know which is worse: sitting in my sea cave with those glaring lights, shivering, being accused of something monstrous, or sitting here in this interrogation room at the police station, also shivering—from the air conditioning—being accused of something monstrous.

"Do you know where Lizzie is?" the detective asks me. I don't even know this man's name. He's not the same one as the one from my cave. He has asked me this same question for, I don't know, maybe the fiftieth time. I am mute. I can't speak. I can't answer because I genuinely don't know what to say.

"You see, we think you took her to that cave. Question is, a little girl like that... how did you get her to swim ten feet down through a narrow four-foot opening? That's a small entryway into the cave... it's not easy getting through that small cavity, and she must've been resistant and very scared. But then again, there was that storm, there's no way you could've gotten through with that heavy weather bashing at the rocks, you would've ended up trapped in there, maybe drowned, so did you hide Lizzie beforehand? If you took her somewhere, we need to know. Where did you take her, Stephen?"

I shake my head. My face is wet. I feel tears rolling down my cheeks.

"Did things get a little out of hand? Maybe, you know, it started as a game or something? Then things got a little out of hand? That can happen with kids, right? But you need to let us know where she is."

I look him in the eye for a second, incredulous that somebody could accuse me of something so crass, so vulgar. But I don't answer because I still don't know what to say.

"That's how it happened. Isn't it? That Lizzie got a little overexcited, or maybe something happened to her and you got scared? Scared enough to hide her, to keep her quiet? If you took her, Stephen, you need to come clean with us now, or things could get a whole lot worse for you." His voice is gentle, persuasive. "I want to be helpful. If you open up to us now, things may even go in your favor."

I say nothing, just wipe those embarrassing tears off my face.

The detective goes on, "Maybe you forgot yourself, got carried away in the moment? Did something you didn't mean to do? That you regretted later? It happens to all of us."

My voice finally finds a little strength. "Where's the lady detective, can I speak to her?"

"Detective Alba? If you think a lady cop's going to be any different from me, you're mistaken."

His accusation baffles me. Truly baffles me. He thinks he can squeeze out information this way? By means of persuasion? "This is how they train you?" I ask him. "To push people into believing they did something when they didn't, by repeating the same thing over and over again until they admit to something they never did?"

"What did you do with Lizzie, Stephen?"

I haven't asked for a lawyer because I don't believe I've said anything that will incriminate me. But it doesn't really matter what I say because they've decided I'm guilty ahead of time. They decided I was guilty the minute they found my sea cave, the minute they found the pink shoe.

"You won't find Lizzie in that cave," I tell him.

"So where will we find her?" the other cop, who has remained silent, suddenly pipes up.

What is it about me that makes people see me this way? All my life... all my life it's been like this. The ostracized one at school in the playground, the one who was called "weirdo" right from the age of... God I can't even remember... since forever.

All my life, all my life... when, when will it end?

I think of that sweet night with Jayne, which feels like centuries ago. We had such fun, we had such a blast. Even if it was wine-induced, even if she was out of her mind and didn't remember the next day, we did have fun, didn't we?

"You see, I think what you did with Lizzie is this. You took her into that cave the way a dog takes a bone and buries it, you know, for later, to enjoy later."

I know what this cop is doing. This man is trying to break me, he's trying to push me... push me and push me until I can't take it anymore. The last police officer interviewing me was so nice and friendly. It's easy to see these methods they use: the easygoing cop, the persuasive, insidious cop. I can't say anything. I can't speak, my mind is in turmoil.

Finally I croak out, "I think maybe I need a lawyer. An attorney."

"That's your legal right," he says, disappointed.

"Don't I get a phone call too?"

"Yeah you get a phone call too," he lets me know in a gruff voice. "It's your attorney you want to call?"

"No, I need to call a friend... well, not a friend, but somebody important."

"Okay, I can arrange that for you."

Maybe once I've made the phone call, all this will be over.

But the terrifying thing is, I have a horrible feeling I've been hung out to dry.

CELESTE

"What kind of relationship do you have with your husband?" Alba asks me.

I look at her but am not sure how to answer. What is she expecting me to say?

"Happy? Close? United? Independent?" she prods.

"We're very close," I say, surprised.

"But he spends a lot of time away from home, right?"

"Business meetings, that's all. He takes providing for his family seriously. Of course I'd love to have him home as much as possible but he's a very busy man."

"Is he a good father?"

"He's the best father ever. Very caring, very hands-on, you know, when he's around, when he can."

"When he can?"

"As I say, he's very busy, but he's wonderful with the children. They adore him."

"Has he ever hurt you or... let me put it this way, has he ever hurt the children?"

"Hurt the children?" My eyes... I can feel them grow large.

"He has never hurt the children," I say with honesty. It's true, the children have never been hurt by him.

"None of them?"

I shake my head.

"Celeste, I need to talk to you about your baby, Violet. She passed away, I believe?"

I bite my lip to stop myself crying.

"I'm so sorry for your loss," Alba says. "Can you tell me what happened?"

I go mute. My eyes film over. Words won't form in my mouth.

"Is there any way either of you could have mistakenly hurt your baby?"

Silence. "Baby?" I mouth, no sound escaping from my lips. I look into the middle space, a squadron of tears forming, my heart thudding.

"I'm sorry, Celeste, but this is important. Any way you might have harmed Violet?"

I still don't respond. A lump in my throat makes it too hard to speak. My mouth feels like cotton candy.

"Since the accident, you find your memory comes and goes, is that correct?"

Now that the subject has veered from Violet, I find my voice. "Yes, some days I can remember absolutely everything... other days it's like... I don't know, like maybe having a cataract or something, not that I've ever had a cataract, but from what my grandmother told me. Like it's hazy and blurry and little chunks of light get in but you don't see the whole picture."

"You remember your baby though?"

I shake my head. I cannot go there right now.

Alba sips in a large breath as if her exasperation is reaching breaking point. "All right, let's get back to Lizzie then. I'd like to go through everything that happened the night that Lizzie went missing again, if you don't mind."

"Okay," I respond, trying to piece together the events, trying to remember what I told her before. It's hard when somebody asks you the same question twice because they assume you're lying if the second time you say something a tiny bit different.

"You said that Jayne dropped the kids off at around seven fifteen, right?"

"If that's what I said, it must be true."

"You can't remember telling me this?"

"Maybe I said seven fifteen, maybe I said seven twenty, I couldn't swear to anything. I can't be expected... nobody looks at their watch around here. I mean, I don't even wear a watch, and I never look at my phone. That's the point of living somewhere like this, we don't go around looking at the time all the time, and the time doesn't matter. Especially in summer. It was before sunset, that's what I remember."

"Okay, so we have Jayne bringing Lizzie and Liam home sometime before sunset. Did she take them upstairs?"

"No, my nurse, Alex, she had some dinner ready for them both."

"You remember what Lizzie ate?"

"Oh goodness, you'd have to ask Alex, but something simple like... I don't know, mashed potatoes and vegan sausages, maybe?"

"Vegan?"

"Yes, Lizzie decided all on her own she wanted to be vegetarian."

"Where did she get this idea from? Are you vegetarian?"

"No, I think she must've picked it up from one of her friends."

"You know which friend?"

"Who knows... when she goes out and plays on the beach."

"Could you give me a list of her friends, please?" For these detailed interviews, Alba is recording the conversation, with my permission, of course. She clearly does not want to miss any detail, any name.

I rub my eyes. "There's a little girl named Miranda who lives about half a mile south of here. It's the pale pink cottage."

"What's the name of this cottage?"

"Probably 'Pink Cottage.' The cottages have very basic names around here. I don't know what the address is, nobody cares about addresses here, we just walk around, or drive from A to B in our golf carts, you know, that's the kind of place this is."

"When did she last see Miranda?"

"I'm so sorry, Detective Alba, but I simply can't remember. I know she has friends all over the island, she's such a chatty, vivacious soul, always making buddies wherever she goes. People of all ages. Everybody warms to Lizzie."

I wonder if the detective notices I am talking about my daughter in the present tense. I am optimistic—hopefully, contagiously so. Yet when I catch Alba's eye, she acts as if my talking about Lizzie in the present tense is heartbreaking.

"Perhaps you should talk to the au pair again? Or my husband... he, he was around a few weeks ago, he took off a couple of weeks from work and he was looking after the children."

Alba nods but changes tack. "Let's get back to the night Lizzie went missing. So you were in the kitchen with Lizzie and Liam, eating dinner?"

"Maybe I was with them for a little bit, but I didn't have any dinner myself. That's right, I was having a bath I seem to remember."

"The way you're telling me this sounds as if it was years ago, this was only a few days ago, Mrs. Wainwright."

"Please call me Celeste. I know I sound vague, I'm so sorry. I can remember things years in the past, but things that happen today or very recently are a blur. I get confused. It... it's a haze, I can't give you details, if I gave you details I would practically be making things up. I mean, little snapshots pop into my consciousness, they come and go."

"Does Ms. Sharpe often look after the children? How come, if you hired Jayne for the summer, the nurse is still minding the kids?"

"Because there are only so many hours an au pair is allowed to work. She's not a full-time nanny, you see, they're very expensive to hire."

"And you have a budget?" The detective looks around the kitchen and her eyes land on the diamond ring on my engagement finger.

I laugh, lifting my ring finger to the light. "This old vintage thing? It was a gift from my grandmother. She loved costume jewelry. Look, just because we own a nice house and a lot of property on the island doesn't make us cash rich, you understand."

Alba looks like she knows a real diamond when she sees one, like she is sure this ring is not a piece of costume jewelry. "You've never thought of selling one of your homes here?" she says.

"Never sell, never sell property, it's the cardinal rule," I answer.

"Did someone tell you that?"

"Somebody did tell me that once, and it stuck with me."

"Oh, yes, who?"

"Is this pertinent to Lizzie's disappearance?"

"No, just me being curious."

"I remember now. After supper Alex brought Lizzie upstairs and Lizzie had a bath with me."

"*With* you?"

"Yes, she likes to get in the tub with me sometimes. I have to make sure the water isn't too hot, so usually she comes at the end of my bath and I give her a nice sudsy back rub and clean her all over and then wrap her in a big fluffy towel. She loves it."

"And your son? What about Liam?"

"He's a little bit old now to take a bath with his mommy. I'm not prudish but you know, he's a little boy and reaching the age where... well, I don't think it's appropriate anymore to have him in the tub with me."

"I understand."

"He told me he didn't need a bath anyway but he was perfectly clean and that he wanted to go to his room, so that was fine by me. There are no rules and regulations in this house with the children in the summertime, we let them be quite free."

"Do you think it's possible, Celeste, that you took Lizzie outside for a walk or something that night? That you had forgotten and took her out to the backyard?"

"A walk?"

"Some people say they've seen you walking at night, in the evenings."

"Who?"

"Neighbors."

"They say they saw me *that night*?"

"I'm not saying that, no."

"So what are you saying?"

"I wanted to ask if it's possible you took Lizzie out and then forgot?"

"There was a storm that night, why would I take her out into a storm?"

"I'm asking. Do you think that's a possibility?"

"That would be crazy, that would be a crazy thing to do... dangerous. Trees... trees could've fallen down on top of electrical wires, anything could've happened. Struck by lightning, even, it would be crazy to take somebody, especially a little one out into a storm like that." My voice is becoming shrill. "Just the thought of it, just the thought of doing something so crazy like that is..."

"After the bath, what happened next?"

"Well, I dried Lizzie, put some cream on her face."

"Cream?"

"Yes, she likes to be a grownup, be like her mommy, so I put a little cream on her face to make her feel special. And then I put her to bed, got her into her jammies, and read her a story."

"You remember what story?"

"*The Happy Unicorn*, it's her favorite."

Alba pauses, as if absorbing what I've said. As if she refuses to believe this nice domestic picture, that the possibility of me being an adoring mother is preposterous. "What about Liam?"

"He was in his room. You know, he's older now, he can entertain himself."

"He didn't want to story too?"

"No, I don't remember him asking me for a story."

"But you're sure he was in his room?"

"Oh yeah, very sure."

"How can you be sure if you were in Lizzie's room, reading her a story?"

"Because by the time she'd fallen asleep I went into check on him."

"Was he awake or asleep?"

"Strange you should ask."

"Why?"

"Because he was fast asleep, already tucked up in bed, and I thought, *What a wonderful thing it is to have this girl, this au pair, because she's obviously tiring out the children*. Liam's very rambunctious, you see, but that night he got into bed all on his own and even turned out the light, the main light, all on his own. It was such a relief, and I remember thinking, *Why haven't I done this before? Why didn't I get an au pair last summer? It would've made my life so much easier*. It's funny, isn't it, when you do something small in your life, when you make a little change, you don't heed much attention to it in the moment and such great things can come of it, such huge things. Anyway I've told you all this before, haven't I, Detective? The events of this evening. I've told you twice before."

"Just checking, covering my bases, in case you missed something. You trust your au pair?"

"She seems great."

"You checked out her references, right?"

"Yes. And the au pair agency does that on our behalf. The girls are screened."

"But if Jayne wanted to come in at night, she could unlock the kitchen latch?"

"Yes, of course. But why would she have come over in the middle of a storm when she was safe and cozy in her cottage?"

"You trust your nurse, Alex Sharpe?"

"Of course. She's been invaluable."

"How well do you know her?"

"Well, the hospital recommended her—she's one of the head nurses there—she came with glowing references, and because she's been so helpful I have no reason to doubt her." And then I add, "Should I? Is there something you know about her I don't?"

Alba ignores my question. "Has she ever been abusive to the children?"

"No!"

"She seems very stern, a little cold."

"She's a bit bossy maybe, but it's her manner. She's efficient, a no-nonsense sort of person. It's a hard job being a nurse, she has a lot of responsibility."

"You trust her with the children?"

"Oh yes."

There is a hiatus, an awkward silence and then Alba adds, "There's something that escapes me."

I lace my hands together, wishing this interview would be over. For a moment my mind slips away to Lizzie, a voice telling me I'm all wrong as a mother.

"There is one thing that I find very strange," the detective says.

Her voice snaps my attention back. "What?" I say, fear nibbling at my heart, making me remember who I am, why a detective is here in the first place.

"You're super calm about this, Celeste. Most mothers would be hysterical, crying, begging me to find their child, and you seem almost distant, cut off."

I consider her accusation, wondering whether I should turn on the waterworks for her sake—full-on, this time—and I think how predictable she is, expecting a woman to react in a certain way under a certain set of circumstances. This detective does not have children of her own. She told me that. She thinks we mothers should be all alike, a cardboard cut-out mom who weeps and sniffles and blows snot bubbles twenty-four hours a day to prove the love of her child. She has already deemed me unfit. There are rules these days about being a mother. Cookie-cutter rules for the way you should think and behave. Deviate a bit, make it up as you go along, let your child be free and discover things for themselves, let them run wild in the backyard instead of hovering over them while they play with their tablet or are glued to YouTube and you're a "bad mother."

"Because," I reply, "I know you're doing your job, Detective, the best you can do. I've done the hysteria thing and it hasn't gotten me anywhere. It hasn't helped us find my daughter, has it? I've cried my eyes out. I've screamed and raged and smashed things. There are no more tears inside me. When I next see Lizzie, when I hold her in my arms... there will be tears of happiness, that I can promise."

THE DISAPPEARANCE

Alba calls Forensics. It has already been established that there are no new fingerprints in the house, or in the shed, or on the swing set in the backyard that cannot be accounted for. The DNA, the same. Alex Sharpe's, Celeste's, Jayne's, Max's, Marjorie's, and of course, the children's. Still, she calls anyway, on the off chance. She has an abounding feeling of uselessness, but also that her second-guessing—which is so part of her nature now, so intrinsic to her very being—is all she has to go on at this point. It is her lifeline, her raison d'être.

"Hey, Sal, it's me, Alba, just checking in."

"Thanks for calling back," he says.

"Calling *back*?" It must've been with a sympathy call on his part; she's been hounding him so hard, probably driving him nuts with her insistence.

"Yeah," he says, "I asked Scully to get you to call me."

"How come you didn't call me direct?"

"We were just talking, him and me, in person. I told him I had something, and for you to call."

"You got something new?"

"Something very major that could affect the whole case, yeah."

"With the DNA?"

"With the DNA. Listen, can I get back to you in five? I need to double-check something."

"What's so—"

But Sal has ended the call, leaving Alba in a state of flux, wondering what in the world they have found.

She and her team have combed through every single backyard and garden on this island. They have inspected each garden shed for Lizzie's DNA, for footprints, for clues. She has interviewed each family, every child. Every friend of Lizzie's and Liam's. Although, the strange thing is that the picture is very different from how Celeste painted it. Turns out Lizzie does not have a bunch of friends her age. Alba is not sure if it's because of other families' preference for privacy, or the Wainwrights themselves, but it sounds as if Lizzie was/is a loner and not encouraged to play with other children. Either that or the islanders are keeping their distance.

From what Alba has gleaned, the Wainwrights believe that their children should be free, but the other parents of the younger kids here don't share that vision of parenting, not only because of Lizzie's disappearance, but because they have a different set of values.

"We never let our little ones run around without supervision," one of them told the detective. "What with the ocean, which can really kick up at any time, and all the people who come and go... well, this year's different, you know, with tourism so down. But this isn't the seventies, is it? We don't have the same kind of parenting techniques as our grandmothers or even our mothers. Things have changed, the world has changed."

And it's true. Few parents have the same attitude as in the olden days, Alba agrees. Even in a laidback place like Cliff Island.

There are no new leads. Every child has an alibi for that night, even the teenagers, which makes sense considering the storm. No fingerprints are showing up in the Wainwrights' home that can't be accounted for. Either the perp was wearing gloves and going around in socks or the perp is someone living in the house. Or—and Alba is considering this possibility more every day—somehow Lizzie managed to get outside on her own.

It is eight a.m. She wants to call Sal back but has hassled him enough already. She'll give him five more minutes.

The sky and the ocean merge into a block of cerulean blue, hard to tell where one ends and the other begins. Alba, looking out toward the ocean, sitting in a lounger, takes a few spare minutes to let her face soak up the early morning rays. She never burns, not with her Puerto Rican heritage, and her body craves a dose of vitamin D once in a while. It feels great on her skin. The day will heat up unbearably—they've had a spate of hot weather—and it's not the greatest thing wearing a uniform, trudging around in the hot sun, but she prefers it to rain and she prefers it to snow. And she prefers it to the "mud season." These Maine winters are cruel and long. And she appreciates summer, every last minute of it, each year a little more as she ages. If you'd asked what she'd be doing when she was forty-plus when she started in the force, she wouldn't have imagined today's scene: alone, confused, not running around chasing her kid playing tag or something, but desperately searching for somebody else's child. It's at times like these that she wants to give up on this case and hand it over to somebody more competent. Scully seems to have confidence in her, and she only wishes she could share that view of herself.

How can she be coming up empty like this? She's gone through every lead, each possibility, interviewed absolutely everybody, not once but twice, or even three times. She's beginning to think... she doesn't even know what she's thinking, she doesn't know who she suspects anymore. But she's close, some voice inside her head is telling her so. *Do not give up. The truth is right before your eyes.*

And now Sal has a lead?

Standing up, stretching her arms and limbs, she notices her morning shadow twisted and sharp, thrown into chiaroscuro relief as if her body has created a piece of art. She keeps wondering about Celeste and her attempted suicide, if that is indeed what happened. Was it an accident? By complete chance there was a bystander who dived in the lake and saved her and Lizzie. The man, a twenty-two-year-old student, got to the car before it sank. Lizzie, strapped in her child seat, was miraculously unharmed, nothing more than a few bruises. Celeste hit her head and broke a couple of ribs.

Her phone rings.

"It's me, Sal."

"You got new DNA, in the house?"

"No, no, everything's the same as it was, but it's a question of Lizzie's parentage."

Alba's ears are burning. Lizzie's *parentage?* "Go on."

"I told you it was big. Get this: Max Wainwright is not Lizzie's father."

Alba's pulse takes a leap. "You're sure?"

"Well, these tests are pretty accurate, so yeah, I'm sure."

Alba's breath catches in her throat. This is not what she was expecting. How is this possible? It feels like every single damn thing about this case has been turned upside down. *Max Wainwright not Lizzie's father?* This is a twist she sure as hell did not see coming.

"Alba, you still there?"

"Yeah, Sal, I'm still here. Thank you so much. Great work. Do we know who the dad is?"

"Nope. He's not in any DNA database. Doesn't show up on 23andMe. No criminal record."

Alba's heart is beating fast. Her mind galloping in different directions, wondering what step she needs to take next. Max Wainwright's disappearance—with him not being Lizzie's biological father—takes on a whole new direction. "Sal. Next time, you call me direct, okay? And keep this to yourself, I don't want the media to get wind of it or all hell will break loose."

"Sure thing, no problem."

"Great job, by the way. This is huge. *Huge*."

Alba marches back to the Wainwrights' house. The sun is heating up now, rising in the sky like a helium balloon, hot, white. It's a beautiful day, and this news makes it even more perfect. She is going to crack this case even if Scully tries to slow her down. He can shove his "kiddo" right up his ass.

Celeste is in the kitchen in her bathrobe, having breakfast. Alex Sharpe is cooking. Still the vulnerable confused Celeste, is she? The nurse fluttering around the "invalid"? Alba now knows Celeste is a great liar, or at least a good dissimulator. Making out that she and Max have the perfect marriage. Celeste had her fooled, that's for sure. The cracks had obviously started in the relationship a lot sooner than was usual with a couple still married, still pretending to be perfect. Especially for people without money worries.

Celeste looks up from her breakfast as Alba knocks and enters the room, pushing open the kitchen screen door. "Detective Alba, what a surprise!"

"Sorry to disturb your breakfast."

"Would you like some?"

"You know what? I would." She isn't going to be the ingratiating detective anymore. Celeste owes her one, big time. Why not eat a hearty breakfast to set her up for the day? "Whatever you've got, bring it on. Eggs, bacon, coffee, all of it, yeah I'm hungry, I won't lie." And she is hungry, "hangry," actually. She can't believe the innocent act Celeste has been pulling all along.

The sweet wife at home with her beautiful linens and candles, playing happy family, but meanwhile her daughter didn't even belong to her husband? And what about Max himself? What the hell game is he up to?

"You got it," the nurse says. "Coming right up."

They are both very genial and friendly, Alba notices. A little too genial. Considering Lizzie is still missing, maybe even dead. And considering what Alba now knows. The nurse is no longer wearing her uniform, her hair is loose. She has a much more casual air about her and looks younger, less stern. Alba is seeing everything in a new light. Like watching a movie that has been restored and is now in HD, showing up the actors' pores. She has so many questions she doesn't even know where to begin. She needs to curb herself, not scare off Celeste. Play it cool.

"You wanted to see me about something?" Celeste asks.

"Yeah, some DNA evidence has come in."

Celeste's subtle yet definite Mona Lisa smile drops. "Oh yes? Anything conclusive?"

"I would say it's extremely conclusive. Not as far as finding Lizzie is concerned but conclusive in another sense."

Celeste's blue eyes widen. "And what might that be?"

"Can we talk candidly here?" She tosses a look at Alex.

The nurse, standing by the stove with a spatula, stops what she's doing for a second. "Would you like me to leave?"

Celeste shakes her head. "No, it's fine. Stay."

Alba pushes a strand of hair away from her eyes, clears her throat and readies herself. It is interesting, to say the least, that Celeste is happy to have Alex Sharpe witness what she is about to say. Are these two closer than patient and nurse? "I might as well cut straight to the chase. We've found out that Lizzie—from her DNA—is not your husband's daughter. Isn't Max's child."

Celeste covers her face with her hands and mumbles through her fingers. "I was wondering when you'd get to that."

"Celeste, I really don't understand why you didn't tell us this sooner, it's putting obstacles in our way, making it so much harder to find her."

"Does it make a difference? Who the father is?"

"In a way, yes. I mean, technically, no, but it does complicate things, and yeah, it makes a difference because—"

"Now you're thinking *Max* could be a suspect?"

Um, yes. "Well, he does have a good alibi for that night," Alba says.

"Yes, he does," Celeste agrees in a low voice as if to insinuate, *His alibi doesn't stand.*

"Could you please explain to me what happened? Why Lizzie is not Max's child when you have a seemingly happy marriage?"

Celeste glances around the kitchen for a moment, chewing her toast thoughtfully, as if to find a direct answer from the old blue fridge humming away, as if the fridge is telling her what lie she should concoct next, what tale should spout from her lips that might sound convincing. She looks up at a chandelier...who has a chandelier in the kitchen? The Wainwrights do. She doesn't catch eyes with Alex though.

She finally comes out with, "I never wanted Max to know, I hope you understand."

"What happened? Please be straight with me," Alba says, her tone a touch bitter, a tired strain to her voice. Celeste has given her the runaround in the politest possible way. Always polite as she spins her yarn, that's the unnerving part.

"It was, well... obviously nearly five years ago. I had a very drunken night. It was at a party with old friends from college. Max had been away a lot. Always busy, always unavailable. He was on a business trip somewhere, I can't even remember where now. Anyway, as I said, I got very drunk and partied too hard and I must've ended up in bed with someone."

"Must have?"

"Yes, I kind of had a blank the next morning."

"You think someone spiked your drink?"

"Honestly? I have no idea."

Whenever Alba hears the words *honestly*, or *trust me*, or *truth be told*, it perks up her ears. It's like the crossed arms when it isn't cold, or the jackhammering leg, or the eye rub.

"I don't *think* anyone put anything in my drink, but it is *possible*."

"You have any recollection whatsoever of having sex with a stranger?"

"Maybe it wasn't even a stranger, maybe it was somebody I knew from college. You know, there were a whole bunch of us there getting back together again, having a blast. I remember flirting with various people, having fun drinking the night away, playing silly games. I think I might've... I simply don't know what happened that night."

"So the next day, what ensued?"

"I had a terrible hangover, felt like hell, drank a lot of liquids, ate some chicken soup, bananas, you know, the kind of things you do after a hangover? I regretted my actions, not even sure what I got up to."

"Did anybody ask for your number the next day? Call? To give you a clue who it was?"

"Not really, no."

"Not 'really'?"

"Nothing I can recall. In fact, no, I remember feeling relieved, like, *Phew, I won't have to deal with some stalker or some trailing puppy dog with a broken heart*. It was a one-night stand, no complications. Until I found out I was pregnant, of course."

"Is there any way the father of the child might've known you were pregnant?"

"God, no. I mean, if they knew I was pregnant they would've assumed it was my husband's baby."

"You never confided in anyone else?"

"No, I was far too ashamed, I didn't tell anyone, not even my best friends. It's a complete secret, the only people that know this are the three of us, in this room right now."

Alba wonders why Celeste is happy to let her nurse in on this clandestine secret. "Max didn't know?" she checks.

"No."

"You're sure he had no idea?"

She shakes her head solemnly, somehow looking like the victim in this, the innocent one.

"Is there any possible chance he could've found out and this is some kind of revenge on Lizzie not being his child?"

"No! Who would want to take revenge on a four-year-old? It's not Lizzie's fault!"

You'd be surprised by the machinations of some people's twisted minds, the detective is tempted to say, but doesn't.

"You think Max had something to do with Lizzie's disappearance, don't you?" Celeste fires out with genuine surprise in her voice, her eyes large and round. The *butter wouldn't melt* look Jayne pointed out, that Celeste has perfected with skill.

Something is not quite right, but again, Alba can't put her finger on it.

"Please, please don't say anything to Max," she begs. "This has nothing to do with finding Lizzie's killer!"

Killer? This is the first time Celeste has used this word. She realizes her blunder too late, and says, "Look, that came out wrong... I don't believe... I believe Lizzie's alive somewhere, and I was so hopeful, but the last couple of days I've been feeling really down about it." She begins to weep.

Alba nods her head in a non-judgmental way. Neutral. But

the thought tumbling around inside her mind is why Celeste said "killer." Is there any way she is referring to herself?

How can a mother, a nice woman like Celeste, with money, status, privilege, be capable of killing her own child?

But she knows it takes all sorts to make this fucked-up world go round.

She needs to talk to the coroner who signed the death certificate for baby Violet. Find out for sure what went down. So far, Carl has not gotten back to her with this. Or he has, but told her nothing has "come up" so far. She wanted to scream, *Things don't just "come up," you have to hunt them down.* She wishes there were more female detectives. She doesn't want to sound sexist—even to herself—but she is pretty sure women have a better nose for detail and get things done more efficiently.

As Alba is figuring out her next move, her boss calls. She can tell by the excitement in his voice that something has changed.

"Alba."

"Yes, sir, what's up?" She still calls him sir, and he still calls her by her last name, never Adele.

"I need you to help out with another case."

"You have a confession? From Stephen Knox?"

"Not exactly."

"What do you mean by 'exactly'?"

"It's in the bag, I can feel it."

"But no confession?"

"No denial either."

"Sir, don't count your chickens."

"This'll be wrapped up soon enough."

"But I still have a lot of work to do. I need to look into baby Violet's death, get the coroner's report, see if this is a coincidence, or maybe murder."

She knows how important the medical examiner's reports

are if, that is, they have bothered to dig into things deep enough. Sometimes these deaths can be explained: underlying biological abnormalities, cardiac disruptions, brain malformations, metabolic disorders. But more often than not these institutions are cash-strapped, so overloaded with work they can't use up their resources in a search for cause of death for every individual baby, especially those whose parents have no record of child abuse, no criminal charges already against them. But if Celeste tried to kill herself and failed, surely it makes sense that she suffocated her baby, and drowned Lizzie. And maybe Celeste herself will be her next victim in another bid for suicide. Alba considers this but is not quite convinced. Something doesn't sit right with her.

Because Celeste did have that chance during the storm. If Lizzie had been with her, Celeste could have killed Lizzie and then herself. Walked them both into the ocean, jumped off a cliff. Alba can still make no sense of this. But she's working on it, and now her boss is telling her she's off the case?

She can hear him chuckle. He is in high spirits, convinced he is hours away from closing this case. "You know how backed up they are? Short-staffed, underfunded, backlogged, overwhelmed. These autopsy reports take months to examine the cadaver. Several months. Besides, Alba, you're barking up the wrong tree."

"But I think I can get an appointment with the chief medical examiner tomorrow. His secretary has promised to try and fit me in."

"You know how incompetent Jackson has been on the Cockburn burglary case? I need you back where you belong, Alba. Till I get this thing wrapped up. You happened to be in the helicopter at the right time and I needed you on that island and you did good, but time's up, kiddo."

She doesn't rise to the "kiddo" bait this time. Taking her off the case, even for a couple of days, at this point feels like he's wielding a great club and smashing her fingers. It is professional bullying.

"Please, give me a couple more days," she pleads.

"Take the rest of the day off and report to me tomorrow morning. Eight a.m. sharp. You're back on burglaries until further notice, no more discussion."

She ends the call without saying goodbye.

JAYNE

Things have gone completely bonkers here. They say Stephen has been arrested for the murder of Lizzie. I don't know much about American law, only what I've seen on TV, but if there is no body how can he be arrested? I know he's a bit of an oddball, and true, I'm not his greatest fan, but I don't think he has anything to do with it.

I still think Celeste did it.

How do I know there's no body? Because I've been watching from afar. Stephen was taken down into what turned out to be an underwater cave. A crowd of us began gathering above, on the clifftops, watching the events unfold. Fascinating. There were divers. Boats. That security police dog—the sniffer K-9—was in one of the boats, but for obvious reasons they couldn't use him. The dog is quite a star. Dune, that's his name, like the movie. We stood there with bated breath waiting... waiting for something conclusive to happen, roasting in the sun, waiting, waiting, on top of the clifftop, watching them from above. Then Stephen went down with a load of divers in wetsuits with bottles and all the gear—although Stephen was in his swimming trunks—and they didn't come back up again. At first it was terrifying, really eerie and weird, and I found out what was going on from one of the policemen in the crowd trying to hold us back.

As you can imagine, Cliff Island has become quite a busy tourist destination in the last few days... well, since Lizzie disappeared anyway. I have become something of a celebrity myself, being the au pair, with people asking me questions about Lizzie. Somebody wanted to take my photograph. I keep having to escape to my cottage and bury myself in a novel.

I'm on my guard and trying to keep my mouth shut. I know how this stuff works; somebody could turn on me and accuse me of being the guilty one. Right now, Stephen is their prime suspect, but how would he have managed to take Lizzie underwater without drowning her first? Unless she was stashed away like booty. Time will tell if he's a killer or not. The whole thing makes me sick, and horribly sad. I watched in shock, my mind numbed in a strange way, still not accepting the reality that Lizzie probably isn't coming back. I keep hoping it will be like that case in Australia where the little girl was found after eighteen days, but that's a one in a million scenario, sadly.

The divers put their professional gear in dry-bags so they were able to swim underwater. Somebody in the crowd explained to me how you can put anything in one of those specially designed bags and not one drop of water will get inside. For a second I had a sick notion that it *was* Stephen and he had put Lizzie into a dry-bag, but that's crazy. Too sick to even consider.

But then again, whoever took her is sick.

Who would've known there's a cave down there?

I've been looking up flights to get back home to the UK, but I don't want to go home. What do I have to go back to? I've been floating the possibility of traveling across the USA by Greyhound. Might as well go sightseeing while I'm here. I'd love to see the Grand Canyon, Vegas, Los Angeles, San Francisco and the Golden Gate Bridge.

But if I leave now, it might seem like I'm running, like I'm guilty. It looks dodgy, doesn't it? Heartless, like I don't give a shit. And I so *do*. I do care, with all my heart I care. All I can think about is little Lizzie and how terrified she must have been... I don't want to even entertain the worst-case scenario, it's too morbid to consider. I should stick around for a couple more days anyway. I also still feel like I must be here for Lizzie in my cottage, just in case.

I decide to go to the main house, to see what's going on. I've never really talked to Sharpie. Not a real, proper conversation anyway. I need to find out what's going on between those women, if Sharpie was in on it too. How well does she know Celeste? Who hired her and where does she come from? I'm assuming the police know all this and do not suspect her, although it's true they're concentrating all their efforts on Stephen. I know nothing about the woman—and I'm curious.

I head over to the main house with the excuse that I left something of mine in Liam's bedroom, in case they ask.

But once I'm there, my instinct tells me to keep schtum. I have this desire, this pull to check out Liam's bedroom. I slip in quietly through the back door, into the kitchen, and hear muffled voices coming from Celeste's bedroom. I pad into the house as quietly as I can, avoiding the creaky floorboards and sticky-outy pieces of furniture, which I try not to bump into. I'm better at navigating my way around this house than I was at first.

There is muffled, dulled but distinct laughter... a kind of chitchat, like between two good girlfriends who have known each other for years. Then it fades. Up the stairs I go, tiptoeing quietly into Liam's bedroom. I need to bring something down to make it look authentic for a reason why I'm here. And it's true, because the last time I was here I came across that drawing with

Lizzie scrawled out in black, in a more than slightly sinister way. He's only a boy, but still, it was a little nasty. But there was another drawing he did for me. A nice one of a boat. He told me it was a present. I'll take that as a memento.

The bedroom is in pretty much the same state it was before when I looked through those drawings. That couple he drew? I wonder why he didn't pick the right color for his mother's hair. I examine the picture again. And the hair is wavy, not straight like his mum's, but then Liam is not very precise. He's not skilled with his coloring: too clumsy, too hurried. Maybe I was like that as a child, too clumsy, not careful enough? That's what was drummed into me by my mother. *You're a clumsy oaf,* she'd say. *A big fat lumbering ham-fisted fatty.*

I look through the closets, not knowing what I'm searching for and not understanding why I feel compelled to rifle around. Sheer curiosity, I suppose. Then something bright catches my eye. A little pink plastic shoe, about Lizzie's size, although I've never seen her wear it before. It sits nestled half hidden under a fallen T-shirt. I don't touch it, I don't dare.

It sends a razor-sharp chill down my spine.

I stand there, frozen to the spot, not knowing where to turn, what to do next. I hear comings and goings from and into the house, and then, a good fifteen minutes later, I detect Detective Alba's voice. I am trapped in the bedroom, eavesdropping on their conversation.

THE DISAPPEARANCE

"Who's upstairs?" It's Celeste calling up from the foyer.

Jayne comes out of Liam's bedroom, the drawing of a boat in her hand. "It's me, Jayne."

"Jayne, what are you doing sneaking around like that?"

"I was in Liam's room getting something." She holds up the drawing. "He did this for me, I want to take it."

Jayne comes downstairs, a slightly sheepish expression on her face like a dog who might have upset the trash and is awaiting punishment. She clutches a crayon drawing as if it's a long-lost relic. And it jolts Alba's memory. How Celeste had told her how she had read Lizzie a story about a unicorn the night of her disappearance, but Alba remembers seeing that very same book in Jayne's cottage early the following morning. Celeste did not read that story to Lizzie. Is it possible Max came into the house that evening, took Lizzie, and that Celeste was unaware of his presence? Because maybe Celeste hadn't done all those things with Lizzie that she said she'd done: putting her to bed, reading her a story. Was Celeste simply doing her own thing? Perhaps she had not been with the children that evening at all. And she felt neglectful and ashamed, so made it all up to pass herself off as a better mother? It might have been easy for Max to slip into the house and take Lizzie. Yet why would he do that? But it would explain why he didn't show for his interview, why he is missing.

Alba's mind is going around in circles. She's grabbing at stubby little straws, her thoughts in turmoil. Somebody is lying. The more Alba thinks about it, the more embroiled she becomes in the tiny details surfacing in her brain, crying out to be heard. After all, in her experience, that's how she has in the past solved cases: the minuscule details that might go unnoticed, that you might toss away without giving them a second thought.

"I have something to tell you, Detective," Jayne says.

Alba takes a deep breath. "Can we talk about this later?"

"No, it's very important. There's something upstairs in Liam's room you should be aware of. I heard through the grapevine one of the reporters telling me there was a pink shoe they found in the sea, nearby the cave. Well, there's a pink shoe up in Liam's room too."

"What were you doing in his room snooping around?" Celeste snaps.

"I wasn't snooping around, I was checking to see if I'd left anything of mine in there. I'm sorry, I didn't mean to... I would've said something, but I didn't want to disturb you because I heard you were busy talking with Nurse Sharpe."

"Thank you very much, Jayne," Alba says. "I appreciate the heads up."

She remembers the unicorn book, wonders if Jayne had gotten her hands on it.

"And there's another thing I'd like to talk to you about," Jayne goes on. "I haven't mentioned it because it felt so terrible saying something negative about a child, about Liam. But he was a little aggressive with Lizzie the day before she disappeared. I didn't pay"—and here her voice cracks—"I didn't pay much attention to it because he's only a child, and children do horrible things to each other without meaning it. But he did throw a stone at Lizzie, called her names."

"Why didn't you tell me this?" Celeste says, her voice a vibrato.

"Because I didn't want to cause trouble. I hadn't been here long and it was something I thought I could handle myself, and I *did* handle it. I got Liam to apologize and everything was fine afterwards."

Celeste chews the inside of her cheek and then puffs out a blow of annoyance. "You should've told me."

"I know, I'm sorry, but I didn't want to cause friction between the children, and I thought... well, Max told me to go with the flow and I just wanted to..." She doesn't finish but breaks into sobs.

The detective's mind is spinning with possibilities. She's wondering if Liam did something to hurt Lizzie and somehow Max found out and is covering up for his own son.

Possible.

But Jayne has been lying. Alba feels it in her bones.

JAYNE

When I first arrived all I could think about, apart from making a good impression and doing a great job, was having time to myself: reading novels, catching up with sleep, and putting my troubles behind me. But with the media and the press hanging around outside my door, I've been holed up in my little cottage, feeling trapped, longing to be outside in the fresh air, desperate to be free without all those sets of curious eyes on me, wondering, gossiping, judging.

I am desperate. And, honestly? I'm angry. I did not sign up for this crap. So when the last ferry leaves the island and the crowds go home—luckily there's nowhere for them to stay here, and camping has been prohibited—I fling my door open.

Outside, the briny air is fresh and I find myself skipping like a child along the sandy path towards the bluff. The three-hundred-and-sixty-degree view clears my head, the wildness of Cliff Island calms me, despite the tragic situation in every blade of grass, in every molecule of every rock and tree. I scramble between the rocks, filling my lungs and let out something between a scream and a groan, feeding it to the elements since there's nobody to hear my cry. *"When will this end?"* I yell from the bottom of my lungs.

Then I spot Stephen, clambering over the terrain towards me. We haven't spoken for a few days. What could I say? Offer my condolences about his near arrest? The last thing I needed was to be associated with a suspect. Although, yeah, I get it, we're all suspects, but up until now Stephen is at the top of their list. Being interrogated by the police has made him look guilty in the eyes of the media, even if he is innocent. These days nobody gets a fair trial. It's not that I haven't felt a certain degree of sympathy for the guy, but I've been keeping a wide berth of him.

He shouts over to me, "Hey, Jayne, wait up!"

I don't really have much choice. I don't want to be rude, make him feel even worse about what's happened. I'm flummoxed as to why they haven't brought Celeste in for questioning. And, where are Max and Marjorie? Nobody seems to have seen hide nor hair of them.

"You managed to get out of your cottage unseen?" he pants when he catches up with me.

"I needed some space," I tell him. "You've been inside all day too, haven't you? Avoiding the media?"

"They're vultures, aren't they? It feels like the only thing that matters to them is scooping a juicy story to sensationalize."

I nod in agreement, dreading what they may dig up on me. Somehow those press people always manage to find stuff, no matter what you're hiding. Are they going to unearth my story? How I gave my baby up at fifteen, the stalking allegations, the legal shit that followed. I can't even go there in my head, can't bear to think of my shame, the choices I made, the screw-up of my life.

I focus back on Stephen. "Is everything okay now? They let you go, the police?"

"They don't have anything on me except suspicion. That

pink plastic shoe that was bobbing around outside the cave. Nothing can be proved. It's all hearsay, conjecture."

I admire his confidence. He almost appears carefree. "Yeah, well, someone's guilty. Unless it was a genuine accident," I say.

"Someone is guilty," Stephen agrees.

The way he looks at me makes me wonder if he thinks *I'm* the guilty one.

I hold my dress down to stop the wind blowing it up. The idea of Stephen seeing my knickers makes my cheeks flush, remembering that disastrous night. If only I'd known. "I just don't understand what happened to Lizzie. You think she drowned?" I ask.

He changes the subject swiftly. "So why are you still here? Still on the island? They told you you have to be here?"

"No, actually, they haven't. I keep hoping Lizzie might show up and... I don't know, it feels like abandoning ship, if you know what I mean. I sort of feel like I have to stay here until..." I sift through my options, wondering. "But I am considering going cross-country or something, checking out America a bit."

"Not a bad idea. Lots of fun things to do, it's an amazing country. Some of the best national parks in the world, nature reserves and stuff. We've got everything in the US, every kind of landscape from Swiss Alpine-looking places to awesome painted deserts. Right here in Maine we have Acadia, which you really should not miss. It's beautiful. Then you've got the Grand Canyon, Yellowstone. You won't be disappointed, it's a good idea."

"I'm thinking about it. Do you think they'll ever find Lizzie?"

"I feel very hopeful," he says. "By the way, I wanted to warn you. I saw that police K-9 heading toward your cottage."

"You're joking? I thought the dog had gone for good! Thought it hadn't found anything and done its job!"

"No. I'm pretty sure they were—well, the dog the handler

and the detective—were making a beeline toward your cottage. Maybe they need to ask you some questions?"

My heart misses a beat. *Oh, God.* "I'd better get back then."

"Good luck," Stephen says, and I don't know if it's my imagination, but with his lips pressed together in confidence, I detect a minuscule Bruce Willis smirk as if he's thrilled the attention has shifted from him to me and he's in on my secret. My stomach freefalls with dread and fear, knowing what's going to happen next. They don't need my permission to enter the cottage and do a search. I'm not an official renter or anything. Celeste will have given them carte blanche, they wouldn't even need a search warrant.

They will have discovered my cache.

It takes me about half an hour to walk home. I'm in no rush, because what's done is done and there's nothing I can do to stop them in their tracks. I observe them from above, swarming around my cottage, yellow crime scene tape fluttering in the late afternoon breeze. I tear my gaze away, looking to the sky for answers, as if Someone Up There can dig me out of my mess. I can't believe I've been so stupid, so idiotic. Thinking that the focus was on Stephen...well, that's just it, I *wasn't* thinking. I did something rash. I don't know what got into my head. Being so upset about everything must have made my brain go mushy. I'm tempted to head to the main house and not deal with this... with that detective right now. I swear I'd get on a boat if I could rather than see this unfold, but the last ferry has gone and it's evident I'm done for.

The only thing is to face the bloody music and deal with it. I know there's going to be a slew of questions and they won't believe my answers.

Fuck!

I approach the cottage and as I draw near, the dog yanks his handler towards me, tail up, all excited like he's coming to greet me but I know what it is: he can smell Lizzie all over me. A shudder runs through my body, my scalp prickles.

The forensic team are here bagging the evidence: Lizzie's clothes, her bunny, a coloring book, a mini pair of leggings. I'd wrapped them in several layers of plastic bags, but obviously not enough to seal in her scent.

I know what's going to happen next. I feel it the way you feel pain and see sprinkles of white stars seconds before you even realize you've bumped your head...

They're going to arrest me for the murder of Lizzie.

JAYNE

"Jayne Smith, we need you to come in to be questioned, make a statement."

The fact Detective Alba says my surname makes my whole body go numb. I feel like I'm floating above myself, looking down on this person called Jayne Smith who has nothing to do with me. Here I am in a foreign country being suspected of murder... this is absolutely terrifying.

"Come in, where?"

"To the station, at our headquarters in Portland, over on the mainland."

My lip trembles. "Why can't you do it here?"

"Well, we can, but it's easier as everything's set up there."

And now I know what's coming. On top of this they will have dug into my past, a backup to their theory, proof of my guilt. The hoo-ha with my baby's parents. The adoption agency, the legal web I got myself into. The stalking. The spying. The police intervention. The embarrassing scenes, but most of all the shame. Giving her up was the worst thing I ever did. I was fifteen, I was unfit to care for a baby, but still, she was *my* baby, she was my world. It makes me sick to think I listened to those who I thought knew better than me at the time. "In the best interests of your child," they purred in such a convincing way. I was too young, too broken to fight for my baby, in too much turmoil, and it all seemed to happen so fast. So fast... but also in slow motion like you're watching yourself from above, a bit like I am now, making the most regretful decision of your life.

Detective Alba is being friendly, very matter-of-fact like it's routine. But I know different.

Now look what I've gone and done.

THE DISAPPEARANCE

Alba and her partner have been questioning Jayne Smith for almost two hours. It is at times like these that your tone of voice is all-important. Too friendly, someone may lose respect, too eager, people back off, too abrupt, people get scared and clam up. Being a detective is all about human psychology. And it is so easy to play it wrong, to screw up.

Jayne has insisted she's innocent, dozens and dozens of times, over and over, pleading with them to believe her. Even to direct questions like, *Did you kill Lizzie Wainwright?* or *Where did you hide Lizzie?* she has professed her innocence.

Alba tries again. "What were you doing with Lizzie's articles of clothing and personal effects wrapped in several layers of plastic bags?"

"How many more times do I have to tell you!" Tears are flowing down Jayne's splotched face, red and raw from the barrage of questions being fired at her. "Like I said, I wanted a memento of Lizzie."

"Because you believed she was already dead, right?" Alba's partner, Carl, cuts in, leaning toward the suspect.

No doubt Jayne can feel his breath on her face as she pulls

her head back and turns her face away from his. "No! I don't… I don't know what happened to Lizzie, but what if she drowned or something? I really honestly have no idea, but I loved that little girl, I *love* that little girl and I never would've hurt her. I wanted something of hers to remember her by."

"You were planning to leave, right? Leave the island? Your suitcase packed?"

"Well, I don't have a job anymore, do I? With both children gone. There's nothing for me to do now, so I thought maybe I might go traveling, get a Greyhound or something. Look, I would never ever harm a child!"

"We found other children's things in your possession. A child's stuffed animal that Celeste Wainwright says does not belong to Lizzie. Who does it belong to?"

"This vicious line of questioning has been going on for hours and whatever I say you won't believe. Look, if you think I'm some kind of child serial killer you've got another thing coming. I told you, that teddy was my sister's. She died when she was a little girl. This is crazy, I didn't do it, I didn't do it, I didn't do it, I didn't do *anything*!"

Alba and her partner exchange glances. They leave Jayne alone in the room while they confer outside.

Alba says, "I know this evidence is stacked against her, but she sounds completely innocent. Besides, unless we get a confession, we're wasting our time. Even if we do get a confession, her lawyer could throw it out in court as not being admissible. What the dog found was after we'd done the searches. They could say the evidence had been planted or tampered with or contaminated to make her appear guilty. You know as well as I do this may not wash. And I think she's telling the truth."

"Why, because she's a good actress?"

"She's distraught, desperate, looks like she's pretty cut up about Lizzie, that she really cares for her, even loves her."

"Yeah, she loved that little girl so much, the way the wife-beating husband loved his wife so much he strangled her to death. Sometimes love kills."

"I really don't think she did it."

"She's the only one who actually has something that belongs to Lizzie in her possession, Alba, the closest thing we got to pure evidence."

"Yeah, but we didn't find it the first time around, she told us it's only been there since yesterday. Dune would've found it first time when we originally searched her cottage."

"But we don't know that. Maybe the stuff was so well hidden that the dog missed it first go."

Alba shakes her head, doubtful. "I don't know. Dune's good at his job."

"Look, the stuff has Jayne's fingerprints all over everything!"

"I do believe her when she says she took the items from Lizzie's bedroom and that drawing from Liam's room when she discovered the pink shoe."

"Exactly, she 'discovered' the pink shoe in Liam's room, you don't find that suspect? Another thing we never found first time around. Weird, don't ya think?"

"But it didn't have her fingerprints on it, so why would there be fingerprints all over these other articles of Lizzie's and not on the pink shoe?"

"Because she didn't think we'd *find* the other articles. She thought we were done with Dune. So maybe she brought the things out of their hiding place, wherever that was, and then hid them in her suitcase."

"But it wasn't the same clothing that Lizzie disappeared in. She was wearing pajamas."

"*Apparently* wearing pajamas, if you can even believe the mother. Celeste Wainwright's pretty flakey, her memory cannot be relied on."

"Until we find a body there's no proving anything, and even if we do find a body, if Lizzie gets washed up, there'll be very little evidence to go on after so many days in the water, or maybe no DNA to go on at all, so then we're all the way back to square one again."

Carl rubs his jaw. "She did it. This au pair did it. Let's not forget she blacked out that night. Let's not forget the coral-pink child's cardigan on her porch."

Alba releases a breath she's been unknowingly holding in. "Why am I not convinced?"

"Because she's a good liar, she seems friendly, and you can't believe that a woman would hurt a child, that's why."

Alba raises a brow. "That's not the reason and you know it."

Alba and Carl are back in the interview room again, Jayne slumped in the chair, her head resting on her arms, which are spread flat on the table, her hair spilling over her wrists, tumbling off her shoulders like a curtain she's trying to hide behind. She looks up when they return, her gaze a swamp of fog, of misery.

"We want to talk to you about your criminal record," Alba begins. "In the UK."

"Criminal record?"

"We have proof, Jayne, from the database. Proof of your conviction for shoplifting, your prison sentence."

"Last I heard I don't have a criminal record, and I certainly didn't spend time in jail!"

"Last you heard?"

"I'm being facetious."

"This is a serious matter, Ms. Smith."

"You think I don't know that? But I have no idea what you're talking about. I've had some run-ins with the police, yeah, and I did shoplift a Barbie doll once, when I was nine. But I don't *have* a criminal record!"

Carl replies in a calm voice as he takes a chair and sits

beside her. "There's no point in you denying it, Jayne, we know everything about you."

"Well, you've got it bloody wrong! I don't have a criminal record! I had a shit life, yeah, I did some questionable things, got into trouble, I had a rubbish upbringing, and once I got a police caution when I was fifteen for graffiti, but I don't have any actual criminal record. I think I'd know if I did!"

Carl gives Alba a look, just short of rolling his eyes. "That's not what we know."

"All right, prove it to me, show me this criminal record you have. Show me the paperwork because I don't have a criminal record, you've got the wrong person."

Carl tosses Alba a narrow-eyed glance.

In Alba's experience people that profess their innocence to such an extent are either mentally ill or often *are* innocent, contrary to what people might believe. It's the evaders, the sneaky ones who avoid giving direct answers to questions—the way some politicians operate, for instance—who are often guilty. Those who give reasons as to why they would never do such a terrible thing but don't actually deny doing what they did, those are the signs to look out for. Jayne has looked Alba in the eye throughout most of this interview and sworn that she did not touch Lizzie, and for some reason, Alba believes her. Still, the evidence is there, and Jayne is the only person so far tied to direct evidence.

"If you were telling the truth," Alba says, "don't you think what you did was extraordinarily stupid? Going into Lizzie's room and removing some of her possessions without asking, bringing them back to your cottage and wrapping them in plastic bags, don't you think that's a pretty crazy thing to do, considering the child is still missing and you're a suspect?"

Jayne fixes her gaze on Alba. "Yes, I think it must be up there with the stupidest most moronic things I've ever done in my life. I totally agree with you there, and I don't know why I did it. I wasn't thinking. I thought the dog had finished and I only wanted something of Lizzie's. A keepsake. And I knew that if I asked Celeste, Ms. Sharpe would be all over it, and I don't know, I just wanted a private moment with Lizzie, and before I knew it I found myself in her room, wanting to feel her for a while, and then I saw the little stuffed toy, and I took it, and then those little itty-bitty leggings and sweet unicorn T-shirt, and then the coloring book... well, that was something I already had at my cottage from the last time she was coloring, and I put them all together and wrapped them up and thought I'd take them home with me. If I'd killed her or harmed her in some way, I wouldn't have been so stupid. I would've been cleverer."

Alba doesn't respond, but holds her gaze on Jayne.

"You said 'killed'?" Carl asks.

"'Killed' because that's what everyone's secretly thinking, isn't it? I mean, let's be honest, everyone thinks someone has murdered her by now, am I right? Or maybe she drowned, got swept away in the storm and, I don't know... I don't know"—her eyes fill up with tears again—"your guess is as good as mine as to what could've happened. Things like this *do* happen, so why are you trying to blame it on me? Have you interrogated Ms. Sharpe? Or Lizzie's mother?"

"Of course we have."

"Well, I suggest you go and interview them again because they're hiding all kinds of stuff, I reckon."

Silence. The atmosphere is charged with mistrust. Anger. Suspicion. On all sides.

"We have here copies of emails back and forth between you and Mr. Wainwright concerning your employment. We have a copy of your passport. Forms you filled out. And here we have the au pair agency's file on you."

"Can I see?"

"Sure." Alba pushes the file over to Jayne.

Jayne scans her eyes across the pages as if she's in a trance looking through the paperwork. Tears drip onto the paper. "In your opinion I'm guilty, so what can I even do?" She slaps her hand on the papers. "Ask for a lawyer? I don't have any money to pay a lawyer. I'm in a foreign country, they don't have Citizen's Advice Bureaus here, do they? I don't even know what to do!"

"Please, take your time," Alba says.

Jayne sifts through the papers. "What's this one?"

"That is the report that came back from the Criminal Records Office in the UK. Your criminal record."

Jayne taps at the paper. "No wonder there was a cock-up. They've got my birthdate wrong."

"What do you mean 'wrong'?"

"They switched it around. I was born on October 1st 1999. They've put January 10th 1999."

Carl takes the paper from her. "How is that possible?"

Alba shakes her head. "We Americans put the month first, then the day. The Brits and Europeans do it the other way round. Day, then month. So when we say 10/01/1999, they would write 01/10/1999."

"Who ran the database check?"

"Scully. Must've jotted down the date the American way."

Carl lets out a false laugh. "Fucking great."

"You know how many Jayne Smiths there are in the UK?" Jayne huffs through exasperated sniffles. "Smith is the commonest name ever known to man in England. My mother tried to do me a favor by adding a Y in my name, and it hardly makes a dent. We are, as you Americans would say, a dime a dozen. I mean, even on Facebook. There are hundreds, maybe even thousands of us. I told you, I don't *have* a criminal record. Whoever did this database check got me mixed up with another Jayne Smith."

THE DISAPPEARANCE

Several days have passed since Max, Marjorie, and Liam left the island, and they are nowhere to be found. Not to mention Lizzie, who is still missing. The police have zero evidence to go on concerning Stephen, apart from a suspicious pink plastic child's shoe that was floating around near the entrance of the cave that Stephen frequented. The shoe is an exact match to the pink shoe found in Liam's room.

The press is having a field day. Scully has put Alba back on the case. Nobody saw Max, Liam, or Marjorie arriving on the mainland. They were last spotted on Max's speedboat.

The investigation notches up to a new level. Conspiracy theories are beginning to take root, especially with the media. The whys and wherefores cannot be a coincidence. And it is now that Forensics finds a couple of things they missed the first time around, simply because they weren't focusing in this direction: Celeste is not Liam's biological mother. But something even more telling is that Marjorie is not Max's biological sister. This is information that Alba would have loved to have gotten her hands on several days ago. She cannot understand how this got looked over. The tests they were doing were to eliminate certain DNA and prints from the possible crime scene, not to check for parental lineage—although they did find out about Lizzie not being Max's daughter—but still, why did nobody notice this discrepancy? Again, this is something that the press and the public will not be able to accept. They have been watching too much *CSI* and believe that the forensic department is infallible, that they always get it right in record time and these kind of things take minutes not days to get processed. In real life, things get tangled and jumbled, and in real life human error and delays are rife. Alba feels the weight of this heavy on her shoulders as if she alone is somehow responsible for all that has gone wrong. Things have come a long way since the seventies when people like Ted Bundy got away with multiple murders from bungled police investigations, but the team should have joined the dots sooner. *She* should have joined the dots sooner about Marjorie and Max.

She repeats this revelation over and over to herself, trying to make sense of it.

Marjorie is not Max's biological sister.

This is not something Alba had cooked up even in the wildest part of her imagination. She has seen all sorts, some things truly beyond belief, but this? This had not crossed her mind. Marjorie and Max have similar features. Both dark, both very attractive, in good shape, They look, by all appearances, like brother and sister. With background checks and social security data, they checked out as siblings. Who could have known? Was Celeste aware of this?

So what is the relationship between Max and Marjorie? It can be only one thing, surely. It doesn't take a genius to figure this out, nor why he married Celeste in the first place.

Money.

In Alba's experience it is nearly always money.

It has to be. If they are parading as brother and sister they must have some master plan in mind. But knowing that Celeste and Max were lying all this time about being a happy couple, which is the chicken and which is the egg? If Max and Marjorie are indeed lovers, how long has their relationship been going on? The fact that Lizzie is not Max's means things had been going badly right from the start. Is it possible Marjorie has been around all along? Even before he met Celeste? And how much did/does Celeste know?

If this is so, Celeste and Max's marriage cannot simply be a case of a man marrying a woman for position or money, because a third party is involved: Marjorie. It isn't the first time Alba has seen a woman become victim to a relationship scam. Billions of dollars every year are lost because of fraud, and relationship scams are the second most costly form of online fraud—after wire fraud. The numbers are huge. A lot more is lost from relationship scams than phishing scams or phony charities. The thing is, because people feel so shamed and embarrassed, a lot doesn't go reported, so the numbers are even higher than anyone can imagine. Only fifteen percent of victims report the crimes to law enforcement.

Was it shame and embarrassment that made Celeste clam up and not report this? It's a classic reaction. Even extremely intelligent people get scammed, especially those looking for love.

Or was it fear?

It is when Alba receives an alert that things get really interesting. They have Celeste's cell phone monitored.

I wired you the money, now give me my kids back.

All in good time.

Don't play games, Max. I've done everything you asked.

So this is what has been going on? *Kidnap?* Things are beginning to fall into place.

Alba's heart is hammering in her chest. The kids are still alive! This is what matters. This is what counts. But at the same time, if Max is capable of kidnap, he is a wild card. He could do anything.

The next steps Alba takes are crucial. She will not be able to live with herself if she blows this.

She has to get this right. Kidnapping is a federal crime. Is it time to call in the FBI?

First things first. She needs to see Celeste.

She ponders her next move and wonders where Max and Marjorie could be. Since that crazy storm last week the weather has settled. It has been perfect for a few days. It would be very easy for Max to have gotten away on his speedboat. A boat is so much harder to track down than a car. There are less controls, no roadblocks, no speed cameras. It is a lot easier to travel incognito. Perhaps they have changed boats? They could be anywhere by now. The Caribbean, for instance, on some remote island, out of US jurisdiction. So Lizzie is with them? And Celeste wants Liam back too?

Alba finds Celeste, not in the house this time, which is unusual, but outside in the backyard, hanging the laundry. She has never seen Celeste in this domestic situation before. Linen sheets—probably Celeste's own brand—are fluttering in the wind. She is hanging them up with wooden pegs, along with clothing from a hamper, including things that must belong to the children. Alba suddenly sees Celeste in a new light. No wonder the poor woman has been so evasive. She was forced into an impossible position, cornered. Her children kidnapped —she must be terrified of everything going belly-up. Max could do anything. Celeste has been too scared to speak up.

"Detective," Celeste cries out in greeting, her head peering over the washing line. "I thought you were taking a couple of days off, away from the island."

"Well, those couple of days are over," Alba answers. "How you doing?"

"Oh, in a terrible, terrible turmoil about Max missing, obviously."

It was Celeste who reported him missing. She let Alba know that she had phoned him over and over again; she wanted to speak to Liam especially. She also called Marjorie. No answer. What is Celeste playing at? Max is stalling for time, clearly. And Celeste has been aiding him. Unwillingly, or on purpose?

"It's not normal. Even when he's away on business he always answers his phone or texts me." Celeste is a good liar, she doesn't flinch.

"When did you last see him?" Alba inquires. She has asked this before, of course, but asking the same question several times over is never a bad idea. She wonders what fib Celeste will spin now.

"Just before he left, when he said he was off to the mainland. He said he was going to Boston, maybe stay there a night and then to our house in Portland."

Alba's colleagues in Portland have already checked out the house. Max is not there, but his car is there, untouched, parked in the same place it has been all week. There are no charges to hotels in Boston on his credit card. He could have paid cash though.

"I'm worried, that's all," Celeste goes on. "I mean, I'm sure there's some explanation."

"I'd like to talk to you," Alba says, the linen sheets a barrier between them. "Can we go inside to chat?"

"Sure." Celeste finishes pegging up the last item of clothing: must be Liam's shorts. Not left soiled in a bathroom hamper but fresh and clean as if she's expecting him back any minute. Alba feels a pinch in her heart. A little yellow dress also flutters in the breeze. Alba needs to play this right. See what information Celeste offers her before she pins her down.

It's always the kitchen in this house, the heart of the home. It looks as if it hasn't been touched for years. Alba wonders how unusual it is not to remodel a kitchen, not to keep things up to date when you have so much money at your fingertips.

"There's one thing I'd like to let you know about," Celeste informs her as if reading the detective's mind. "Our money."

"Money?"

"Maybe you're not aware of this but, well, our money is—"

"Yours? You're the family provider," the detective interjects.

"You know?"

Alba gives her a look that says, *We're the police, it's our job.*

Celeste's jaw slackens in shock. "Our private finances got *investigated*?"

Alba nods very slightly.

"You're allowed to do that? Isn't this kind of thing prohibited under some act, some data protection law?"

"When a child is missing and there's an Amber Alert, yes, we have the jurisdiction to go in and investigate."

Celeste sips in a breath. "Well, Max... at least, I'm assuming it was him, unless he got involved with criminals or something. Max cleaned out our bank account."

"How much?"

"There was nine hundred and fifty thousand dollars in a savings account, and we had some stocks he cashed in and then, well, nearly two million has gone, just sort of disappeared, got transferred to an account I don't recognize."

"Can you give me the account number?"

"Of course." Celeste plucks her phone from the kitchen table, goes to her online bank and punches in her passwords. Her phone pings with a security code—double verification, and she taps in another code, another password. Finally, she takes a screenshot of the transfer and sends it by airdropping it to Alba's phone. Alba is impressed. Celeste is pretty au fait with technology. She had a notion that Celeste was flighty and vague. Not so.

Not so at all.

Alba asks, "So you think Max made off with the money and wants to start a new life?"

"Your guess is as good as mine."

Alba does not react, her expression flat. But one thing is for sure: Celeste is a liar and is hiding the truth at any cost. She starts with one of the lies, the omittances, not mentioning the kidnap for now. "Why didn't you tell me, Celeste, that Liam isn't your child?"

"But he *is* my child."

"Not your biological child."

"Your reaction, Detective, illustrates my point."

"Your point?"

"People love to differentiate between people's biological children and adoptive children and it really grates on me."

"But this is an investigation, these details are—"

"I'm sorry for my lack of transparency, but I really didn't feel it had any bearing whatsoever on Lizzie... Look, I apologize, but if you knew anything about children, Detective Alba, you'd know blood isn't what makes someone a parent, doesn't dictate how much you love a child. Liam is my child, just as Lizzie and—"

"Violet?"

Celeste goes quiet. Alba has been pressing and pressing for the pathological report on Violet, and so far, nothing has come up. Another element in this convoluted case that makes no sense.

"Max was married before?" Another lie. The "wife" didn't show up in their investigation. It is hard, at this point, to know where Max Wainwright's lies end and where Celeste's begin.

Celeste sighs. "Yes. His wife passed away. Look, I don't differentiate between being a mother and a stepmother. I don't like that word, 'stepmother.' It sounds like a baddie in a fairy tale. Liam was a toddler when I married Max. As far as he's concerned, I'm his only mom."

Alba raises her chin. "But you haven't been straight with me, have you? Haven't drawn the whole picture clearly?"

"You never brought it up. I assumed you knew and it was unimportant."

Alba clenches her jaw. Something she discovered (when she dug a little deeper, and which Scully had missed at first) was that according to Celeste's father's will, Liam would never inherit money from Celeste's father, but Lizzie and Violet would. And if anything happened to the girls, the money would pass down to Celeste. "And there's something else I'd like to talk to you about," she adds. "Marjorie. Did you know that Max isn't related to her, that he isn't her brother?"

"What? That's *crazy*! Are you sure about this?"

"The DNA tests don't lie."

Celeste's blue eyes grow round. She looks like her daughter in this moment. She stands, her chair goes flying to the floor. She wrings her hands together. *An act? Or real shock?* "But surely there's been a mistake?"

Alba shakes her head. "No mistake. You didn't have any idea?"

"No! Course I didn't, how would I know that?"

"Because you must've met his family?"

"No, I haven't. We had a very quiet wedding. He told me he had a sister but she couldn't come. She was living abroad, in Singapore. I never saw any photos of her... well, once, a blurry old snap from years ago. Other than that, I never saw photos, so when Marjorie turned up, I... well, I took her for who she said she was... his sister."

"No suspicion?"

"No. Besides, after the accident my memory was coming and going, and it made sense I didn't recognize her because I hadn't seen her before, so I took her to be his sister. They look alike. Both with dark eyes, dark hair, why wouldn't they be brother and sister? I had no reason to doubt him. I mean, if someone introduces their sister to you, the last thing you imagine is that they're making it up! I can't believe this!"

"You had no idea they were... a couple?"

"God, no, no! It's so shocking, and to be honest, to be frank, I'm completely devastated! Why would he do this? Why would he?"

Contrary to Celeste's protestations and raised voice, Alba remains calm. "There's something else, Celeste."

"Oh, Lord, what now?"

"We know what's going on," Alba says. "That Max kidnapped Lizzie."

CELESTE

"Max kidnapped Lizzie," Detective Alba just said. I was wondering when she was going to arrive at that. I go back, picking over every thread of conversation with Alba, rolling all of it over in my mind, wondering how many of the clues she picked up along the way. When was it we had last spoken about Max? I remember her asking, *Tell me about your marriage.*

The perfect family. The perfect life. I wonder if Alba has some inkling, some instinct that I have been lying to her about our marriage all along? About Max, about me, about how much I love him.

I glance at her now, but her face gives me no clues. "I'll make some fresh coffee," I suggest. "I'm exhausted, and this revelation about Marjorie has come as such a shock."

"Did you have any idea Max was capable of kidnap?" she asks.

There's something about Alba that unnerves me. I think she has a gift for reading people's minds, so I shake my head no, get up, turn my back to her and busy myself in the kitchen. Dig out some plates and chocolate chip cookies—Lizzie's favorite kind—turning over everything in my head. The lies I've told for my own self-preservation, the intricate mess that was me and Max. I needed to keep this woman in the dark. So yes, I have lied.

It's true I was head over heels in love with Max when we first met, completely bowled over. Max was so accomplished, courteous, well-bred, a real gentleman, a fantastic conversationalist, even spoke French and knew all about wine and food. He was sporty, too, played tennis, did fun things like skydiving... I mean, he could have been cast as James Bond. He drove a beautiful car, wore tailored, bespoke suits, Italian ties, handmade shoes. How on earth was I to know that he wasn't who he said he was? I had led a pretty sheltered life. I hadn't had many relationships, no serious boyfriend, so when Max professed his love, I believed him. I took him for who he was, at face value. He was attentive, drank in every word I uttered. He really listened. I had never met anyone like him. He was so different from other men I had known. That was what made me fall for him. The attention he paid me, the way he gazed into my eyes and listened when I spoke. He was so *present*. If only I'd known what was to come after he had already hooked me in.

The first red flag—which I took for love—was how he didn't want to "compromise the relationship," by sleeping with me even after we were engaged. He was too "respectful" for that. Ha! Of course he didn't want to sleep with me, he was sleeping with Marjorie! How was I to know? He rhapsodized, told me how he'd fallen in love with me, that this had never happened to him before, that I was his godsend, his soulmate.

Of course his ultimate plan was to scam me for my money, but I was too blind to see. He peppered the conversation with little hints about how wealthy he was. His financial assets, and money he would be inheriting. This was before we tied the knot. A double knot, I found out, virtually impossible to unravel. One of those trick sailor's knots that I had tied myself and couldn't fathom how to disentangle. I had never discussed money—I'd been raised not to—nor even asked him about any of this money talk, but he dropped it into the conversation: property he owned, stocks and shares, land, how he was going to inherit this and that one day. It was such a warning sign. Another crimson flag, but I didn't see it. You don't when you're in love, do you?

A little lamb being led off to the slaughterhouse, that was me. Max—although of course Max was not his real name—duped, not only me, but several women before me. When I realized he wasn't quite the wealthy investor he told me he was, he admitted he had gotten a bank loan to fund his charity fundraiser at the Met. The one he set up to impress me, to woo me. Then I discovered that of course he hadn't gotten a bank loan—no bank would've lent him money—it was the woman before who had unwittingly bankrolled him through his scheming and conning. There were several of us, but I was the real prize. The women before me had been a warm-up. But the worst of it? He and Marjorie worked as a team. I was their "mark," they called me. Their target, I was nothing, nothing to him whatsoever, except one big walking, talking, breathing dollar sign—or rather, dollars, *plural.*

"You honestly had no clue at all that your husband and Marjorie were in a relationship?" Alba asks me again.

I shake my head. Fill the cafetière with coffee. "You must think me really naive."

I remember how I felt: *disbelief, guilt, shame.* Like I was caving in on myself. I had nowhere to go, nowhere to hide my shame.

Max left a trail in his wake. Before me he drained a particular woman's bank account—Liam's mother—undermining her sense of what actually happened, knocked her reality out of kilter, ruined her credit score, trashed her life, and then, just like that, she died. Before her there were others. The interesting thing is that not one of these women before me was dumb. Not at all. Liam's mother was the CEO of her own pharmaceutical company. One was a doctor, one an IT manager, and another an engineer. It was almost as if Max got a thrill by preying on the smart, well-educated ones.

He told me he was an investment banker. True, he wasn't lying about that one; he *was* investing.

Investing in *me*, banking on *me*.

Had I looked Max up online after we met?

I had!

I had done my homework, I *had*. Even though I'm not the greatest internet sleuth, I gave it my best shot. But he was so smart, that man. He had all sorts of websites and Google entries about what a great guy he was, and how he was doing this and that, donating money all over the place. It's easy to set that kind of stuff up if you know what you're doing; things on Google, I discovered, are rarely verified. Max was a pro, a professional conman. He conned me, sucked me right into his game.

When we met he had nothing but debts. Although I was in the dark, of course. He should have won an Oscar he was that good. He even had my father fooled, which is saying something.

I thought I was going crazy at first, and it was only when one of his exes reached out to me via Facebook, warning me, that I realized what I'd gotten myself into.

The kettle boils and I fill the cafetière with boiling water, my back still to Alba. I don't want her to see the bitterness on my face, the big lie.

She asks, in a quiet voice, "You have any idea where they could be? Any clue at all? A cabin in the woods, for instance? We need to locate Lizzie and Liam, and you *have* to tell me what you know. No games, Celeste, this is imperative if you want to see your kids alive."

"Of course I want to see my kids alive," I retort. "You think this has been easy for me? Doing everything Max asked and waiting like this until he decides to let me know where my children are? It's torture!"

"Did you know he was capable of this? Of kidnapping your children? Celeste, it feels like there's a whole lot you're not sharing with me. When did this start? It must have dawned on you at some point what kind of a man Max was, surely? There must've been some clues? Is that why you fell into the arms of another man? Lizzie's biological father? You caught on to Max, didn't you, not long after you were married, isn't that true?"

I close my eyes in shame. Still, it is the shame that trips me up. The notion that I should have known, I *should* have seen him for who he was. Remember Paul Newman in *The Sting*? Leonardo DiCaprio in *Catch Me If You Can*? Add Max to that list. These are the types of men who are conmen. Charming, affable, easygoing, intelligent. Their rakish smiles raking you in, beguiling you with their undivided attention. Professionals. The best in the game.

I planned to divorce Max and saw a lawyer the second I wised up. I told him so. That was a mistake: to forewarn him. It gave him ammunition. But the really foolish thing I did was go and see a psychiatrist, a real one, not someone like Stephen... that's another story. I was given antidepressants because I was so devastated by what he had done to me. It was a perfect moment for Max to strike, and boy, did he strike.

I was complicit in my own victimization. I aided and abetted him and made it all possible.

I should have seen the signs.

"He married you for your money, didn't he?" Alba probes.

I bring the coffee and cookies to the table, still not looking her in the eye. Boy, was I naive. You would think, wouldn't you, that if somebody asked for your hand in marriage and was as romantic as Max, he'd be madly in love with you? I felt like I was the luckiest woman in the world, the pulse of adoration and love thrumming through every fiber of my being, only to discover there was someone else.

"Did Max marry you for your money?" Alba asks again, more softly this time.

I nod but say nothing.

One of the first scams he pulled on me was medical costs. His "mother" wasn't able to make it to our wedding because she was ill in the hospital. Her insurance didn't cover her costs. He showed me photos of her, even text messages... all kinds of things to tug at my heart... my God, I even spoke to her on the phone. Her wobbly, weak voice. Never asking for a thing herself, and strangely, Max didn't ask for anything either. Smart. But I wound up doing a bank transfer to his mother (Marjorie, as it turned out) to help pay for the medical bills, because Max's money was "tied up in investments." I was a fool. But when you're in love you don't imagine anybody is capable of doing this kind of thing. Even when you're *not* in love you don't imagine anybody is doing capable of doing this kind of thing. But this was Max, this was the man I married. He was a master at telling people what they wanted to hear.

I felt so ashamed. I couldn't tell my parents I'd been taken for such a ride. I just wanted it to all go away. I decided I would divorce the second I could. By the time I got around to seeing a lawyer and sorting it all out... well, the rest is history, you can guess what happened next.

But it's not even the money, it's the humiliation, the act of your faith being broken. And when someone as handsome as Max is the perpetrator, people can't believe it. They *won't* believe it. It took *me* a long time to believe it, even when the truth was smacking me in the face.

And here Detective Alba is... believing it, wanting me to share my story, to open up.

But I can't. It's too late.

I can't tell her anything.

DR. STEPHEN

I'm back on the island, shellshocked. Truth is, I don't have anywhere else to go. This is home, for now, anyway. I had to lawyer-up in the end. A friend from college who's an attorney. I had no choice but to make that call. Irony is, he knows Max, or used to. Hates the guy. His name is Owen. He's a criminal lawyer and had quite a bit of success in the past. I don't know how I'm going to pay him, I don't have a budget for this kind of shit, this is not what I expected to happen.

And here we are again, Owen and I, me reeling from the police interrogation as he tries to prepare me if I get called in again. It helps that we're not at the police station anymore, but here, in the comfort of my cottage.

"You've got to tell the truth." Owen's voice is a touch solemn, but even. Calm.

"I can't, not yet."

"You've gotten yourself into a real bind," he says, stating the obvious. "You don't owe this family anything, I don't know why you're protecting them."

"Because that's the way I am," I tell him.

"You can't keep doing this, you have to put it out there in the open."

"It's just not in my nature."

"But as far as other people are concerned, your nature is a whole lot worse than reality. Their imagination is running wild, you know that don't you? The media, even the foreign press are getting interested."

I sigh. Owen is right. "I know."

"You got yourself into some real deep shit, didn't you?"

I wish he'd stop rubbing salt in my wound. "I guess so."

"Guess so? Know so."

I stare out the window. The sun is high. I wish I could be outside but don't dare risking people's eyes on me.

"That fuck Max," he says. "I always hated the guy."

"I know you did, do, did."

Owen is "smooth," that's the word I think of to describe him. Or "suave" maybe. Combed-back hair, old-fashioned style, but a WASPy version. Slick, his clothes immaculate, not a crumb on his lapel, not a grease stain on his knife-pressed chinos. He smells of exclusive aftershave and soap and money. The kind of guy I wanted to be, the kind of guy I would never be. I have a reputation I'll never be able to shake off.

"You know we never actually had sex," I tell him, changing the subject entirely, my mind jumping to something else altogether. "Me and Madison. It was a platonic relationship, not that anybody would believe that, least of all her parents. And least of all Madison herself, judging by her blog."

Owen locks eyes with me, and I'm not sure if he's even following my train of thought.

I muse some more over Madison, the schoolgirl, my impressionable student who had decided she was so in love with me. The poem she wrote for class, the one I said had such a promise. I had no idea the poem was about me.

Looking into your eyes is like seeing the ocean
Twinkling sapphires in the mist
What have I missed?
When I see you
I feel true.

Madison's life has been defined by me. She has a blog with thousands of followers hanging onto her every word. It is so sad. For her. But especially for me. I am ostracized. But it was completely out of my control, then and now. All I can do now is wish it away. Sometimes I still wonder if something had happened: some kind of sexual contact, because she is so convinced of it herself. Of *course* I did not have sex with a sixteen-year-old! I didn't even find her sexually attractive, how could you, how could you, as a grown man find a teenager attractive in that way? I simply wanted to help her because she had talent, she had promise. You don't stand a chance these days as a man. If you get accused of something, you are already guilty before you've even had a trial.

I know there is something about me, about my face... something in the planes of my face makes me look guilty even when I'm not. The jury tapped into it. The judge. I was done for before I even opened my mouth. All I've ever wanted is to do the right thing, be a decent guy. Why does it always go so wrong?

I tell Owen, "Madison was delusional, but of course I found it flattering the way she was so in love with me. I was a fool not to set things straight right from the beginning, be 'cruel to be kind.' Isn't that what they say? She was such a good student, and I was helping her so much with her work, her future career. It *mattered* to me, so we spent much more time together than we should have after class. It didn't look right, it didn't look normal, I'm the first to admit it. And look where it got me."

"Yeah, well, you had a shit attorney representing you. He really screwed up big time. You should've called me."

"That's why I called you now, so I didn't land in the bog again."

"Well, if you'd told the truth from the beginning—"

"Don't chastise me, don't patronize me, Owen. I think we should let things play out and see what happens next."

"They're going to haul your ass back in there any second if you do that."

"They have nothing else to go on. They have no proof."

"They need you as a scapegoat even if they have no proof. What the fuck was that shoe doing floating around anyway?"

"I swear I think someone planted it there."

"How can you plant a shoe in the ocean?"

"I don't know, someone threw it down from the cliff, made it look—"

"How did they even know you were there in that cave? And why didn't you spot that damn shoe yourself?"

"Somebody wanted it to look like I was guilty, to hide their own guilt."

"It was Celeste, wasn't it?"

"She wouldn't do that though, she wouldn't."

"How do you know?"

"I can't believe it, not after all I've done for her."

"Make sure nobody comes near this cottage, you don't want them planting some kind of evidence."

"It can't have been Celeste," I ponder, still rolling all this around in my head. Mainly, how I've gotten myself into this mess in the first place.

"Max?" Owen suggests. "Look, we could make this all go away if you tell them what the hell is going on."

"I can't. A promise is a promise. I'm not that kind of guy."

"What does that girl Jayne know, the au pair?"

"Nothing, she was wasted, drunk out of her brains, she can't even remember what conversations we had."

"I can only do so much if you don't want to talk," Owen says.

"I know, I know you're doing your best under the circumstances."

"I got you out of that interrogation room, but next time it could be a cell, you get that don't you?"

"But they have nothing on me."

"For now. For now, that's true, yeah, but things could change."

"I need to speak to Celeste," I tell him.

"Are you crazy? With that detective all over her like a cheap suit? She's got eyes in the back of her head, that woman, plus you don't know who else is watching, waiting. All those rubbernecking tourists all over the place, you don't know which one of them is a plain clothes cop. The reporters are like vultures too. Keep your goddamn mouth shut."

I keep thinking I should get away from here, go to a hotel somewhere, but I don't want to look guilty, like I'm running. That shit when you don't have money. Which brings me to the big question. "How am I going to pay your fee?" I ask Owen.

Owen temples his fingers, brings them to his lips and breathes on his hands. "Don't worry, I have an idea."

Before I can stop him, he pulls out his phone and dictates a message. "I know everything. And by the way, I'm expensive."

I feel the veins in my body heat, and my pulse rate quickens. A rush of blood fizzes through me. "What the fuck did you do that for?"

"You'll see how this pans out."

"I'll see how that fucking Detective Alba will pan out! All this is going to implode, Owen! They've probably tapped our phones, have you thought of that? However they do it with cell phones these days, which I think is pretty easy, isn't it, for the police to do that kind of stuff?"

I now regret getting involved with this schmuck in the first place. I should've bided my time and they would've let me out soon enough without any evidence. What a mess this whole thing is... what a freakin' *mess*.

CELESTE

"What would I have done without you?" I ask my old school friend Alex.

"You'd be dead," Alex tells me simply.

"I would be, wouldn't I? How do you think he would've done it?"

She tops up her wine, and mine. "Overdose, probably. Or he might've smothered you with a pillow at the hospital itself, or the second you got home."

"You don't think he would've killed Lizzie first, then me afterward?"

"No, he would've wanted you out of the picture first, Lizzie a while later to make it look authentic... Or maybe you're right. Maybe he would've set it up so it looked like you killed her yourself. Of course. That way he would have gotten the girls' inheritance. But you know, that's why I kept an eye on Marjorie whenever she cooked. A couple times I even made Lizzie and Liam trade plates in front of Marjorie, to be sure. I knew Max would never have harmed his own son. His ego was too big for that."

I roll the stem of my wine glass between my fingers. They

are shaking somewhat. All this intrigue and excitement. All the lies I've had to keep tabs on has taken its toll on me. "The bastard got what he deserved."

"He did, he really did. He had it coming."

"Ms. Sharpe," I say with a laugh. "You saved my life."

"No, that student saved your life when he jumped into the lake. I prolonged your life is all."

"True. Poor Jayne, she wound up at the police station being grilled. And Stephen too. I feel guilty about that."

Alex's mouth lifts into a small smile. It's nice seeing her smile after the tight-lipped role she's been playing so well. "Well, it all sorted itself out, didn't it? The distraction was just what we needed."

"Idiot, I can't believe Jayne did that. Going into Lizzie's room and Liam's room and gathering those things. She should've asked."

Alex takes a sip of the Burgundy and swallows, her eyes fluttering with bliss, savoring every drop. "Jayne has issues, anyone can see that."

"Poor girl, though. Maybe we went a little far planting the cardigan, and poor Stephen with that pink plastic shoe."

Alex shakes her head. "We had to stall for time, had to tangle up the investigation a bit, we had no choice." She yawns, stretches her arms. "I'm beat. All the drama, jeez Louise. It was hard work not letting you out of my sight, not letting Max near you. I felt like a guard dog."

"I know, you must be wiped out. I sure am. Well, now he's gone for good, we can relax."

"Yeah, except for that irritating detective, she's still sniffing around. What are we going to do about her?"

"Leak 'the story'"—I reply, using air quotes—"to one of those reporters hanging around, that eager newscaster with the big fat mic, that's the easiest way. Observe calmly while it snowballs. Then we can sit back and watch the show unfold from the comfort of our armchairs."

"Armchairs?"

I laugh. "I'm not being literal."

"Well, at least you won't have to be holed up in bed any longer, playing sick, playing whacko. The money's been transferred into 'his' account already, right?"

I can't help but proffer a little smirk. "So many different offshore and shell accounts en route it'll make their heads spin. But they won't be able to trace it to its final destination... there's no FATCA treaty, so no way Uncle Sam can track it. I think Alba bought the kidnapping story. It'll show him up as the gold digger he is. Or was. And when the FBI start digging into his past, which they will, the 'kidnap' will match up perfectly."

"Clever. You always were top of the class. By the way, where's your diary?"

I raise a brow. "Oh, I've got it, don't worry. I had such fun writing those pages, about how in love with Max I was, especially. I *knew* he'd sneak a read when I left it 'hidden' for his benefit. I knew he couldn't resist. *Oh, dearie me, there's something wrong with my head, my memory is so shot, my, oh, my, I've forgotten everything! I'm so in love with my husband!*"

"You really think he bought it?"

"I do, don't you? His ego certainly did, or he wouldn't've had the gall to bring Marjorie into the house and pass her off as his sister."

"I don't know. It might've given him a thrill, blatantly shoving her under your nose like that."

"I'm not so sure. I think he did believe me, weirdly enough. Enough to keep him off my case anyway, enough to make him believe I wasn't a threat for the time being. And enough to keep the detective in the dark, had she decided to delve into my 'private' musings."

"You think she read your diary?"

"No." I laugh. "She's too upstanding for bad behavior antics like that."

"I can't tell you how good it feels having that asshole gone. '*Out, out, damn spot!*'" Alex says.

"Yep, we did it. Now we need to let the rest of it fall nicely into place."

ALEX SHARPE

Celeste and I go back a long way. We went to high school together. I was the scholarship kid, the skinny nerd with Coke-bottle glasses and crooked teeth. It was a private school. I didn't have the right clothing, my parents were blue collar, I had never been to Europe like they all had, or a Broadway show. I didn't even have the right taste in music. I was mercilessly teased to the point of pain. Along came Celeste. She wanted some help with Biology one time, and I reluctantly agreed. I suspected she was probably using me, but, flattered, I went along with it. Soon we became friends. Not best friends, but she turned my life from hell to suddenly being respected by the gossip girl queens. I was no longer the freak but simply the nerdy friend of Celeste's. She changed everything for me. Then, as life often goes, we lost touch after we left high school, until she showed up on a gurney at the hospital where I worked, after an attempted suicide, her blood toxically laced with a cocktail of sedative-hypnotic drugs. I had dealt with many suicidal patients over the years, and this seemed casebook at first, until slowly Celeste recovered, and with that recovery came a revelation that her husband—who had been visiting her every day with flowers, expensive chocolates, and fresh fruit (such an adoring spouse)—had tried to kill her, spiking her morning Thermos of coffee with enough medication to put a stallion to sleep. It was no wonder she suffered from drowsy driving and, knowing the route she took over the bridge every day crossing the lake, it sounded plausible that he had planned her car crash. The chances that she'd fall asleep at the wheel with that mélange of legal but lethal medications were extremely high.

Max did such a beautiful job of playing the attentive husband, the loving father, the man who would do anything for his ailing wife that if I hadn't known Celeste personally I might have found it hard to believe her. At first I thought she might be genuinely brain-damaged after the accident. But soon, after a CT scan, I knew there was nothing wrong with Celeste's brain at all; she was in shock, and rightly so. It was blamed on her depression. Suicidal tendencies, postpartum blues, postpartum psychosis. Max was so quick to package it all up beautifully in a little parcel for the doctors and anyone who would listen, making himself seem like such a wonderful caring husband and so concerned for the wife he so adored. Thank goodness I was there by her side.

It was then that Celeste hired me to help her get her life "back on track." I took the job because Celeste was my friend. She had done so much for me at school, I owed her one. On top of that the money she offered was too good to turn down, and if she was right I knew I would never forgive myself for not agreeing to protect her. It's amazing what a tight bun and pair of glasses can do. I transformed myself into the strict, no-nonsense nurse to be feared. My job? To keep Max away from Celeste, make sure he didn't spike her food, her drinks. And to collaborate in making sure Lizzie and the baby were safe. It was twenty-four-hour-a-day care, being a watchdog really, not letting him near her, administering her medication, although of course the heavy medication was just vitamin pills for the most part.

The thing I still don't understand is how he was willing to murder a child. Lizzie was meant to be dead after that car accident. Violet too, along with her mother. When the little girls were alive, thanks to that student who saved their lives—it was a miracle, it really was—Max must've been beyond surprised.

There was no SIDS death on Violet's part. It was all an act. But knowing how Max didn't give a damn, and how his plan was to get rid of the children and Celeste anyway, I picked a day when he was away, got my brother to pose as a doctor in a white coat, to come to the house, to "file a report" and I left with him, baby swaddled in my arms, brushing Marjorie aside with my brisk, get-out-of-my-way, I'm-a-professional-nurse demeanor. Meanwhile, Celeste was feigning hysteria, although some of it was half real. She was beside herself with worry, about to be parted from her baby for a week or two. All this for the benefit of Marjorie. We knew she'd report it all to Max. Max had no reason to suspect a thing. He must have been thinking "one down, two to go." What did Max care that Violet was dead? I showed him a falsified coroner's report. Not that he even asked for it. He didn't check it out, didn't even care about arranging a funeral. Violet wasn't even his own, what did he care? And by this point, he believed that Celeste really was suffering from traumatic brain injury, because I kept reiterating this, assuring him that although it didn't show up in the CT scan, Celeste was most likely suffering from brain trauma. I am a nurse. He bought it. He had no idea we had gone to school together.

I took Violet to her father, who also happens to be Lizzie's father too. Eric Lawson. Celeste's boyfriend, the children's sailing instructor, the man I tried to keep away from the island, whom I told off and had to shoo away, in case he messed up our plans by making things too obvious.

And as for Lizzie? That was a whole lot more complicated. We knew we had to get her off the island fast, before Max became suspicious or did something drastic. We were aware from the weather forecast that a storm was coming, but we had not anticipated it would be that dangerous—nobody had. If we'd known, we would have held back. But it was serendipity as it turned out. Celeste had hired a private helicopter (and a pilot who signed a non-disclosure agreement and was handed a wad of cash—a trusted friend of my brother's) to pick Lizzie up on the north side of the island, where she was passed over to Eric, and where they boarded the helicopter. The moment it was airborne I called 9-1-1 from the house's landline, pretending to be Celeste, and reported Lizzie as missing. We didn't know that Detective Alba happened to already be in the air, only twenty minutes away. But it wound up in our favor. People who heard the helicopter believed it was one and the same, a rescue vehicle scouting the island.

Luck was on our side.

I behaved dishonestly, true. Did things to put the police off the scent. Planted that cardigan at Jayne's house, threw the pink shoe weighted down with a few pebbles in the toe and hurled it onto a rock near where Stephen swam. I wasn't prepared for the ramifications of that one.

I felt bad for Jayne going through that nasty interview, but really, what was she thinking gathering bits and pieces of Lizzie's and hiding them in her suitcase? And poor Stephen. Both were put through the wringer. It's been hard biding my time in this collaborative effort. Celeste asked a lot from me, and even from Stephen. He spotted Celeste and Lizzie that night but swore he'd never tell. By that time, he was aware of what was going on with Max, what a charlatan he was, what a murderous gold digger. Max needed to pay for what he'd done to everybody, particularly Celeste. And his co-conspirator Marjorie, she was no less despicable. You'd think conmen, con-women, and con-people in general would be a thing of the past, sort of like Raymond Chandler characters out of crime novels, but they do exist in everyday life, some small fry, others... well, they're pretty good at what they do, and Max was a pro. He had me fooled at first.

Celeste did a great job acting, pretending her mental health was in jeopardy, pretending she couldn't remember a thing. I honestly think Max actually bought it. When he read that diary full of reminiscences and her undying love for him, I believe he thought he'd gotten away with everything and was waiting to try again.

Well, Celeste got there first.

CELESTE

Have you ever been gaslighted? I'm not talking about the white lie kind, the *You were the one who didn't lock the front door!* type of thing or, *You were the one who came up with the big idea!* But things like when your whole psyche is turned inside out, upside down… like when somebody tries to kill you and everybody is telling you you're crazy, that it's in your imagination.

That is what happened when I landed in the hospital after the car crash. They blamed me for the drugs in my system, tried to convince me I had tried to kill myself. I was told by all the powers that be—the doctors, the nurses, and my very own husband—that I had tried to take not only my own life, but the life of my daughter and my unborn child.

Of course my hysteria took root, because I knew it was a lie. After they pumped my stomach, I awoke to my own hysteria. They had proof that I was crazy, proof because I was so manic. "Of course I didn't try and kill myself!" I screamed, arms flailing, kicking, screaming. They went ahead and diagnosed me with postpartum psychosis. My world splintered into shards.

There was Max, always by my side. The loving husband, the picture of sincerity, kindness, and concern.

It was him, I knew it. I thought my coffee tasted strange that morning.

Of course it was him, but nobody would have believed me judging by the state I was in, by the tests that showed all the drugs in my body when I was brought by ambulance, wheeled in on a gurney. But by a miracle, one of the head nurses, Alex Sharpe, hearing that I was there, having known me from high school, came to my bedside. She listened. Finally, she believed me. If it hadn't been for her, I probably would've ended up in a psychiatric hospital, I was that desperate and scared and crazed. She was the first person I confided in about Max. The charade was over.

He had tried to murder me.

I related to her the whole story of my marriage and how deep the problem was. How, after I had been admitted to the hospital, he whispered in my ear, *You breathe a word of the crazed idea in your brain, and watch what happens to Lizzie, for real this time.*

There was no way I could press charges. I didn't dare. Especially while I was holed up in a hospital bed, recovering. I knew I needed to take control, take my power back, in a different, cleverer way. Alex, luckily, had not taken a vacation for three years, and the hospital has a policy of vacation carryover from one year to the next. I offered her any sum she named to look after me, to keep me safe, and we arranged for her to come home with me to Cliff Island, to help me with my recovery, look after me, my baby, and Lizzie. But mostly, to guard me from my husband, to play the role of a strict, busybody nurse. I knew what Max was planning to do next: get rid of Violet, Lizzie, and then me so he could inherit everything. He already had infiltrated his way into some of my bank accounts because he'd become an expert at forging my signature.

It sounds crazy to some. All this instead of simply pressing charges? Because Max wrapped things up so tightly with a white silk bow, had so many contacts—judges, lawyers, even people in the mafia (which later turned out to be to my advantage)—I didn't have the time to do things legally or by the book. With my history of depression, that was another weapon in his arsenal. I was twenty when I spent a stint in a psychiatric hospital. And now this "attempted suicide" on top of that?

Alex, and later Stephen, and of course Lizzie and Violet's biological dad, Eric, helped me set things straight.

THE DISAPPEARANCE

There is no way to trace the source of Max's messages to Celeste's phone because they were sent from a burner. No possibility of knowing if he has fled the country or not, or if he has double-crossed Celeste by taking the kids with him.

Alba had a hunch about Violet and it turned out she was correct. There is no autopsy report for the baby, because an autopsy never took place. Her team were searching for something that never existed, so no wonder it took so long. No funeral. No death certificate. The baby never died, or if she did, it was not reported. The baby, like Lizzie, simply vanished.

And when Alba thinks about it, Celeste never actually discussed Violet with her. Celeste avoided answering questions. Clever. Celeste never "lied" about her baby, just skirted the topic. Who took Violet, and where she is now, this is the question.

Alba has a pretty good idea who has the answer: Celeste herself.

Either Celeste is brilliant or she has been scammed completely. The money's final destination is untraceable. And legally, because Max is Celeste's husband, unless Celeste presses charges against him, there is nothing the police can do. It is not technically theft. She transferred the money without involving them. She is not even asking them to catch him, to pursue this. All she wants is her children back.

And there is someone else pushing Celeste into handing over money: Owen, Stephen's attorney. He hasn't technically broken any laws either. The *I know everything. And by the way, I'm expensive* message he sent her is not a direct threat, at least, not in a court of law. Although, were Alba to pursue this, she could argue it was incriminating. She probably wouldn't get very far though. This sharkish lawyer has a reputation that precedes him. The plot is dense enough as it is, she doesn't need to wade into the mire any further.

All Alba can do is wait. Wait until Celeste receives another message from her husband telling her the whereabouts of the children.

Alba is pretty sure there is more to the story. A lot more. But at this point all she cares about is the kids' safety.

Finding them alive and well.

CELESTE

Alba is back in my kitchen while we wait for the next text from Max to find out where the kids are.

Alba is still in the dark, although maybe she can read between the lines? She has stopped grilling me about our marriage. Perhaps she wants to spare me more woulda-coulda-shoulda humiliation? It's always easy in retrospect, in hindsight, isn't it? To dissect relationships after the fact? To rail at yourself for being gullible? But it's what happens, isn't it, in real life? Those kick-ass heroines only exist in comic books and detective shows. In real life we're all vulnerable when it comes to love, aren't we?

And even if we do then get it right, there'll be several wrongs trailing behind us in our wake. Trial and error, we are only human. Even Judge Judy got divorced. We are all fooled every day even in small ways. We never really know people, not really. Facebook, Instagram. Everybody's hiding something, everybody's dissimulating. The picnic, the soccer game, the outing to the museum. Nobody shows the kids screaming and sulking, the parents giving each other dagger eyes seconds before the camera points and it's all smiles and sweetness and oh, such a loving, happy family.

I was no different, but I didn't do it on social media, I did it behind the scenes, the way Max did it behind the scenes. But his scam was so much bigger than mine. And he was the one who got the ball rolling, not me.

The question was, what was I going to do about it? I guess nobody could imagine how far I would go in the end. To protect my family, my loved ones, to come out on top as a survivor myself.

Alba and I sit here in silence in my kitchen, her questions all dried up. For now, anyway. I bide my time, waiting patiently for her to leave so I can get back into action and put an end to this fiasco.

I can't put a foot wrong.

As I make us some sandwiches and coffee, she pipes up: "I'm curious, Celeste, at what point did your marriage with Max start to show cracks?"

Cracks? That's a polite way of putting it. It was the Grand Canyon. But I don't tell her this. As sympathetic as she is, she's a cop, and I cannot trust her.

"Oh, I don't remember," I lie, serving her a sandwich and topping up her coffee.

But I do remember when it started to go so wrong, or rather the moment when I realized the man I had married was one big walking lie. He didn't waste his time either, letting me know who he was. A week and a half after the wedding I heard him talking on the phone: *"I promise, darling, it's going to be all right."* I wanted to know who this "darling" was, because it sure as hell wasn't me. He'd already grown cold, literally the day after our honeymoon, even *on* our honeymoon. He was distant, texting all the time, pretending he was busy doing business.

What *was* this business he was so busy with?

That was another big lie: he didn't even have a job. It all

started coming out in the filthy, soiled wash. My father happened to become very ill at this point: he was diagnosed with lung cancer; it had spread everywhere. I didn't have the heart to tell him about Max. My father was so proud of me for getting married, so proud of me for starting a family, even though Liam wasn't my own child, but Papa was excited about the prospect of more children on the way, of being a grandfather. I couldn't take that away from him, tell him I wanted a divorce a week after the wedding, not when he was dying.

So I stayed in the marriage, swallowed it all down and got on with it. It wasn't long before I found out who the "darling" was. At first I assumed—even hoped—it was Max being a womanizer. *That* I could have understood, or vaguely accepted. Max, handsome, dashing, having all these women throwing themselves at him. But no, it was *one particular woman*, which made it so much more painful, so much harder to bear.

Marjorie.

Three's a crowd is one thing. But three in a marriage? Princess Diana had a point.

Marjorie was always there during their scams, waiting like an actress in the wings to play her part. She had never left Max, not for one second. I did not understand how she could accept me. How could she bear it that Max had married another woman? *Her blood runs iced in her veins*, I decided. After the car "accident," Max took it a step further, dared to parade his partner in crime in front of me, bringing her into my home while I was recovering. What gall. As if I'd believe she was his sister! But I played along, played the hysteric, the invalid with brain trauma, pretending I believed him as I bided my time. Was Marjorie at our wedding, among the guests? That's why I needed to find our wedding album, to see if she was there. I was so happy on my wedding day, in my beautiful, beaded white dress, so in love.

Alba finishes her mouthful. "Did you never think about divorcing him?"

Why didn't I untangle myself from his web a lot sooner? Good question. "My parents were, well, very conservative," I tell her. "I didn't want to upset anybody, you know. Marriage is what you make of it, really. Have you ever been married, Detective Alba?" I throw the ball in her court and only half listen to her answer. *No longer married, no kids.*

I think back to my father's illness and, despite what the doctor said—that he had nine months to live—Papa actually kept getting better. A strong old boot, my dad was, nothing could keep him down. But then my mother also became ill. The last thing I was going to do was shove a divorce in their faces. I did not want to hurl my baggage at them, burden them with my own problems, break their hearts. I'd sort it out later, I decided. At a later date.

"Marriage takes work," I throw out at Alba now, taking a sip of coffee. "Nobody said it was easy, or if they did, they were lying."

"But you chose not to let Max know that Lizzie wasn't his, right? He believed, and still believes, that Lizzie is his child?"

I nod at Alba vaguely and pretend to check my messages. I knew Lizzie wasn't Max's and Max knew she wasn't his too because we hadn't had sex for ages. He didn't *want* to have sex with me, he was disgusted by me. He had been disgusted by me right from the start.

He wasn't disgusted by my money though.

"And you told me Max was a widower, right?" Alba asks.

"That's right." I don't give her more. Max had wheedled money out of his and Marjorie's last "mark," the woman who was Liam's mother. They hadn't gotten married, but she had left him everything in her will. Did he kill her? It was a "boating accident." Not hard to deduce. And when I laid eyes on that poor little boy, I knew Liam needed love. At first I simply took him for a needy child who had lost his mom, but when I found out who Max was my heart went out to Liam even more. It wasn't his fault he was the product of fraud, of Max's scheming. He had only just learned to walk. Liam needed me and I vowed to be a good mom to him, no matter what became of me and Max.

I was brought up to never flash my money, to never show that I was independently wealthy, but Max had done his research. I am not the kind of woman who has a thousand pairs of shoes in her closet, and I would never travel by private jet or even attach my name to a large charitable donation. I prefer to donate anonymously. Our money is hidden, "discreet." We Wainwrights have land all over the world; my cache on Cliff Island is the least of it. Oh, and that's something else I don't brandish. Wainwright is *my* name, not Max's. Max took my name when we got married. It was my father's idea, actually. He refused to let his daughter be a Dickman. Papa had a lot to answer for. I blame him for not being more on the ball, more savvy. Not insisting I get a prenup. Because the bulk of the money skipped a generation, Papa didn't think it mattered. He wasn't worried about Max marrying me for my money because it would be my children benefitting from the inheritance, not us.

Max had us *all* fooled. He was a pro. Everything: the gala dinners, the wining and dining, the gifts, the daily postcards, all were a ruse to win me over—or rather, to win over whichever of his suitors came up trumps. I was the "winner," the fool who rushed in.

I found out, a couple of years later, that I was not the only woman on Max's list of heiress candidates. It was Max's ambition to marry money, then abscond with as much as he could get his hands on. He'd lined up all his prospective targets at that gala dinner to see which one of us he would play with, which one of us was the most suited to his needs, which one of us would fall, hook line and sinker for his charms.

And there was I thinking I was the luckiest girl in the world.

I had no idea there was a third party, another woman waiting in the wings for her cut of the money, waiting to be reunited with her love when it was all over. "It" being me. When *I* was over.

Dead.

But it wasn't enough me being dead, he then discovered. He needed to kill the girls too, since they would be the inheritors of my father's fortune. With all of us dead and gone? Max would get the lot.

I flick a glance at Alba now, feeling bad for spinning so many lies. But I couldn't tell her or she'd disrupt my plan. *Our marriage is solid*, I remember telling her. *Very stable.* But then it came. The thing I had been dreading. Waiting for. I knew the police would find out the moment they tested the children's DNA.

But I'm not going to share any of this history with Detective Alba—why should I? If she can't work it out herself, too bad. She's an intelligent woman. I can see it in her eyes, but every time she gets close to the answer her boss pulls her away, steers her in the wrong direction. Typical. That dunce of a boss pulled Alba off the case just when she was on the verge of having it all wrapped up. Why is it that Alba isn't leading this case? I mean, *properly* leading it... she's being used like a puppet, having her strings pulled by a man, because that's the way the world works. However far we women may have come, we have so much further to go.

I am done being controlled by men.

My father, the patriarch in our family, and the controller of all controllers, was over the moon when I married Max. He believed a woman needed a man to look after her, and he couldn't see my life as being fulfilled until I found a husband

and was ready to start a family. Another reason why I didn't divorce Max while Papa was still alive: Papa would not have tolerated a scandal. He preferred whitewashed lies and deceit to any whiff of a scandal. Families can be so toxic. You play your role within the family structure because you know anything else is tantamount to betrayal in their eyes.

Detective Alba finally gets up to leave. We say our goodbyes and she thanks me for the sandwich and answering her questions. She is polite, professional as always, and, as always, I have no idea what is going through her mind. I think I have evaded her scrutiny but I can't be sure. I will find out with the next step I take. A risky endeavor that could put me behind bars. But I have no choice.

After she leaves, I go upstairs, run myself a bath and pour in some lavender salts. It may be summer but I love a good soak in the tub, a glass of wine by my side, a good book.

I lie back, letting the warm water soak into my weary bones, muscles tight and contracted from all my lies, and from all the detective's questions. I sip my wine, put the glass down and take in a deep calming breath.

I pick up "Max's" burner phone and send myself the last message:

Thanx for wiring the money. The kids are all yours. You can find them at the sailing club.

I know, within seconds, Alba and her team will have every sailing club in the radius of a hundred miles alerted. They have my smartphone tapped.

I am relaxed about this. The kids are with my boyfriend, Eric, happy as anything... Stephen's been keeping me posted. He and Eric have a private, coded exchange, by email, keeping me up to date with the latest developments. It's been hard being without the children for the last eight days, but it is certainly worth the sacrifice. The most painful thing of all has been being parted from my baby, from Violet. I have felt like a monster at times, putting the kids through all this. But for them it's been a vacation. They adore Eric. Alex's sister, also a nurse, was hired by me to look after Violet. They've all been living at Eric's sister's apartment. Spoiled as anything. Pizzas and video games for Liam, with major bribes to keep his mouth shut, if and when it comes to that.

Besides, that slimy attorney, Owen, whom Stephen drummed up and who then wheedled his way onto my payroll, is on standby for when the media circus hits, which, I'm assuming, will be any minute because I've tipped off the reporters. They'll be so ecstatic, so thrilled to see the children reunited with their mom. The kids, apart from a few minor bruises Lizzie sustained from her sailing classes, are in great shape. Owen won't allow anyone to ask the kids a thing. Or me.

I can just say, "I'm thrilled to have the children home, please respect our privacy at this monumental time of our lives."

I finish my chilled Burgundy with a little edge of satisfaction, dismantle the burner, pluck out the card—I'll throw it into the ocean—and then my phone rings. I know exactly who it is without even looking at the screen.

Detective Alba.

She'll be wondering where Max and Marjorie are. I won't offer her any clues. The beauty is that when someone has dealings with the mafia, even in small, rather pitiful ways, it's so easy to snitch on them and inspire wrath from the powers that be, stir up trouble. Max had been playing with matches. I offered a flammable straw. And I know how that lot are experts at making people disappear. And if their bodies wind up washed up on some shore? Who am I to speculate about what happened after what he did to me, did to the children?

Everybody was told that Max and Marjorie had taken Liam away from the island to go sightseeing, to keep him safe. I am the one who arranged for Liam's safety. I meant it when I said I consider that child my own. It's not his fault that he's the product of one of Max's scams. Will he miss Max? Of course he will, but I know Eric will make an amazing stepdad when the time comes. He's a decent, kind man. Liam thinks he's great—he'll be a wonderful father figure.

I pick up my phone, lie back in the tub. "What a relief," I say to Alba. "The children are okay."

"You know which sailing club he's talking about?"

I tell her the address.

"I'll send you a boat," she says, and I feel a tinge of guilt. I have used up great chunks of police and government resources in the search for Lizzie. But when the police department get my check, my donation, they'll be flabbergasted, I'm sure they'll let any suspicions slide. I'm counting on it. I'll also be counting the money I paid myself into those untraceable shell accounts.

THE REUNION

The bar is packed, every seat taken, as bodies gather around the TV to soak up today's news, which has been on a loop—the same story—for hours. Alba is with George—K-9 Dune by his side—celebrating. Not only the "success" with the case, but her promotion. It isn't official yet, but Scully has told her he is retiring and has nominated her for his job.

Maybe she'll miss being called kiddo, after all.

But she is excited. Not "counting her chickens" as she herself would advise anyone, but calmly pressing her hands together in a prayer that everything will pan out.

She lifts her eyes to the giant TV, amid the cheers of the customers, the clinking glasses, the laughter. Everyone is smiling. The whole nation is smiling, and above all, Celeste is smiling as she hugs Lizzie and Liam, holding Violet in her arms. The perfect mother. Something in that woman's eyes confirms to Alba that Celeste was the biggest scammer of all. No proof, just a hunch. But Alba won't breathe a word.

She knows how important it is for a woman to win.

"Cheers," George says, winking at her, and they clink glasses.

Alba smiles and raises her eyes to the screen as the reporter gushes on:

"In this incredible turn of events, and seemingly against all odds, little Lizzie Wainwright has been reunited with her mother, after her alleged father, Max Wainwright, along with his clandestine lover, Marjorie—posing as his very own sister, no less—kidnapped not only Lizzie but their baby Violet, extorting money from his own wife, and most likely fleeing the country in Max Wainwright's private speedboat."

Alba mulls this over. They never did run tests on Violet's DNA, did they? Too late now. She wonders whom the baby belongs to. Oh, well, does it even matter? She feels proud of that, that the press never got ahold of the DNA data proving that Lizzie wasn't Max's.

Alba turns her attention back to the TV.

"The family's lawyer has asked for privacy at this sensitive time," the newscaster continues, "as mom and children get ready to return home, escorted by the police to spend happy moments of celebration at their home on Cliff Island, which for security purposes will be closed off to tourists and non-local visitors until things return to normalcy. But one person has agreed to share a few words with us. Jayne Smith, the Wainwrights' British nanny."

The newscaster shoves the mic in the au pair's face. "Jayne, firstly, how are you feeling right now?"

"Elated." Jayne bites her lower lip as if to stop herself from crying.

"Were you surprised that Max Wainwright had kidnapped his own children?"

"Gobsmacked. He seemed like such a nice man. I'm honestly lost for words."

"Will you continue to work for the family?"

"If they need me, I'd be honored."

"Can you tell me about the children?"

"Just how great they are, you know, sorry... I... I feel a bit emotional." She wipes her cheeks of tears and turns away from the camera.

A man butts in. Owen, the slimy attorney, dressed in a sharp gray suit, a brash vermillion tie swinging from side to side. "Excuse me. We are in negotiation for a future book deal, an auction, actually. Any new offers, please come forward. Ms. Smith will be relating the relevant information in due course. For now, we ask for your patience and understanding at this emotional time. The family asks for privacy, too, but we promise... stay tuned, we won't let you down."

Alba can't help but laugh. She'll stay tuned all right. She'll sing along with the melody.

A LETTER FROM ARIANNE

Dear reader,

Thank you so much for choosing *The Breakdown* and reading it until the very end. If you are new to my books, I hope you had a fun ride and that I was able to offer an escape from the real world for a while. I have other books too, so do check them out. And if you are a return reader, wonderful! Thanks so much. I can't tell you how much I appreciate your trust in me as a writer to deliver an entertaining story.

I have more books in the making, so if you'd like to be the first to hear about my new releases, you can sign up using the link below:

www.bookouture.com/arianne-richmonde

During these difficult times, many of us haven't had the opportunity to travel as much as we'd like, so I hope you have enjoyed this trip to Cliff Island in Maine. However, I have taken quite a bit of poetic license adding all sorts of things to *The Breakdown* that, to my knowledge, do not exist in real life. The sea cave, for starters. So, if you are from Cliff Island, please forgive my run-wild imagination. It comes with the job!

I saw a TED talk with an FBI agent saying how on average we lie ten times a day, and this was one of the things that sparked the story for *The Breakdown*. Lying is an ongoing theme that fascinates me: how people are not what they seem, and how we all fib every day, even in small ways, and how people's true identities are easier than ever to hide or dissimilate in today's world.

Thank you so much for joining me on this adventure. If I have entertained you in these oddball Covid times, and with all the great books and shows to choose from, I am honored. If you have a few minutes please do leave a quick, spoiler-free review, even just a couple of lines; we authors are so grateful when people spread the word.

I love hearing from readers and having an online chat so don't be shy to reach out on social media.

Take care,

Arianne

facebook.com/authorariannerichmonde

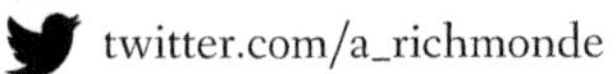
twitter.com/a_richmonde

instagram.com/arianne_richmonde

ACKNOWLEDGMENTS

I am so grateful to my pal and ex homicide detective and author Suzie Ivy, who checked over Detective Alba's chapters… thank you! Any mistakes or bad calls on my character's part are my own. Thanks so much for answering my barrage of cop questions.

A big shout out to my editor and publisher, Helen Jenner, for helping me be a better writer and reining me in when I veer wildly off track, and making my stories shine, and to everyone in the fabulous Bookouture team, including many other authors in the Bookouture family who have been so supportive. And a big thank you, too, to Becca Allen for your talent, and to Anne O'Brien for your skillful copy edit, you are just the best. Also to Lisa Horton for such a stunning book cover. *The Breakdown* has been a real team effort.

Another author and friend helped me no end: Nelle L'Amour. A million thanks for your generous time and energy concerning this book and for reading everything I write. For your honesty, your enthusiasm, your eagle eye, your ideas, and above all, your sense of humor. You have been with me on my writer journey; I can't tell you how much you mean to me.

I am so grateful to all the bloggers who spread the word about my books. You work so incredibly hard, squeezing in our books between your busy family lives and day jobs, how generous you are with your time! Thank you so much.

Last but never least, my animal children, my family, who

surround me as I write, and my husband for all my morning coffees and meals while I'm writing away.

Printed in Great Britain
by Amazon